LAST LIVING WORDS:
THE INGEBORG BACHMANN READER

Translated from the German by Lilian M. Friedberg

With a Critical Introduction
by Dagmar C. G. Lorenz

Last Living Words

The Ingeborg Bachmann Reader

GREEN INTEGER
KØBENHAVN & LOS ANGELES
2005

GREEN INTEGER
Edited by Per Bregne
København / Los Angeles

Distributed in the United States by Consortium Book
Sales and Distribution, 1045 Westgate Drive, Suite 90
Saint Paul, Minnesota 55114-1065
Distributed in England and throughout Europe by
Turnaround Publisher Services
Unit 3, Olympia Trading Estate
Coburg Road, Wood Green, London N22 6TZ
44 (0)20 88293009

(323) 857-1115 / http://www.greeninteger.com

First Green Integer Edition 2005
Stories and poems [with the exceptions listed below] are
published here through agreement with Piper Verlag, München.
©1978 by Piper Verlag GmbH, München
"The Thirtieth Year," "Everything," "Among Murderers
and Madmen," "A Wildermuth," and "Undine Quits"
are published in new translations by permission of Holmes & Meier Publishers
and the poems herein are published in new translations by permission of Zephyr Press.
The translator would also like to thank *Chicago Review*, *Denver Quarterly*, and
Trivia: A Journal of Ideas in which some of the stories first appeared.

English language translation copyright ©2005 by Lilian M. Friedberg
Introduction ©2005 by Dagmar C. G. Lorenz
Back cover copy ©2005 by Green Integer
All rights reserved
The translation of these works was made possible, in part, by a translation grant from
the Eugene M. Kayden National Translation Award Committee

Design: Per Bregne
Typography: Kim Silva
Cover photograph: Stefan Moses

LIBRARY OF CONGRESS CATALOGING IN PUBLICATION DATA
Ingeborg Bachmann [1926-1973]
Last Living Words: The Ingeborg Bachmann Reader
ISBN: 1-933382-12-0
p. cm – Green Integer 136
I. Title II. Series. III. Translator

Green Integer books are published for Douglas Messerli
Printed in the United States on acid-free paper

Contents

Acknowledgements	7
Introduction, *by Dagmar C.G. Lorenz*	11

Stories

The Ferry	31
In Heaven and on Earth	39
The Thirtieth Year	46
Everything	120
Among Murderers and Madmen	155
A Wildermuth	202
Undine Quits	266
Manners of Death	284

Poems

Voyage Out	325
The Mortgage on Borrowed Time	328
Wood and Shavings	330
Theme and Variation	332
Early Noon	335
Everyday	338

Message	339
Night Flight	340
Psalm I-V	343
In the Storm of Roses	346
Viennese Panorama	350
Curriculum Vitae	355
You Words	357
No Delicacies	360

Acknowledgements

A work of this nature is never the product of one mind or the result of one person's efforts. The first order of thanks is due the Eugene M. Kayden Translation Award Committee at the University of Colorado-Boulder and Douglas Messerli at Green Integer. The ongoing support of the Bachmann heirs and of Piper Verlag has been crucial. The Europäisches Übersetzer Kolloquium, Robert Bosch Stiftung and Deutscher Literaturfonds made valuable research opportunities available, and the Robert Kauf Memorial Fund of the University of Illinois-Chicago supported related research activities. Michael Hammond of Shakespeare & Company, the Boston Playwrights' Theatre and Massachusetts Museum of Contemporary Art (MASS MoCA) are also due special consideration for their production of "Undine's Valediction" and excerpts from "Among Murderers and Madmen." Special thanks is due Marilyn Gaddis Rose, Ingeborg Majer-O'Sickey, and Gisela Brinker-Gabler of Binghamton University. Other individuals who have lent various forms of support include Lise Weil and the editors of *Trivia;* Jorun Johns and Donald Daviau of Ariadne Press; editors of *Denver Quarterly* and editors Andrew Rathmann, Eirik Steinhoff, Andrea Scott and W. Martin of *Chicago Review;* special thanks to Stefan Moses for the use of his photograph as a cover image; Robyn Schiffman, Monika Schausten, A.P. Marki, and Markus Schaeffer. Peter Höyng and Amanda Norton provided valuable insights into the text of "The Thirtieth Year." Peter Jansen has been an important source for literary allusions and an astute analyst of difficult issues in translation. Curdin Ebneter, Claudia Arlinghaus, Stefanie Schaffer-de Vries, Malte Krutzsch, Jeanne Haunschild, Peter Torberg, Biene van de Laar and Reinhard Streit provided indispensable insights into nuances of the German originals in final revisions to the poems, special thanks is due Zephyr Press for permissions to print new translations of the poems, to Holmes & Meier for permission to publish new translations from *The Thirtieth Year,* and to Jeffrey Ankrom for consultation and advice. Dagmar Lorenz, Helga Kraft, Sara Hall, Sander L. Gilman, the Graduate College, the Center for Research on Women and Gender (Alice J. Dan Award) of the University of Illinois-Chicago have provided generous financial, professional and personal support.

Though many people have commented on these translations, offered advice and consultation, the ultimate responsibility for any errors, omissions, infelicities, or excessive liberties remains, of course, mine alone.

This work is dedicated to Dr. Hilde Bacharach

Introduction

Among scholars and students of literature the name of Ingeborg Bachmann (1926-1973) is well known. A path-breaking postwar Austrian poet, playwright, and prose writer, she played a major role in shaping literary discourse in the German language after World War II. She was among the first to problematize the impact of lingering pervasive authoritarian and racist structures, the much-debated phenomenon of everyday fascism, in post-Shoah Central Europe. In Germany and Austria the publication of the *"Todesarten"-Projekt* in 1995 led to a highly publicized controversy and elicited renewed interest in an author whose works had consistently been a major attraction for the West German publishing houses of Piper and Suhrkamp. Yet, Bachmann, surprisingly, has remained relatively obscure in the Anglophone world. Now, more than a quarter of a century after her untimely death in 1973, it is time to acquaint a wider readership with her challenging and inspiring work. Bachmann, very much a daughter of her own time, was at the same time a keen and sensitive observer of evolving social trends.

The chaos and barbarism of World War II and the catastrophe of the nuclear attack on Japan were still fresh in people's minds when Bachmann emerged as one of the most talented postwar writers in Europe. A native of Klagenfurt, a town in the southeastern Austrian province of Carinthia, she began her career in Vienna working as a scriptwriter and editor for the Austrian radio. She was encouraged and supported by members of the postwar literary elite, including Hans Weigel, one of the few returned exiles, whose mission was to rebuild intellectual and literary life in Austria. She made her debut in 1952 in Niendorf at a meeting of Gruppe 47 (Group 47), an association of predominantly West German writers, whose coveted prize she won the following year. Because of her affiliations with the Gruppe 47, her work was read more in the context of postwar German than Austrian literature, and her rich poetic literary voice, together with her indebtedness to the cultural heritage of the Danube monarchy, set her apart from other Austrian authors. Like many Austrian intellectuals, Bachmann took up a life of travel and displacement, and was often considered a member of the international intellectual jet set and a representative of artistic chic. Not unlike some of her literary protagonists, she became the object of prolific gossip because of her relationships with men, among them the Romanian-born Holocaust poet Paul Celan and the Swiss author Max Frisch. Bachmann's supposedly extravagant lifestyle attracted attention that focused largely on her self-imposed exile from Austria and Germany and her sensationalized "drug addiction"—a dependency that was actually caused by errors in medical treatment. Her death as the result of complications from burns sustained in an accident in her Rome apartment in 1973 gave rise to wild speculation and added to the aura of mystery surrounding the author.

Bachmann began her career as a writer after 1945, in the aftermath of fascism and Hitler's "Total War." Bachmann became increasingly aware of her and her contemporaries' association with a history of crime, and it is no accident that her initial conceptualization of "Manners of Death" coincides with the Eichmann Trial (1960-62) in Jerusalem and the Auschwitz Trials (1962-64) in Frankfurt.[1] These high-profile trials generated renewed interest in the Holocaust and the Nazi era on an international scale, reflected, for example, in Hannah Arendt's *Eichmann in Jerusalem* and the ensuing controversy involving, among others, Günter Anders and Saul Friedländer. Countless works dealing with the Shoah appeared in German-speaking countries, and Bachmann's interest in these controversies and her reading of the Nuremberg Trial transcripts are well-known.

During Bachmann's lifetime, her works had already been translated into many different languages, including Italian, French, and English. In this award-winning translation, Lilian Friedberg shifts from the recent focus on Bachmann's posthumous legacy back to works the author published

---

[1] Much, perhaps too much attention has been paid to Bachmann's involvements with men. Thus Sigrid Weigel, in her extensive Bachmann book focuses on issues related to the author's work and production without getting caught up in the discussion of what amounts to little more than gossip. Sigrid Weigel, *Ingeborg Bachmann: Hinterlassenschaften unter Wahrung des Briefgeheimnisses* (Vienna : P. Zsolnay, 1999).

during her lifetime, that is, texts over which Bachmann exercised complete authorial control. Thus *Last Living Words* highlights and celebrates Bachmann's literary achievements during her lifetime in the attempt to present Ingeborg Bachmann as a life-loving, rather than a death-driven author whose writing represents an indefatigable and brilliantly orchestrated struggle for life—her own life, that of others, and the life of her work.

Lilian Friedberg is emerging as an expert in the field of literary translation with special focus on Bachmann. Her careful selection of texts in *Last Living Words* reveals Bachmann's range of genres, topics, and literary styles and underscores Bachmann's responses to the ongoing debates of her time. Thus, certain core motifs are cast and recast, locations and character constellations are revisited. The carefully crafted intertextualities between individual works call to mind the methods of production and literary strategies of other Austrian authors such as Veza Canetti, Heimito von Doderer, Robert Menasse, and Marlene Streeruwitz where a similar predilection for sequential writing can be found. Once created, their characters appear or are alluded to in different works, moving into the foreground in some or fading away in others.

Bachmann writes about Austria and the Austrians with the intimate knowledge of an insider who wants out. In her writing she expresses the inner conflicts arising from having to reject her native culture on moral grounds. She saw Austria inextricably linked with an imperialist and genocidal past that had its beginnings long before the Nazi takeover in 1938. Nonetheless, as a writer Bachmann remained tied to Austria by language and socialization, and her works struggle with this conflicted tie.

Through her personal acquaintance with survivors of racial persecution and genocide, Bachmann had come to empathize with the victims and survivors of the Nazi Holocaust. She incorporated the position of disenfranchisement into her texts, but to her credit—as a non-Jew—she did not seek to write a "Jewish" book or assume the voice of the Nazi victims.

Becoming a poet at the end of the world war amid the ruins of Central Europe meant, for Bachmann, coming to terms with the physical and ideological devastation of her childhood. Having been raised and educated during the Nazi era she experienced the total invalidation of everything she and her peers had been taught when the occupation forces brought western-style democracy and information about Nazi atrocities to the people of Austria and Germany. Increasingly dismayed by the continued self-imposed ignorance embraced by an Austrian public that subscribed to the official historical narrative of Austria as the first victim of National Socialism, Bachmann abandoned the confined and confining literary circles of postwar Vienna.

Rather than assume a position of moral indignation towards the past, Bachmann explored in her radio plays and narratives the multi-layered relationships between perpetrators and victims, including those of sexuality and marriage. Her works reveal that emotional ties as well as social conditioning and gendered class structures cause victims to become accomplices in the destruction of others and in their own demise. Such is the case, for example, in "The Ferry" where, notwithstanding the sentimental embroidery provided in the young Josip Poje's musings, the woman is clearly an object of communication and trade between him and the Lord of the manor. At the same time, unaware of her actual condition, she plays into the hands of both men.

Her relentless search beneath surface structures distinguishes Bachmann from many German and Austrian postwar writers who portrayed the Nazi era and the postwar period in black-and-white while fundamentally accepting the binary structures of race and gender underlying authoritarian and fascist thinking.[2] Bachmann did not believe in a constitutional difference between victims and perpetrators. Neither did she consider National Socialism a historical aberration. Her texts are disquieting precisely because they describe the close proximity in which the power brokers live with those they exploit, the negotiations that take place between unequal partners and the crimes that are committed under the guise of cooperation and mutual consent.

---

[2] See, for instance, the discussion of the authoritarian personality in Theodor W. Adorno, Else Frenkel-Brunswick, Daniel J. Levinson and Newitt R. Sanford, *The Authoritarian Personality* (New York: Harper, 1950).

These crimes, the expression of a pervasive "everyday fascism," remain indiscernible to the public and impossible to prosecute.[3] Bachmann portrays fascism as the logical extension of capitalism and patriarchy.

In the poem "Viennese Panorama" the narrative of Vienna's rich history is evoked only to be undermined by the speaker's own narrative as it directs attention to signs of destruction such as withering trees, oil wells driving the onset of spring from the open fields, and wheels that have ground to a halt. In rapid succession the emblems of the "city of waltz" pass in review—kissing couples, the Ferris wheel in the Prater amusement park, Roman ruins, and the church of Maria am Gestade, all reminders of the human domination of nature and each other.

---

[3] Dan Bar-On introduced the concept of a double wall to describe the barriers that prevent perpetrators of and eye-witnesses to atrocities from relating their experience, and the barriers that prevent listeners to reports about Nazi crimes from processing the information in "The Holocaust Perpetrators Feel Guilty in Retrospect?" in *Der Holocaust. Familiale und gesellschaftliche Folgen*, ed. Dan Bar-On et al. (Wuppertal: Universität Wuppertal, 1988), 33-55.

The church, once by the banks of the Danube, now surrounded by the city, recalls the man-made modifications of Vienna's river banks. The giant Ferris wheel, erected in 1896/7 for the World's Fair, once considered the height of technology, stands in the midst of what used to be meadows and woods. Roman edifices dating back to the time of the fortress of Vindobona call to mind a history of imperialism, as do the fake Roman ruins at Schönbrunn castle built for the edification of the Habsburg rulers. All these structures, no less so than the couples' furtive kisses, appear commercialized and degraded: life in the tenements is sterile, the chestnut tree blooms without scent, the eternal light in the church is extinguished, and the fish are dead. Bachmann's Vienna, swollen with memory, is a city dead and devoid—a ghost town portending disasters yet to come. This portrait of Vienna as a "city without warrantee" resurfaces in prose form in "The Thirtieth Year."

Not only did Bachmann consider the attempt to eliminate the baggage of the past from her German language and literary tradition futile in an environment where every stone and every street represented a historical marker, she was aware that the defeat in 1945 had given Central Europe and particularly the former fascist nations an opportunity for transformation. The poem "Message" reads like a commentary on different postwar discourses—those of renewal and rebirth as well as those of survival. In allusion to the "grave in the breezes" assigned to the murdered Jews in Celan's famous "Death Fugue," Bachmann asserts that all that history has in store for the "fallen," perpetrators and bystanders alike, is not "immortality," but merely a grave from which there can be no resurrection.[4]

Like other critical thinkers, Bachmann soon realized that the opportunity provided by the defeat of Nazi Germany was slipping away: only a superficial restructuring of the former authoritarian patterns was taking place. By keeping the foundations of the protofascist mentality of the prewar era intact, the opportunity to encourage a renewal of those cultural, religious, and ethnic traditions that the National Socialists had attempted to erase

---

[4] Paul Celan, *Poems. A Bilingual Edition*, trans. Michael Hamburger (New York: Persea Books, 1980), 50-53.

passed by as well. The Jewish exiles were not invited to return to Austria, and those who did return were expected to live as Austrians rather than as Jews.[5] Socialism, a strong movement of the interwar period, had been dismantled in the 1930s, and its legacy was shunned and repressed in the postwar republic which came under the spell of an anti-Communist paranoia not unlike the one that initiated the infamous McCarthy era in the United States. Many critical intellectuals who began their careers in postwar Vienna—Ilse Aichinger, Paul Celan and Jakov Lind—soon realized that the formal end of the Nazi regime was not a new beginning and they left Austria. Indeed a continuity existed linking pre- and postwar Austria in terms of mentalities and personalities.[6]

---

[5] Dagmar C. G. Lorenz, introduction to *Contemporary Jewish Writing in Austria* (Lincoln: Nebraska University Press, 1999), xii.
[6] Klaus Amann and Albert Berger, introduction to *Österreichische Literatur der dreißiger Jahre,* ed. Amann and Berger (Vienna: Böhlau, 1985), 8.

Bachmann's earliest poetry is already distinct from the terse writing of her German contemporaries. Her poetic vocabulary summons up Romantic as well as Art Nouveau and Surrealist imagery. Her proficiency in traditional representational strategies and awareness of recent ideology, pre- and postwar, and her profound disillusionment distinguish her work from that of other prominent writers of the same period such as Heinrich Böll, Günter Grass, and Max Frisch. Moreover, she obviously shares in the creative imagination of Existentialism and the Beat era. For example, the image of the lover who "sinks in the sand/ rising around her flowing hair" in the poem "The Mortgage on Borrowed Time" calls to mind Samuel Beckett's image of a similarly oppressed woman drowning in a sand dune in his play *Happy Days* (1961).[7] Coming from a different point of departure, she reaches the same conclusion about human relationships as other writers associated with the literature of the Absurd. Love, intimacy, and friendship are represent-

---

[7] Samuel Beckett, *Happy Days: A Play in Two Acts* (New York: Pergamon, 1983).

ed as the illusions of bygone eras.

The ominous opening and concluding line, "There are harder days to come," in Bachmann's poem demonstrate how acutely aware she was of the difficulties lying ahead. Bachmann looks ahead to the post-Shoah era with considerable pessimism because she did not believe that the devastation wrought by National Socialism could be easily overcome nor did she accept uncritically the political and cultural impulses from the victors, particularly the United States. Her apocalyptic poems evoke the chaos of the Nazi era, as does "Early Noon" through the proximity of the idyllic linden tree to a German sky that "blackens the soil." They also foreshadow the horrors of new wars, "no longer declared, merely perpetuated" ("Every Day"). The European intellectual elite, including Bachmann, never believed in the notion of a "war to end all wars." Revelations about the Holocaust and the bombing of Hiroshima and Nagasaki by the United States resulted in an increased awareness of the fragility of human existence and the murderous potential of the human species. Bachmann and her colleagues, the first generation living with the knowledge of industrialized genocide, gas chambers and the atomic bomb, were distrustful of the future and particularly suspicious of the seemingly normalized sphere of everyday life. They were especially wary of their average fellow citizens who, as they well knew, had taken part in organized mass murder. Bachmann expresses this sentiment in numerous texts, including the poem "Wood and Shavings" with its admonition "Make sure you stay awake." Not unlike Ilse Aichinger and Erich Fried she was convinced that it would take several generations to overcome the damage wrought by National Socialism.

Bachmann was not a victim of Nazi persecution, but she did take the side of the victims and survivors. Her erstwhile mentor, the poet Ilse Aichinger, her friend the survivor and poet Paul Celan, and the eminent existentialist critic Paul Améry, former victims of National Socialist racial and political persecution, had been instrumental in creating an oppositional consciousness that kept Jewish memory and the legacy of the Shoah alive. Moreover, authors who had been persecuted under National Socialism were keenly aware of the exploitation of minorities worldwide. Many among them maintained their ties to Austria, and were active participants in the intellectual life of the Second Republic: Elias Canetti, for example, who examined the phenomena of mass manipulation and power in a global context, and Erich Fried, who discussed the atrocities of the Holocaust alongside the oppression of Palestinians in Israel. Similarly, Bachmann took up the theme of privilege by birth and position early in her work, as for example in "Theme and Variation": "He is a stranger to suffering, the one with the world at his hands,/and was anything not handed him?" In the same text she addresses the possibility of resistance on the part of the most powerless, the bees and the workers, calling attention to the vulnerability of the powerful, be it the human species or those humans who wield power over others.

Bachmann's skepticism toward Germany and Austria grew over time. In "Manners of Death," her last and most controversial project, she articulates her worst suspicions and fears about the far-reaching legacy of post-National Socialist Germany and Austria in the form of an economic and cultural world order that encourages homogeneity and shuns diversity. The story of Franza, a woman born—like Bachmann—in Carinthia, and identified with the culturally oppressed Slovenian minority, who is destroyed by the machinations of her husband, a medical doctor of the Nazi era specializing in the long-range effects of the Holocaust on its victims. Bachmann's text suggests that the totalitarian structures from which National Socialism and Fascism drew their power are identical to those underlying racism, ethnocentrism, and misogyny everywhere. She represents them as part and parcel of Western civilization and a common trait of human males. Bachmann's work is replete with instances of abuse: abuse of the weaker group by the stronger, of people of color by whites, of the underprivileged by educated professionals, of women by men, of animals by humans. "Manners of Death" furthermore makes transparent the collaboration between various complicit parties of the supposedly non-political sphere of society, the "private sector." In her view this sphere is optimally insulated against intrusion by state authorities, thus sheltering the most heinous abuses, including those of husbands against their wives and those of the professional elite and corporations such as Hoechst and Bayer against disadvantaged groups and third-world populations.

Ingeborg Bachmann's voice deserves to be heard, not only in Europe where her significance as one of the most influential writers of the twentieth century is firmly established. In German-speaking countries, her works are still widely available in bookstores. This is not the case in the Anglophone world. Although her major works are taught in German and Austrian Studies as well as Women's Studies programs, often in translation, they have remained relatively obscure and unappreciated outside the university setting. The fate of Bachmann's writings in English translation is not unique. With a few rare exceptions, German authors, including the most illustrious classics, have not fared well in English-speaking countries. To explain this phenomenon, one could point to cultural barriers, differences in sensitivity, value systems, and reader expectations, but a major factor seems to be the quality of the translation itself.

Different translators have translated Bachmann

into English, but the translations have failed to resonate with the wider public. Indeed, to produce a literary translation of an oeuvre as seemingly simple and straightforward and at the same time as complex and tied in with the cultural discourse of Bachmann's era presents a tremendous challenge. In addition to being a writer and poet Bachmann was an intellectual, a language critic and theorist, and an academic. Her disillusionment with Heidegerrian Existentialism as expressed in her doctoral dissertation was resolved in part by a growing interest in Austrian philosopher Ludwig Wittgenstein, whose *tractatus logico philosophicus* substantially influenced her relationship to language. Bachmann's poetic language is reflective, equally conscious of what to avoid after the world war—sentimentality and pathos—and what to strive for. The latter leads her on a quest for a woman's voice in an era of conservatism and a critical and self-critical stance to resist residues of fascism in her wording and her intellectual approach. In her critical essays she addresses the topic of writing and poetic practice in her time, and her literary prose opens up perspectives into modern subjectivities. Obviously, the range and diversity of genre characteristic of Bachmann's oeuvre present a challenge for any translator and call for a native command of German and English as well as familiarity with the cultural codes that inform her writing and the target language, English—and, with this volume of translations, that challenge has been met.

—DAGMAR C.G. LORENZ

The Ferry

In high summer, the river, a thousand-voiced song carried by a steep incline, fills the entire countryside with the sound of rushing water. But near the riverbank, it is quieter, murmuring more as though immersed in itself. It is broad and its strength, settling into the land, signifies separation. To the north, the valley is dark and dense, hill set near upon hill, vaulted forests cascading down from above, and in the distance, steeper heights rise, building a gentle arc into the land on nice, bright days. Across the river, the manor is situated in the first darkness of the wooded passage. The ferryman Josip Poje sees it when he takes people and cargo across the water. It's always there in front of him. It is blazing white in color and appears suddenly before his eyes.

Josip's eyes are young and sharp. He sees from afar when branches bend in the brush, he catches his ferry guests' scent, regardless of whether they are basket weavers seeking switches on the opposite shore, or craftsmen. Sometimes, too, a stranger comes, or entire societies of laughing men and gaily clad, cheerful women.

The afternoon is hot. Josip is completely steeped in solitude. He's standing on the small bridge that leads from the river's bank across the long stretch of soft sand. The boat landing has been built in the middle of the solitary brush, a flat surface of sand and stone that stretches to where it eventually turns to prairie and field. There is no clear view of the riverbank, every attempt to see it drowns in the brush and there are small, barely beaten paths worn like fresh scars in between. The play of clouds on this fickle day is the only variability. Aside from that, the calm is tiring, and the silent heat presses its mark on every last thing.

Suddenly Josip turns. He looks over at the manor. There is water between, but he can still see the "Lord" standing at one of the windows. He, Josip, can stand or lie still for hours on end, he can listen to the same water day after day, but the gentleman in the white house, a place they sometimes call the "castle," must have restlessness in his blood. He stands first at one window, then another; sometimes he comes down through the woods, making Josip think he wants to cross the river, but he declines as best he can above the water's roar. He strolls aimlessly along the riverbank, then turns back. Josip watches this often. The Lord is quite powerful, he spreads dread and perplexity in everyone around him, but he is a good man. Everyone says so.

Josip doesn't want to think about it anymore. Searchingly, he peruses the paths. No one is coming. He laughs. He's got his little pleasures now. He may be a grown man, but he still enjoys seeking the flat stones from the sand. His steps are measured in the damp, yielding sand. He weighs the stone in his hand, testing it; then, bending over, he swings his arm and the presumptuous thing whizzes over the waves – skipping once, then again and yet again. Three times. After he's been at it a while, the stones skip eight times. They just can't be too round.

Hour after hour steals by. The ferryman has long been a taciturn, withdrawn dreamer. The wall of clouds above the distant hills grows higher. Maybe the sun's semblance will soon disappear, swirling golden seams in the fog-white palaces. Perhaps then Maria will come. She'll be late again, bearing berries in her basket, or honey and bread for the Lord. He'll have to ferry her across the river and watch as she walks toward the white house. He doesn't understand why Maria must bring everything to the Lord's door. He should send his hired help.

The late afternoons bring confusion. His misgivings vanish with weariness. His thoughts are traveling secret paths. The Lord is no longer young. He'll never harbor any desire as painful as young Josip Poje's. Why does Maria have to think about him when he doesn't even look at her, but is thinking instead of great things that are incomprehensible and obscure to her! She can go to him time and again, he won't so much as see her if she doesn't say anything. He won't be able to read her eyes and will send the girl without words away. He'll know nothing of her sadness or her love. And the summer will pass and in winter, Maria will have to go dancing with him.

The little mosquitoes and flies that come to life after sunset are already swarming. They always probe the air, flying in leisurely circles until they suddenly converge. Then they separate and continue hovering until the cycle repeats itself. Somewhere, birds are still singing, but one can hardly hear them. The river's roar is expectation that suffocates everything else. It is a loud noise, filled with fear and arousal. Coolness blows in and with it, a troubling thought. Even a blind man would still see the white spot of the wall shining through the woods from the opposite bank.

Evening has come. Josip thinks about going home, but waits a little longer. It is hard to make a decision. But then he hears Maria coming. He doesn't look her way, he doesn't want to look at all, but the approaching steps say enough. Her greeting is hesitant and helpless. He looks at her.

"It's late." His voice is filled with reproach.

"You're not making another crossing?"

"I don't know," he responds, "where do you want to go at this time of day?" He is seized by a strange implacability. She doesn't dare answer. She's fallen silent. His gaze is a judgment. He notices that she isn't carrying anything. She doesn't have a basket, or a purse, not even a bulging scarf. She brings only herself.

She is a foolish girl. He is full of wonder and

doesn't understand her and even despises her a little. But the clouds now have their glowing golden seam. The waves in the current are more measured and wider than by day, the eddies within them darker and more dangerous. No one would dare cross the water by boat now. Only the ferry offers security.

The wind caresses Josip's forehead, but it remains hot nonetheless. An impulse erupting within him plunges him into confusion. The ferry's rope creates a connection, dissolves the groundlessness and points, straight and unerring, toward the opposite bank, to the white manor.

"I'm not crossing," he snubs Maria.

"You don't want to?" The girl is beginning to sense something. She holds up a small pouch, enticing him, "But I'll pay you double the fare!"

He laughs with relief. "You wouldn't have enough money. I'm not crossing anymore."

Why is she still standing here? The jingle of coins fades away. Trust is in her face, and entreaty. He reiterates his refusal, and his reproach.

"The Lord won't even look at you. Your dress is not fine enough, and your shoes are heavy. He'll send you packing. He's got other things on his mind. I know, I see him every day." He is intimidating the girl. After a minute replete with reflection, her eyes fill with tears.

"In winter, the Lord won't be here any more. He'll quickly forget about you." Josip's comfort is cold. He is troubled. He'll take her across the current after all. Increasingly, perplexity spreads across his face. He looks to the ground. But here is nothing save the abundance of sand. A beautiful plan washes away in the wasteland of rigid indecision.

As Maria slowly turns to leave, he does not understand her for the second time this summer evening.

"You're leaving?" he asks.

She stops once more. Now he is happy. "I'll be leaving soon, too."

"You will?"

He busies himself with the ferry. "I'm thinking about wintertime. Would you go dancing with me?"

She looks down at the tips of her shoes. "Maybe...I want to go home now."

A little later, she's gone. The ferryman Josip Poje thinks that she might be sad after all. But it's bound to be a merry winter. Josip picks up a stone and slings it across the water. The river is oddly murky, and, in the dull of evening, not a single wave has its foaming silver crest. It is nothing more than a gray surge of water that thrusts itself into the land with its broad strength signifying separation.

In Heaven and On Earth

A red shadow ran across Amelie's forehead. She stepped back from the mirror and closed her eyes. The streak Justin's hand had drawn across her face disappeared for a moment. He had hit her only once, then hastily retracted so as not to betray himself too soon. A storm had been unleashed within him that a thousand strikes to Amelie could not have stilled.

"Oh, God," he muttered and washed his hands. As a matter of principle, he only used "God" when he believed nothing else would suffice for expressing his emotional state. Amelie was too shocked to come any closer; but she knew it did him good to be asked, so she asked, from the other side of the room, quietly: "What?..." But she didn't dare ask: What is it, what has happened you, who has insulted you?—for she was no doubt the reason for his bitterness. After a while, she got a hold of herself and blushed. "Can I make it up to you?"

"No," Justin screamed, unrestrained, "the lost money, you can't..." he broke off, exhausted, then, derisive, took up the thread again, "Make up for it! Make up for it! You must be mad. You sure as hell can't get the better of those scoundrels!"

"Has someone swindled you?" she whispered.

"No," he responded, "I swindled them, just as they deserve. I took the money they don't deserve. Do you understand that? They don't deserve it."

"Yes," she answered and, relieved, watched the wrinkles fade from his forehead.

A little later, he left. Amelie pulled out her work and tried to turn to account the many hours in which he forced her to partner his monologues. Her fingers stumbled across the silk she had to stitch with bright colors. Now and again, she looked hastily up at the clock, and amid the wishes that he might come home early, another one mounted, that he would come home late. But all her desires amounted to hoping and praying for the best for Justin. Around midnight she tried to straighten her back, but it had grown stiff and she took this as a sign to continue working. A strange sleepiness trickled into her joints and when Justin's footsteps became audible, she tried to get up, but was unable. She stared at him.

"Why don't you go to bed?" he asked, smiling a smile that made her forget everything. She leaped up in a fit of joy, and hit the floor hard. She struggled against his hands trying to help her. "It's nothing," she stammered.

His face stood dark before her. "You haven't fallen ill, have you? You'd best not cause me any trouble!"

"I've just grown very stiff from sitting so long," she placated him.

"Amelie," he said, and, his voice rising with waking distrust, "do you mean to deny that you only stayed up waiting because you wanted to know when I would come home?"

She fell silent and reached for the scrap of silk that had fallen from her hands.

"You've been drinking again?" she said, bravely.

"Did you wait up for me just to figure that out?" he asked, more urgently. "I've lost my last damn dime and you're sitting here waiting to take me to task?" He grew ever louder to drown out her silence.

"Amelie," he said, gently, as if to a small child, "Let's be reasonable. This can't go on, with you sitting here at home, just adding to the load on my back and holding it against me. Can't you see that?"

She nodded in consent and stared at him in admiration.

"I think I've been slaving away long enough now on this barbaric fairground of life!" He threw himself into an upholstered chair, reached into the pockets of his coat and turned them inside out. "Plundered, pillaged," he concluded and laughed in a way that made Amelie's blood freeze. Then she went silently to the cabinet and fetched a thin envelope from beneath her lingerie. She quickly pressed it into his hand. "That's all there is. I've been sewing while you weren't home."

He tucked it away. "Since when?" he asked.

She didn't answer and lay down on the bed. After they'd turned out the light, he took a deep breath. "I am deeply shaken by the way you could keep something secret from me for so long"—he cleared his throat —"deeply shaken," he repeated, emphasizing each syllable. She turned the light back on and looked him in the face with wild determination. She got up and set herself back to work.

"It doesn't make any sense at all for you to keep

working now. Surely you're not hoping to elicit my sympathy that way," he said, coldly, without turning toward her. She kept sewing for a while, then had to stop because too many tears ran down her face and she didn't know how she should hide them.

"Come here," he said, calmly.

She obeyed.

He pressed a key into her hand. "You go to my old factory now and retrieve from the safe in the office my black attaché case I forgot to take when I left."

"The brown attaché case," she corrected him.

"A black attaché case," he repeated, "I just purchased it not long ago."

"There won't be anyone there now," she pointed out.

"Yes, of course," he responded, distracted, "but you'd be doing me a great favor if you would go now anyway. It doesn't matter because they know about it."

"Try to sleep," she admonished, then quietly ran out of the room...

When she returned, she was amazed to see him still lying awake. She discovered that her willingness had appeased him and dared, bright-eyed and with a soft melody on her lips, to put her sewing away. She went to bed quietly, whispered him a "Good night!" and was happy to hear her greeting returned.

The morning was nice and sunny. The doorbell rang. Amelie placed the flowers in the window and then went to open the door. Cordially, she answered the questions asked by the three policemen and invited them in. Justin, still sluggish with sleep, joined them, acted surprised and stayed out of the conversation. Amelie's imperturbability amazed the officers, and now one of them was asking if she'd stolen the attaché case from the office. "No," she responded, "I went and got it last night."

Justin was irritated to no end by Amelie's innocent eyes. The officer ordered her to come along with him, but she refused to comprehend. She smiled at him indulgently, and turned, still smiling, toward Justin. Then the innocence plummeted from her eyes and was replaced by an abyss of awareness that suddenly engulfed him and her and the very fabric of their relationships. She ran, without needing to ask or wanting to know another thing, to the window and leaped to the dark courtyard below which, like a shaft, held a small square open to the sky...

"Oh God, oh God," Justin muttered, because, as a matter of principle, he only used "God" when he believed nothing else would suffice for expressing his emotional state.

The Thirtieth Year

When a man enters his thirtieth year, people don't stop calling him young. But even though he discovers no changes in himself, he becomes unsure of himself; it seems to him as though he may no longer be entitled to pass himself off as young. And one morning he wakens to a day he will live to forget and lies there suddenly, unable to rise, struck by harsh rays of light and stripped of every armament and every last ounce of courage to face the new day. When he closes his eyes to shield himself, he sinks back and drifts from consciousness, taking with him every moment ever lived. He sinks and sinks and his scream remains inaudible (robbed of everything, even this!), and he falls headlong into the bottomless abyss until his senses abandon him, until everything he believed himself to be has been dismantled, desolated and destroyed. When he regains consciousness, trembling to his senses and returning to his body, to the person who must get up shortly and go about his day, he discovers in himself a miraculous new capacity: the ability to remember.

For him, remembering is no longer what it was, unforeseen or willful recollections of this thing or that. Now, rather, it is laden with a painful compulsion to remember all the years, shallow and fallow, and all the places he has inhabited over the span of those years. He casts the net of memory, flings it over himself and draws himself, predator and prey in one, over the thresholds of time and place to see who he was and who he has become.

Because until now, he has lived simply from one day to the next, trying something new each day, unsuspecting and carefree. He has seen for himself so many possibilities and thought, for example, that he had the potential to become almost anything: a great man, a beacon, a paragon of philosophical insight.

Or an able man of action: he saw himself building bridges, laying roads; he saw himself traversing the terrain, surveying the land in sweat-soaked khakis, spooning thick soup from a tin can, drinking schnapps with the workers, taciturn. He never knew himself to be a man of many words.

Or a revolutionary setting fire to the rotten wooden planks of society; he saw himself filled with ardor and eloquence, inclined to take every risk. He aroused enthusiasm, served time in prison, suffered, faltered and rose to his first victory.

Or an idle lover of leisure born of wisdom—seeking every pleasure and nothing but pleasure in music, books, in ancient manuscripts, faraway countries, leaning against the columns. He had, after all, but one life to live, but one self to fritter away, craving for happiness and beauty, made for ecstasy and addicted to all that glitters!

So, for years he wasted his time on the most extreme thoughts and fantastic plans, and, because he was nothing if not young and healthy, because he still seemed to have so much time, he accepted every passing job. He tutored school children in exchange for a hot meal, sold newspapers, shoveled snow for five shillings an hour while studying pre-Socratic philosophy. He couldn't afford to be choosy, accepted an internship at some company, then quit when he landed a job at a newspaper; they had him writing reports about a new dental drill, about research into twins, about the restoration of St. Stephen's Cathedral in Vienna. Then one day, without a penny in his pocket, he embarked on a trip, hitching rides and using addresses from some guy he barely knew who had obtained them from a third party, stayed here and there, then continued on his way. He hitchhiked through Europe, but then—following a sudden change of heart—turned back and began preparing for tests that would lead to a practical vocation. He would not, however, see this as his final aim in life, but he passed all the tests. At every opportunity, he said yes—to a friendship, a love affair, to the most preposterous proposal, and he did it all on a lark, on a trial-basis. The world seemed to him terminable; he himself terminable.

Never, not even for a moment, had he feared that the curtain might rise as it did now on his thirtieth year, that his cue might come and he might have to demonstrate all he was capable of thinking and doing, that he might have to finally concede to what really mattered to him. Never had he imagined that, of the thousand-and-one possibilities, a thousand had perhaps already been squandered and let slip—or that he might have to let them slip because only one was right for him.

He never thought....

He never feared anything.

Now he knows that he too has fallen into the trap.

This year began with a rainy June. He used to be in love with this month—the month of his birth—in love with early summer, with his astrological sign, with the promise of warmth and with the positive influences of the stars' constellations.

He's no longer in love with his sign.

And it will be a warm July.

He is overcome by restlessness. He's just *got* to pack his bags, terminate the lease on his room, his surroundings, his past. It's not just that he needs to *get* away, he needs to go away. He has to be free this year, give up everything, change places, change his own four walls and the people around him. He needs to pay off old debts, register his departure with the police, bid farewell to a patron and to his drinking buddies—so he can be free and clear of everything. He has to go to Rome, back to where he felt freest, where he'd had his awakening so many years ago—the opening of his eyes, as if from sleep, the awakening of joy, of his measures and his morals.

His room is already cleared out, but he doesn't know what to do with some of the things still lying around: books, pictures, brochures from coastal landscapes, city maps and a small reproduction from who knows where. It is a painting by Puvis de Chavannes, called *'L'Espérance'* where Hope is perched upon a white drape, chaste and squared, with a branch blossoming timidly in her hand. In the background, there is a smattering of black crosses; in the distance—solid and statuary—a ruin; hovering above Hope—a dusky pink strip of sky, for it is evening, it is late and night is closing in. Although night is not in the picture—it is sure to come! It is sure to break out over this picture of Hope and even over the hopes of childhood and blacken this branch till it withers.

But this is just a picture. He throws it away.

Then there is still a fine silk scarf lying torn and perfumed in dust. A few shells. Stones he picked up when he wasn't roaming the countryside alone. A dried rose that he hadn't delivered while it was still fresh. Letters beginning with "Dearest," "My dearest," "Dear, my one and only dear." "Alas." And they are consumed by the fire of one hasty "Alas." It curls and crumbles their thin ashen skin. He burns the letters—all of them.

He'll break away from all the people around him—if possible, without turning to others. He cannot live among people anymore. They paralyze him; they have fashioned him to suit whatever they saw fit. As soon as a person has been in the same place for a while, he begins circulating in too many different guises, images drawn from hearsay, and increasingly, he loses the right to appeal to his own authority. That is why he wants to show his real face from now on and forever. Here, where he has been settled for so long, he can't even begin, but he will when he gets to the place where he is free.

He arrives in Rome and meets the person he had been and had left to the others back then. The person he used to be is imposed upon him like a straitjacket. He thrashes, lashes out, struggling in self-defense, until finally he comes to grips and quiets down. No one allows him any freedom because when he was here in his younger days he had taken the liberty of being a completely different person.

Never and nowhere will he ever be able to free himself and begin anew. Not at this rate. So he decides to wait and see.

He runs into Moll again. Moll, always in need of help. Moll, ye of little faith in mankind; Moll, always hell-bent on testing your limits; Moll, whom he'd lent all his money a long time ago; Moll, who also knew Elena…Moll, in the money now, doesn't repay the loan, so their relations are strained and Moll is easily offended; Moll, whom he had introduced to all his friends in his day; Moll, for whom he had opened every door because Moll had been a friend in need; Moll had since established his roost all over the place and had ruined his reputation with carefully measured stories told second-hand and laced with slightly fraudulent distortions. Moll calls him every day and shows up wherever he goes. Moll frets over him, wheedles confessions from him under false pretenses, then turns around and tells the first person he meets on the street corner, and still calls himself his friend. Even when Moll isn't there, his shadow looms, more gargantuan and threatening in his thoughts and imagination. Moll without end. Moll's terror. But in reality Moll is much smaller than that, he is just incredibly adept at exacting revenge—all the more so because Moll knows he is somewhat in his debt.

This year gets off to a bad start. He comes to realize the way these dirty little tricks can spread and their potential to hit him, that he has in fact often come so close, but this time they descend upon him full force and suffocate him. And suddenly it dawns on him that this dirty little trick will have a long history; it will burgeon and pervade his entire life. Its bitterness will wear away at him again and again, burn him like acid just when he is least prepared. He wasn't prepared for Moll.

But he will have to prepare himself for many Molls—he already knows too many of them here and there; it is only now in his encounter with this particular Moll that he realizes Moll is but one of many.

This year, he will go crazy wondering whether he has ever had any friends, whether he's ever been loved. A lightning bolt illuminates all his commitments, all his circumstances, his farewells, leaving him feeling deceived and betrayed.

He runs into Elena again. Elena, who makes

clear to him that she has forgiven him. He tries to be grateful. She herself barely comprehends the fact that she had blackmailed and threatened him, that she had completely lost her senses in her rage and sought to destroy his very existence—and yet it was only a few years ago. She is open to friendship, amiable, and speaks intelligently, indulgent, nostalgic—for she is married now. They had separated briefly at the time and he had, as he was the first to admit, betrayed her in the basest of ways. He is reluctant to think about the rest of the story: her revenge, his flight, his losses, the subsequent conciliations, shame, even regret, and the courtship renewed. Now she has a child, but when he unsuspectingly asks her about that, she admits—hesitant and smiling—that she had already gotten pregnant while they were separated. She seems saddened for a moment, but no longer. He is amazed by her calm, her composure. Callous and emotionless, he thinks that her anger, then, was merely feigned, that she had no justification for her self-righteousness, no basis for the blackmail he had simply acquiesced to because he had considered himself the only one at fault. (Until now, he'd thought it was only *after* his departure that she'd turned to someone else, perhaps in order to forget him). All this time, he thought he was to blame and she just let him believe in his own guilt. Quietly and emphatically, he exhales, expelling the guilt, thinking: I was ill-advised in my despair. But, I'm even more ill-advised now that I've been set straight. I'm freezing. I would rather have retained my own guilt.

There is destruction underway. I'll be lucky if this year doesn't kill me. I could visit the Etruscan tombs, drive out to the Campagna for a spell, roam aimlessly about.

Rome is big. Rome is beautiful. But it would be impossible to live here again. Here, like everywhere else, friends mingle with pseudo-friends and your friend Moll cannot stand your other friend Moll and both of them are relentless in their treatment of a third friend named Moll. From all sides, you are under fire, pressed up against the wall where you seek shelter. Even though you often feel wanted and needed, even though you sometimes manage to feel affection for others and to need them, all the gestures are awkward and you cannot bear to go around anymore with these constant headaches; even they are at once construed as deliberate displays of offense. You can't leave a single letter unanswered without being charged with arrogance and indolence. You can't even arrive late for a date anymore without provoking outrage.

But where did it all begin? Hadn't this oppression, this derogation of his person by the networks of friends and foes already set in years ago, shortly after he had gotten so caught up in society's dealings and disputes? Hadn't he, in his cowardice, begun cultivating a double life since then, a multiple life, just so he could go on living at all? Wasn't he really deceiving everyone and anyone and often even himself? He had been blessed by birth with a predisposition toward friendship, toward trust. His greatest longing had always been the barbarian desire for inequality, highest reason and insight. All he had gained from experience was the knowledge that people would trespass against you and that you would yourself trespass against them and that there are moments when you would turn gray with insult and injury—that everyone is insulted and injured to death by others. And that everyone is afraid of death which is the only escape from the abominable insult and injury that life is.

August! There they were: days made of steel that had been brought to boil in the forge. Time droned on.

The beaches were besieged by bodies and the sea no longer charged the shores with its armies of waves but feigned exhaustion instead—deep and blue.

On the grill, in the sand, roasted, inflamed: highly perishable human flesh. On the shore of the sea, in the dunes: the flesh.

He was frightened by the way summer had exhausted itself. Because that meant fall was soon to come. The month of August was full of panic, full of the compulsion to take the reins and live life in the fast lane.

In the dunes, all the women eagerly fell into his arms—behind the cliffs, in the bath house cubicles, in cars parked in the shade of pine trees; even in the city, behind Persian blinds lowered for the afternoon, they surrendered themselves in half-sleep or, an hour later, got their high heels stuck in the yielding asphalt of the stagnant street on the Corso and, seeking support, reached for any outstretched arm.

Not a word was spoken that summer. Not a name uttered.

He commuted back and forth between the sea and the city, between light bodies and dark; from one gluttonous moment to the next, between the sun's sprays and the night's shore, he was taken—hide and hair—by summer. And the sun rolled up more quickly each morning and plunged ever earlier before his insatiable eyes into the sea.

He prayed to the earth and the sea and the sun that plagued him so dreadfully at the moment. The melons ripened; he dissected and devoured them. He was dying of thirst.

He loved a billion women, all at the same time and indiscriminately.

Who am I then, in golden September, when I strip myself of all they have made of me? Who am I when the clouds take flight!

The spirit my flesh houses is an even bigger swindler than its self-righteous keeper. Meeting that spirit is what I need fear most. Because nothing that I think has anything to do with me. Each of my thoughts is nothing more than the germination of foreign seeds. I am not capable of thinking anything that has ever moved me and I think things that have not moved me in the least.

I think in political terms, in social terms, and in terms of a couple other categories, and now and then my thoughts are solitary and futile, but I always think within a game with established rules and only perhaps once thought of changing those rules. But not of changing the game itself. Never!

"I", this bundle of reflexes and a well-trained will of its own, this "I"—nourished by history's rubbish heap, by scraps of desire and instinct, this "I" with one foot in the wilderness and the other on the main street headed for eternal civilization. This *impenetrable "I"*, an amalgam of materials, matted together in a cloak of nepotism and corruption, insoluble, yet readily extinguished by one blow to the back of the head. A silenced "I"—an *"I" born of silence.*

Why have I sought destruction all summer long in this intoxication or in intoxication's steady increase? Only to avoid facing the fact that I am but an instrument that someone abandoned a long time ago after using it to strike a few chords, chords I vary helplessly in the mad attempt to produce a piece of music that bears my signature. My signature! As though anything depended on something bearing my signature! Lightning has struck trees and split them. Men have been stricken by madness and torn apart by it. Swarms of locusts have befallen the fields and left trails of devastation in their ravenous wake. Floods have laid hills to waste and raging rivers ravished the precipice. Earthquakes have been without respite. *Those* things alone bear signatures!

Had I not delved into the books, into stories and legends, into the papers and the news, had not everything that is communicable ripened within me, then I would be nothing, a collection of incoherent incidents. (And maybe that would be good because perhaps then something new would occur to me!) The fact that I am able to see, to hear, I don't deserve that, but my feelings, these I truly deserve—those herons crossing the white sands, nocturnal wanderers, hungry vagabonds who take my heart as their highway. I wish I could call out to all those who believe in the singularity of their own minds and the hard currency of their own thoughts: remain steadfast in faith! But they have been withdrawn from circulation, these coins you clink together, you just don't know it yet. Put them out of commission together with the skulls and crossbones and the eagles imprinted there. Admit that it's all over for Greece and the land of Buddha, for the Enlightenment and alchemy. Admit that you are merely inhabiting a land furnished by the ancients, that you are merely renting your opinions and the images of your world are tenured by lease. Admit that when you really pay with your life, you only do so on the far side of the barricade, after you've bid farewell to all that you cherish—on the landing strips, at the airbases—and it is only from there that you embark on a path of your own and your own journey from one imaginary station to another, travelers just passing through, for whom arrival is beside the point!

Experimental flight attempt! Another experiment in love! There is an enormous uncharted world at the disposal of your despair—go ahead, let goods and kindred go!

Feigned sleep, shadowy, winged merriment hovering above the chasms. When one human being no longer entwines the other, but lets him go, quietly and on his own, when the human octopus retracts its tentacles and no longer engulfs its neighbor…

Humanity: the ability to maintain one's distance.

Keep your distance from me, or I'll die, or commit murder, or suicide. Stand back, in the name of God!

I am outraged, with a wrath that has no beginning and no end. My rage dates back to an early ice age and now it is turning against this age of ice…Because if the world is going to end—and everyone says it, believers, nonbelievers, scientists and prophets alike: it will one day come to an end—then why not before it stops rotating altogether or before the big bang or Judgment Day? Why not let it end in wrath inspired by discerning judgment? Why shouldn't this race be able to conduct itself morally and end it all? Put an end to sainthood, to infertile fertility, to true love between people. There would, incidentally, be nothing to speak against it.

He awoke with increasing difficulty each morning. He blinked in the dim light, turned away, buried his head in his pillow. He begged for more sleep. Come, beautiful fall. In this October of last roses…

There is, however, an island someone once told him about—in the Aegean Sea, where there are only flowers and lions of stone; the same flowers that blossom unpretentious and briefly here come into bloom twice a year there, big and brilliant. The scarcity of soil, the repellent rocks incite them. Impoverishment drives them into the arms of beauty.

He generally slept until late afternoon and helped himself get through the evenings with his hobbies. By sleeping in like this, he abandoned more and more of his misgivings and slept himself to strength. Suddenly, time no longer seemed precious, nothing to waste or while away. Nor did he feel the need to do anything in particular in order to be satisfied; there was no wish or ambition he felt the need to satisfy in order to go on living.

What was peculiar about this waning year was the stinginess of light. Even the sunny days were clad in gray.

He always went now to the small squares, to the ghetto or to the coachman's cafés in Trastevere, where he drank his Campari slowly, day after day at the same time. He picked up habits, nursed them, even the slightest of the slight. He took pleasure in looking upon these, his own indurations. On the telephone he often said: Sorry, love, I can't, not today. Maybe next week.—The following week, he disconnected the phone. Even in his letters he stopped offering any promises or explanations. He had spent so many useless hours with others, and even though he wasn't making use of the hours now, still, he was bending them to suit himself, taking in their scent. He came to enjoy time; its taste was pure and good. He wanted to withdraw entirely into himself. But no one noticed or no one wanted to believe it was true. In the minds of everyone around him, it seemed as though he were as extravagant as ever—a real Johnny-on-the-spot—and sometimes he ran into his own shadow in the city, where he greeted it, reticent, because he recognized it from before. His shadow was not a thing of today. Today he was a different person. He felt good to be alone, he had no more demands to make, had dismantled the house of desire, abandoned all his hopes and became simpler day by day. He began thinking of the world in more deferent terms. He sought a sense of duty, wanted to be of service.

Plant a tree. Father a child.

Was that modest enough? Was that simple enough?

If he were to look for a plot of land and a wife—and he knew people who had, in all modesty, done just that—then he could leave the house at eight in the morning and go to his job where he would occupy a place in the social machinery, taking advantage of payment by installments for furniture and federal tax allowances for dependent children. He could see the fruits of his education rewarded monthly in banknotes and use them to plan a relaxing weekend for himself and his family. He could stimulate the circle, circulate within it.

That would appeal to him. Especially the part about planting a tree. Season for season, he could watch the way it took on rings and could let his children climb it. He would relish the harvests. Apples. Even though he doesn't even like eating apples, he insists on an apple tree. And having a son—that would be in line with his tastes even though when he sees children it makes no difference to him what sex they are. The son would in turn have his own children—sons.

But a harvest so distant, outside in the garden,

one that others would reap, far off in the future at a time when he would no longer be alive! What a horrific thought! And here is a whole planet full of trees and children, scraggly, stunted trees, starving children, and no amount of assistance will suffice in helping them to a dignified existence. Nurse a wild tree, take on the care of these children, do it, if you can, prevent just one tree from being felled and then let's see what you have to say!

Hope: I hope nothing happens the way I had hoped for it to happen.

I hope against hope that, should I ever be blessed with a tree and a child, it comes at a time when I have lost every hope of its occurrence and every ounce of modesty. Only then would I be prepared to tend to both of them properly and with a sense of purpose; only then would I be able to leave them in the hour of my death.

But I am alive now. I'm alive! That is an unshakeable fact of life.

Once, when he was barely twenty years old, he had thought everything through to its ultimate end in the Viennese National Library and had come to realize that he was truly alive. He was bent over books like a drowning victim, and thinking, there amidst the little green lamps burning and the readers slinking stealthily about in soft-soled shoes, quietly coughing, quietly turning the pages as though they were afraid of waking the dead dwelling between the book covers. He was *thinking*—as if anyone knew what that actually meant! He can still remember precisely the moment when he pursued a certain epistemological problem and all the concepts were ready at hand in his head. And while *thinking* and *thinking*, soaring higher and higher as though on a swing without getting dizzy and, just as he gave the swing the most marvelous push, he felt himself hit a ceiling that he just had to burst through. He was gripped by a feeling of happiness he had never known before because in that moment he was on the verge of understanding something that related to everything, even to the last things. The breakthrough would come with his very next thought! Then it happened. He was struck and shaken by a blow to the inside of his skull; a pain arose and drew him to a halt—his thinking slowed, he became confused and leapt from the swing. He had overstepped his capacity to think or perhaps had reached the point where no one could go on thinking. Something began to click at the crest of his head, on the roof of his skull; it was a frightening click that didn't stop for several seconds. He thought he had lost his mind and clutched his book in his hands. He let his head sink forward and closed his eyes, fainting, yet fully conscious.

He was at wits' end.

He was more at wits' end than he had ever been with a woman or when all the circuits in his brain had been momentarily interrupted and he'd hoped for his own destruction, when he felt he was no longer an individual member but had become just a category of the species. Because what was destroyed here in this grand old hall by the light of the little green lamps in the solitary solemnity of letters being savored and swallowed was a being that had elevated itself to the highest heights, a winged entity that sought the source of light in the dusky blue corridors and, to be precise, a human being no longer an adversary but a potential accessory to creation. He was destroyed as a potential accessory to the crime and from then on would never again be capable of climbing to such heights and touching the logic that holds the world suspended in its place.

He knew he'd been dismissed, incapacitated, and from that hour on, science and scholarship were a torment to him, because he had spent himself on them, because he had gone too far and been destroyed in the process. All that was left for him to do was to learn another thing or two, to become a stooge and keep his mind agile, but he had no interest in that. He would have gladly assumed a post somewhere on the periphery where he could gaze over the fence and from there, reflect on himself and the world and its language and every condition. He would have gladly returned with a new language, one that would have sufficed to express the secret he had discovered.

And so it was that it was all for naught. He was alive, yes, he was alive, he felt alive for the first time in his life. But now he realized he had been living in a prison, that he would have to make himself at home there, that he would soon fly into a frenzy and be forced to speak this rogue language—the only one at his disposal—so he wouldn't feel so forsaken. He would have to face the music and, on his last dying day, appear as a profile in courage or in cowardice, either hold his tongue, or abhor and address God himself in a rage—God, whom he couldn't find here and who barred his admittance there. Because if He had anything to do with this world, with this language, then He was no God. God cannot exist in this madness, He cannot reside here, He can only have something to do with the fact that this madness exists, that there is this madness and that there is no end to this madness!

In winter of the same year, he went to the mountains with Leni, to the Rax on that weekend—oh yes, he remembers it well. Only now does he remember exactly. They were freezing, shivering, clinging to one another in fright on that stormy night. They had passed the shabby, threadbare blanket back and forth, then torn it away from each other in half-sleep. He had gone to see Moll just before and had confided in him. He'd run to Moll because he didn't know where else to turn, he didn't have a clue about this stuff, didn't know any doctor he could ask, didn't have a clue about himself and Leni, or about women in general. Leni was so young, he was so young, and all the savvy he flaunted to try and impress her stemmed from Moll who did have a clue, or who at least pretended to have a clue. It was Moll who had procured the pills he had ordered Leni to swallow that night in the ski lodge. He had discussed it all with Moll, and, as miserable as he was, relished the envy it spurned in Moll. (A virgin, now that's something that has yet to cross my path in this city, do tell, my friend, do tell!) He had been drinking with Moll and, in his drunken stupor, had breathed in Moll's views. (Make sure you call it quits in time. There is only one thing to do. Extricate yourself from the affair. Think about the future. About the millstone around your neck.) But, in that snowy night, he was horrified by himself, by Moll, by Leni, whom he didn't even want to touch now that he knew what lay in store for her. Never again would he want to so much as touch this angular, bone-white body, this odorless girl of a woman, and so he got up in the middle of the night and went downstairs to the guest room, where he sat at an empty table feeling sorry for himself until suddenly he was no longer alone, until the two blond skiers came and joined him at the table, until he was drunk and went upstairs with the two of them, bringing up the rear like a condemned man, to the same floor of the building where Leni lay awake crying or was crying in her sleep. When he was in the room with the two girls and heard himself laughing with them, everything seemed so simple and easy. Everything was there for him, he could demand everything; it was so easy, he just hadn't yet found the right way to put it in perspective, but he would find it, any minute now and he would have it forever from that moment on. He felt privy to the secret of ease, of tawdriness and of deprived depravity. Even before he had begun kissing one of the girls, he'd given up on Leni. Even before he had overcome the remnant of resistance and shame and ran his hands through the other one's hair, he had made short work of his fear. But then he paid dearly since he couldn't close his ears to the shrill words and confused stammering surrounding him. There was no turning back and he couldn't close his eyes, paid with his eyes the price for everything he'd had the privilege of seeing and was yet to see during those nights of burning the midnight oil. The next morning, Leni was gone. When he returned to Vienna, he holed himself up at home for a couple of days; he did not go to see her—he never went back to see her and never heard from her again. It wasn't until years later that he again set foot in the building in the Third District where she had lived; but she was no longer there. Even now, he didn't have the nerve to inquire as to her whereabouts, and he would have left immediately, would have fled the scene if she had still been living there. Sometimes, when the hobgoblins of his mind were active, he saw her floating down the Danube with a bloated face or pushing a child in a stroller through the city's central park (and on days like that, he avoided the park), or he envisioned her childless—because, of course, there was no way that the child could have been alive—standing as a sales clerk in some store, asking, even before she saw him, if there was anything she could help him find. He also imagined her happily married to some sales representative in the province. But he never saw her again. And he buried it so deeply within himself that it only rarely crept to mind—the image of the snowy night, of the storm, the snow drifts heaped to the sills of the little cabin windows, the light that had burned above three intertwined bodies and that giddy laughter, those cackling giggles and that blond hair.

When for want of a nail even God's kingdom has been lost, when someone has fallen into the grave he dug for another, when all the proverbs have come true and all the prophecies about the changing of the sun and moon have been fulfilled—in a word, when the account has been settled, momentarily at least, and when everything slated to fly like dust to the wind is in flight, then he is compelled to shake his head and wonder what kind of age he is living in.

Like everyone else, he is ill-prepared for this; he knows but a slight fraction of it all and of course, everyone only knows the slightest fraction of what is going on.

He happens to know there are robots that do not err and he knows a streetcar driver who once acted in err with regard to the departure time and the right of way. Perhaps even stars and comets are wont to err when too much gets in their way, confused by diffusion and fatigue, and because they are distracted by the old poetic diction of their light.

He would rather not be up there on top, but he doesn't mind knowing there is something beyond the top because up there is the same thing as down below—that is, everything goes on all around us and there is no stopping it. No one can stop it. You cannot stop your thoughts nor the tools used to expand them. And it makes no difference whether you soar through space to the left or to the right because everything is in flight, even the earth, and if even flight itself is in flight, all the better that everything is in flight and constantly turning, that way you know how much it is turning and that there is nothing to hold on to, not in the star-spangled sky up above…

But deep within yourself, where you rarely come to life and just barely soar along, where there is nothing to hold on to either, but there is a dauntingly tenacious hodgepodge of old questions that have nothing to do with flying nor with launching pads, where you can barely jerk the rudder in reverse and where the moral to the whole of history is made because there is no moral to the story where you seek the morality of morals and the account does not add up

Where someone digs a grave and falls into it himself, where you cling and writhe and keep clinging and can't go on

Because no light has gone on in your head (and what good is it to you then to know all there is to know about the speed of light?), because no light goes on in your head to illuminate the world and yourself and the whole spectrum of life, of all the undead and the dead

Because there is nothing but martyrdom here, because you cannot seem to find the right words in this rogue language and cannot solve the world's problems

The only problem you are able to solve is the equation of the world itself

Even the world is an equation that can be solved to make gold equal gold and dregs equal dregs

But nothing equals what is within you and nothing equals the world inside you

If you could give that up, if you could step away from your old familiar anxieties about good and evil and quit prodding the hodgepodge of old questions, if only you had the courage to step into progress

Not only in the progression from gas lighting to

electricity, from hot air balloon to rocket (subaltern advancements)

If you were to give up on Man, the old Man, and adopt a new one

Then, when the world refused to budge between man and woman, as it does now, between truth and lies, today's truth and today's lies

If you could just say to hell with all that

If you could trash the account you value so much and re-calculate it with the intent of calling yourself to account for it

If you were a pilot and could fly into the curves without wavering, if you could simply report the news, not the whole of history together, your (his)story and that of another and yet a third party

Then, if you were still whole, no longer wounded, outraged, craving purity and vengeance

If you quit believing in fairy tales and no longer feared the dark

If you need not dare take any risks nor to win or lose, and instead simply made things happen

Make it happen, get a handhold on that higher order, think orderly thoughts, if you could place yourself in order, in a balanced account, boundless order would go on like a light

Then, when you are no longer convinced that things must be better "in light of the circumstances," that the rich should no longer be rich and the poor no longer poor, that the innocent should no longer be condemned and that the guilty should be tried

When you have lost the need to comfort and to do good deeds and no longer demand comfort or help

When both compassion and suffering have gone to hell and even hell has gone to hell, then!

Only then, when the world has been grasped in the only place it can be grasped, where the secret of its revolution is revealed, where it is still chaste and has not yet been deflowered or defiled, where the saints have not spoken on its behalf and the criminals have not shed a drop of blood

When a new status has risen

When not a soul alive would think of acceding the succession

When at last the everlasting arrives

Then

Then get up again and tear the old ignominious

order to shreds. Then change yourself so that the world will change, so that the direction changes, at long last! Then fall in line!

When he enters his thirtieth year and winter arrives, when November and December are braced together by a bracket of ice and his heart shivers, his misery puts him to sleep. He flees into sleep, flees backward into awakening, flees at home and on the road, wanders through the desolate ruins of small towns and cannot turn a single doorknob, cannot send his regards to anyone because he doesn't want to be seen or spoken to. Like an onion, like a root in the ground, he would like to crawl beneath the earth's surface where it has retained its warmth. He would like to go into hibernation with his thoughts and feelings. To keep his shrinking mouth shut. He wishes that all he has said, all the insults and all the promises he has ever issued would be declared null and void, that everyone would forget them and forget him.

But no sooner has he settled comfortably into silence, no sooner has he envisioned himself safely cocooned, than he discovers he was wrong. A cold, wet wind blows in and sweeps his lack of expectations around the bend, to a flower vendor's stand selling funeral wreaths and evergreen. And suddenly, he is holding snowdrops in his hand, things he hadn't wanted to buy—he had wanted to go empty-handed! The snowdrops' bells begin tolling, wild and silent, and he goes to the place where his doom awaits him. He is filled with anticipation, and filled as never before with expectation and the desire for deliverance he has been waiting for all these years.

Only now, after he has calmed down and thanked his lucky stars, after he has survived every imaginable experience, does unimaginable love come to him. With the rites of death and the ritual worship of pain that takes a new turn every day.

From this moment on, even before the flowers reached the woman who would receive them, he was no longer his own master; he was, rather, in surrender, damned, and his flesh pulled him along straight into purgatory. He went to hell for a week and, after the first break-up and attempt at reconciliation, he was shot to hell for yet another week. There was no room for sympathy, blessings, or satisfaction. She wasn't a woman who looked like this or like that, who was this kind of woman or that; he couldn't speak her name because she had none—like happiness itself—happiness that ruthlessly wore him down. He was in a state, beside himself, where he couldn't sense the taste of a mouth, where not a single gesture left time for anything, where love became an act of vengeance for every thing that was bearable in the world. Love was unbearable. It expected nothing, demanded nothing and yielded nothing in return. It didn't let itself be fenced in, tended to and sown with the seeds of emotion, but rather overstepped the boundaries and trampled every emotion to the ground.

He had never been without feeling, without complications, and now, for the first time, he was empty, wrung out, and all that was left was a profound sense of gratification in the way he felt a wave pick him up in brief intervals and throw him against the cliff, only to sweep him out again.

He was in love. He was free, robbed of all his personal idiosyncrasies, his thoughts and his goals in this catastrophe where things were neither good or bad nor right and wrong, and he was sure there was no way to proceed and no way out—at least none that could be called a "way".

While the others anywhere and everywhere else were at work, concerned with some specific task, he was just perfectly in love. That required more energy than living and working. The seconds burned like coals, time turned into the blackened trail left in their wake and he emerged, from one second to the next, ever more vividly, an entity made of sheer determination in whom but one element prevailed.

He packed his bags because instinctively he knew that even this first hour of love had been too much, and he mustered his last ounce of strength to seek refuge in goodbyes. He wrote three letters. In the first, he blamed himself for his failings; in the second he blamed his lover, and in the third, he refrained entirely from seeking to place blame, and left his address. "Please write me care of general delivery in Naples, in Brindisi, in Athens, Constantinople…"

But he didn't get far. It occurred to him that everything would fall apart with his departure; he didn't have much money left, had spent the last of it to pay the rent on his apartment in advance so that he could hold on to it—to have, in spite of everything, one place he could hold on to. He loitered around the harbor in Brindisi, pawning off all his worldly goods but two suits, and went in search of work on the black market. But he was unfit for that kind of work and the dangers he could get himself into now. He didn't know what to do next, he slept under the stars for two nights, began fearing the police, fearing the filth, the misery and demise. Yes, he would go under. Then he wrote a fourth letter: "I have two suits left, both of which need ironing, my two pipes and the lighter you gave me. There is no lighter fluid left. But, if you don't want to see me by summertime, if you can't break up with N. before summer comes…"

Before summer comes!

"And if you still don't know by then with whom and why and what for, my God…But even if you knew, perhaps I would not, and I'd be in an even sorrier state of mind. No matter which way I look, I can't see any way out. We shouldn't have survived it."

Before summer comes! By then he would have atoned for this year and everything he may have been able to make of the stuff of these thirty years promised to be altogether commonplace. Oh, but must we really grow old, ugly, wrinkled and senile, narrow-minded and tolerant in order to fulfill our own destiny? Nothing against the elderly, he said to himself, it won't be long before I am an old man myself, and even now, I shudder at the thought of what the passing years is sure to bring upon me. Soon. But now, I am still holding my own, still refusing to believe that this light can be extinguished, the shining light of eternal youth. But, when it started flickering with increasing shortness of breath and hunger and all his attempts to find work or to gain passage on a ship—all these nonsensical ventures that would have been more becoming of a younger person or a crazy man—had failed, he wrote home. He almost wrote the truth and asked his father for help for the first time in his life. He was feeling so miserable because he was thirty years old and, in the past, had always managed to get by somehow. Never had he been so listless and helpless. He admitted his own collapse, broke down and asked for money. Never had he received money so quickly. Barely had he recovered from the breakneck bailout before he was on his way back. He returned via Venice.

He arrived there late in the evening and headed

toward the Piazza San Marco. The stage was empty. The spectators had been swept from their seats. The sea had surpassed the sky, the lagoons were aflame with flares from the flambeaus and lanterns that had flung their light upon the water.

Light, lucid light, far removed from the shady characters. He flitted through like a phantom. From the very beginning, he had been driven to seek shelter in splendor, in spectatorship, and, when he came to rest, watching, he would say to himself: How splendid! That is simply splendid, splendid, it is splendid. Let it always be this splendid and let me fall into ruin if I must for splendor's sake and what I mean by that is, for the splendorous, for this "far surpassing…," for this spectacular success. I know of no paradise I would like to enter after all that has been. But my paradise is wherever splendor prevails.

I promise not to dwell on it, because splendor is suspect, no longer a shelter, and the pains are already on another course.

He didn't used to know how to travel. He boarded trains with a throbbing in his heart and little money in his pocket. He always arrived in cities at night, when throngs of circumspect strangers had long since snatched up all the hotel rooms for themselves and his friends were already asleep. Once he walked around all night long because he couldn't find a bed. When he sailed on ships, the throbbing in his heart was even worse, and on airplanes, the sheer thrill of it took his breath away. This time, though, he had read the train schedule, had counted his new bags and hired a porter. He had reserved a seat and brought along something to read. He knew where he wanted to change trains and this time he didn't run out of money even before leaving the platform where he'd stopped for coffee. He traveled like a man of distinction and remained so cool and collected that no one could tell what he had planned. He was planning to put an end to this vagrant life. He wanted to turn around. He went back to the city he had loved most and where he'd had to pay taxes, tuition, and the price of lessons learned the hard way, among other things. He went to Vienna—still, he hesitated to speak in terms of "home."

He lay down in the compartment with his head resting in contemplation on his rolled up overcoat.

He would roll along the tracks through Europe on this camp he'd pitched, he would be startled from sleep by dreams, would freeze when he approached familiar mountain ranges, doze off, tormented by memories. He wanted to return to the place where it all began because he had seen enough of what was called "the world."

He found lodging at a little hotel in the city center near the post office. He had never stayed at a hotel in Vienna. He had been a sub-letter, with or without bathroom privileges, with or without telephone privileges. Staying with relatives, with a single nurse living alone who could barely stand the smell of his tobacco, with the widow of some army general whose cats and cacti he had to care for when she went off to some health resort.

For two days, he was so indecisive that he didn't dare call anyone. No one was expecting him; there were a few people he hadn't written for far too long, still others who had never answered his letters. He suddenly felt his return was impossibly preposterous for many reasons. He had as much right to come back as a dead man. No one is allowed to continue where he left off. There is no one, he thought, no one who is still counting on me. He went out to eat, to a restaurant he had never dared frequent before, he read the menu with more ease than he would anywhere else; he thought he would be moved by the name of every specialty dish he'd been missing for so long, but he wasn't. He recognized the old peal of bells chiming at noon he had missed so much. A deathly silence was left within him. He happened upon acquaintances along the Graben, ran into more acquaintances, and, encouraged by these momentous coincidences, he fell in with everyone—overly eager and awkward. Unsure of himself, he began telling about his life elsewhere, then quickly broke off because it dawned on him that the others considered the life he'd led elsewhere a betrayal that was better kept to himself.

He stopped at a bookstore and bought himself a guide to the city whose every scent he knew and about which he knew little that was worth knowing. He opened the book, sat down with it on a rain-soaked bench in the city's central park, but then, fearing he might freeze to the bench, following the asterisks, he went to the grand palace with the Collection of Arms and Armor and to the Museum of

Art History, to the Gloriette and to the churches with the baroque angels. That evening, at sunset, he hiked up Kahlenberg mountain and looked down at the city from an observation point recommended by the travel guide. He covered his eyes with his hand, thinking: This is simply not possible! It is not possible that I once knew this city. Not like this.

The next day, he met some friends. He had absolutely no idea what they were talking about, but he was familiar with all the names they mentioned, and even though he couldn't quite picture the faces behind them—he knew them all. The labels had stuck. He nodded to confirm everything he heard, yet it seemed to him so unreal that all this had transpired: an old girlfriend's new children, career changes, corruption, scandals, premieres, love affairs, business dealings.

(My plan: arriving!)

So he runs into Moll again, the wonder boy, the genius Moll, who had dazzled everyone by the age of twenty, the pure intellect Moll who had, in his day, given his highly acclaimed studies on socio-economic decay and cultural crisis to the editor of a Christian publication in exchange for a bread-and-butter pittance. Moll has since turned ironic and takes in the highest of fees, rushing from convention to convention; Moll, the one people poke fun at and who even pokes fun at himself; Moll, who now lives off the fat of former fortune at roundtable discussions and considers the world unworthy of a single new idea. Moll, meeting with the French ambassador in the evening and, the next day, serving on the board at a conference; Moll, still one of the youngest in the bunch, slippery as an eel, expounding opinions but having none of his own; Moll, always living sunny-side up; Moll, who despises any dubious character, and yet who is among the most dubious of characters himself...Moll advises him: "Get on board with us." (The rogue language perfected!) Moll and his superiority complex, Moll who has since developed a taste for everything and everyone he would have despised years ago. Moll's handshake, reserved, yet firm. *"Allora,* bye bye. Take care of yourself. See you then. Think it over. Write if you need anything."

He says goodbye to Moll, returning the reserved handshake with reserve, and goes back to his favorite old café. The headwaiter is taken aback, recognizes him, the charming, melancholy little man. And this time he doesn't have to talk, nor shake hands or take any pains; he is spared the clichés, a smile will suffice: they smile at each other foolishly, two men who have seen a great deal pass them by in their day: years, people, good fortune and bad, and everything the old man could hope to express—joy, remembrance—he shows him by placing in front of him precisely the same newspapers that he used to request and read.

He is obliged to reach for the stack of papers, he owes the old man that much; and he is glad to be in his debt. Here, finally, a debt he is glad to pay without begrudging it.

He begins reading at random, the headlines, local news, culture, miscellany, the sports section. The date is irrelevant, he could just as easily have exchanged this paper for one issued five years ago, he is only reading the tone of voice, the unmistakable print, the composition and layout. He knows like he knows nothing else what should be discussed in the upper left and the lower right-hand sections, what is considered good and bad form here in these papers. It is only here and there that a new word manages to creep awkwardly into the text.

Suddenly, there is a man standing in front of him, about his age, who greets him; he ought to know the man, but he just can't seem to recall who it is—yes, of course, it's Moll standing there and he feels obliged to eagerly offer Moll a seat at his table. Moll—that shy, culture-crazed guy who had once sought to discover the secret of the newest style and who had since found it. Moll, who now knows how one is supposed to live, paint, write, think and compose. Definitive, resolute. Moll, once groping, seeking, feeding on the knowledge and insights of a generation that went before him, had digested and regurgitated everything he devoured. Moll's system. Moll's infallibility. Moll as art critic. Moll, the implacable, *odi profanum vulgus,* Moll who had been struck dumb by the loss of his own language and would now compensate for it by strutting around like a peacock parading the laurels of two thousand other languages on his tongue. Moll, who can't read novels anymore; Moll, for whom poetry has no future; Moll who advocates the castration of music and wants to estrange the paint from the canvas. Moll—rabid, ruthless, misunderstood and always referring to the greatness of Guillelmus Apuliensis (circa 1100 AD)...Moll, who considers Erhard Schön the most astonishing of all painters. Moll the trailblazer. Moll, silent with indignation whenever the discussion centers on a subject someone else knows well, deprived low-level civil servant, collector of obscure books, a man neglected and overlooked. Moll, enviously intent on proving that he has been misjudged and discounted, avenges himself in acidulous bitterness, punitive stares directed at every pretty woman he sees, at every Sunday, every fruit, every act of goodwill. Moll, the martyr. And of course, Moll despises him, too, Moll's old friend, because he's just glanced at the clock and noticed that it's time to go. Moll, who lives according to his own inner clock, one that just winds his stringent spirit ever tighter, letting the tick-tick-tick of privilege keep on ticking...

And the day goes by with these clashes and collisions which he suffers and endures in a world where all the people have become ghosts to him. He is ill-equipped to defend himself against ghosts. And the day after would make that clear.

So he runs into Moll again because everyone's world is full of Molls. But he can barely remember this particular Moll. It's that do-you-remember-the-good-ol'-days-Moll. It's of no use to him to feign ignorance because that just makes Moll remember all the more. Moll reminds him of the way he, as Moll's schoolmate, had gotten drunk for the first time and had slurred his words to senseless babble, the way he'd had to retch and let Moll take him home. Moll still remembers the day when he, Moll's friend, made a terrible fool of himself, and he thinks to himself, "Moll, who holds the negative highlights of my life ready in hand, faithfully keeping in store all my flops and failures, my vulgarities. Moll, my buddy; Moll who had been with me in the army at eighteen, Moll who, reminiscing now, is in the 'service' again; Moll, who rambles on in a language that makes me want to vomit because it's supposed to lead me to believe that I once rambled on in the same language. Moll who had helped me out of a scrape or two." Moll, the strongman, he, the weakling. Moll, who could call a spade a spade: whatever-happened-to-the-blonde-baby-doll?-Marriage!-that-would-be-the-last-straw!-Moll, who knows how to place a bribe, knows his stuff, who won't let anyone pull the wool over his eyes, who can lay the bitches the way they want to get laid, and who can let the bosses take a hike; Moll, who knows how to get at both the bastards and the bitches. Moll, for whom everything is political and who doesn't give a damn about politics; Moll, the fly in the ointment; Moll, who thinks the war hasn't yet been lost, at least not the next one, who considers the Italians just a pack of thieves, the French emasculated wimps, the Russians a subspecies of man, and who knows what the British are really about and what the world is really about, a commercial transaction, a deal, a joke, a mess. Moll: "But I still know you from before, don't try to pull one over on me, you can't pull one over on me!"

How do you avoid Moll? What is the point of trying to decapitate this Hydra of a Moll when you know ten heads will grow in place of the one!

Even though he cannot recall ever having conceded to Moll's memory of a single one of these incidents, he knows what the future will bring: Moll will show up in every nook and cranny, again and again.

Stand back or I'll commit murder! Keep your distance from me!

At the end of one of those nights in which the reunions passed judgment on him and the others, he was standing in front of a bratwurst stand with three characters and a young woman whom he'd once pursued unsuccessfully for a while. Earlier, he had danced with Helene at a night club, had caressed her shoulder with his lips. He couldn't bring himself to kiss her on the mouth even though he was certain that he could get away with it this time. Nonetheless, after they had said goodbye to the others, he had gone with her to her apartment for coffee. She had a vague way of speaking which he quickly absorbed himself. He had probably spoken with her that way in the old days, using nuances, practicing half measures and suggestive ambiguities so that now, nothing could be straight and clear between the two of them. It was late, the room was filled with smoke, her perfume had dissipated. Before he left, he took her in his arms, hesitant and eroded by exhaustion. He was very polite; he turned back on the landing and waved, as though it were hard for him to leave. That was his last act of hypocrisy, and the look he saw on her face, rigid and withering, scared him off. Outside, day had broken—or what passed itself off as day: dawn, fog. He reached his hotel, exhausted yet shrinking from sleep, and bedded himself down like a sick patient, took two sleeping pills, then finally succumbed to sleep. He didn't wake up until it was evening again, warm and with a stale taste in his mouth from sleeping too long, a taste he'd had in the city. He packed his bags, haplessly tossing shirts, brushes and shoes together as though he were in a great hurry and orderliness no longer mattered to him. It wasn't until he arrived at the train station that he looked for a train, running his index finger along the list of departures.

He wound up taking the worst possible train, a local train that stopped at every station; then he had to spend half the night pacing up and down in front of a closed waiting room in the middle of winter at some small town train station in the province, stamping the ground with his feet and clapping his hands together. He would have liked to have boarded a freight car and slept forever. But he wasn't cold enough, wasn't tired enough to do that. This desolation wasn't bad enough to merit such an end.

When the journey resumed, he listened to a fellow traveler tell tales about the percentage of crazy people who consider themselves Napoleon, the percentage who consider themselves the last Emperor, Lindbergh, Hitler or Gandhi. It sparked his interest and he asked whether one might come away unscathed if one just considered oneself himself or whether that too wasn't some form of insanity. The man, presumably a psychiatrist, emptied his pipe, changed the subject and began talking about various other percentage rates and the therapies available for treating this percentage and that. He picked his nose with a pipe cleaner and said: "You, sir, for example, you suffer from…But you're making too much of it…we all suffer from that, of course, it's nothing special."

The next train transported him through a hair-raising night—the wheels switched tracks with a shudder when they rolled through larger stations, bitter with resentment, while he—crammed in among ten other people in the compartment—struggled for air, looked away when the aging woman beside him began breastfeeding her baby while her husband, the greensick guy sitting opposite him, spat phlegm after every coughing attack and he almost went nuts over another man snoring beside the door. All their limbs and legs were entangled, everyone fought for inches of space and tried to encroach on the others. Suddenly he discovered that he too was elbowing his way around in the attempt to crowd out the woman with the baby. Here he was again, in the midst of living human beings, fighting tenaciously for his position, his place, his life. At some point, he briefly drifted off to sleep. In his dream, the city was falling down around him, with St. Karl's Cathedral the first thing to go, together with its grand palace and parks and entire sections of streets; the dream probably lasted only a second, because he was woken from it, scared to death, by a blow to his head. He knew immediately, without having to think about it, that the train had collided with another. A suitcase had sprung from the luggage rack and hit him. He knew right away too that the collision was only minor because the time was not right for anything to happen to him. There would be no untimely grand finale. No untimely exit. No heart-striking tragedy. After a couple hours, they were able to continue on their way and were all relieved, as they would be following a mild heart attack. No one was injured, the damage was minimal. He tried to remember the dream about the city triggered by the two trains crashing or which had perhaps preceded the jolt, and it was as though he would never have to see the city again, but from now on, he would forever remember how the city had been and the way he had lived there.

City without warranty!
Let me speak not of just any city, but of this one city that has captured in its net all the hopes and fears of so many of my years. I can still see it sitting by the broad, placid current like a fat, slatternly fisherwoman hauling in her silvery spoils or putrid prey. Silvery the fear, putrid the hope.

Beside the blackwater of the Danube, against the backdrop of chestnut trees vaulting the moldy green patinas of the domes:

Let me retrieve from the dust the spirit she has shown in times of amity and surrender to ash what arose in times of enmity! Then let the wind come and wipe out any heart that was haughty and hurt here!

City of flotsam!

Because entire countries and the goods they produce have washed up on her shores: the Slovakians' cross-stitch embroidered cloths and the pitchy Montenegrin mustaches, Bulgarian egg baskets and a refractory Hungarian accent.

City of Turkish moons! City of barricades!

So much crumbled stone, so many hollow walls that you can hear it in a whisper from long ago and from far away.

Oh, all the nights that sprang up in Vienna, so many bitter nights! And all the days that threw you for a loop with the buzz of schoolhouses and sanatoriums, old folks' homes and hospital rooms, poorly ventilated and rarely whitewashed, all those days embraced, adored and courted by the bashful blossoms on chestnut trees! Oh all those windows never opened, and all those gates—as though there were no gate leading out, as though even heaven did not exist!

Terminal city! As though this were the end of the rail!

The threadbare politics of *Hofrats* and has-beens in the chancelleries. Never a harsh word in the anterooms, always an insulting, injurious one.

(Always keep them waiting, never dismiss them outright.)

That is the question: whether to love or not to love something you have no desire to love, but the city is splendid and there was a long-winded poet who once climbed St. Stephen's steeple in homage to it.

It is all a question of giving way; one of endorsement. But there are some who drank of the cup of hemlock without asking any questions.

So slander is in league with the tender heart. But there were some whose hearts were equipped with wildly sinuous muscles and a manner of speaking that might have sufficed in Rome. They were hostile, loathed and lonesome. Their thoughts were precise, they kept their hands clean and left the lemmings alone.

There were some with words at their disposal which they set free like fireflies in the falling night or shot across the borders. And one of them had a forehead burnished tragic and blue between the tides of speechlessness.

City of the burning stake! where the most magnificent works of music were thrown to the flames, a city where whatever came from the die-hard heretics—those impatient suicide mongers, those painstaking discoverers—was spat upon and vilified, together with everything that was so intellectually straightforward.

City of silence! Stoic Lady of Justice in the Court of Inquisition with that noncommittal smile.

——but the sucking sound loose cobblestones make when someone staggers across, young, pilloried by the silence, murdered by the smiles. Where do you go then with the scream rising from tragedy?!

City of fools! City of a few flippant, frilly angels and a handful of pawnshop-ripe demons.

Bashful city in dialogue, blushing bud of a conversation that will take place in the future.

City of jokesters, sycophants, trucklers and associates. (Truth can be sacrificed to punctuate the punch-line, and words that please have half deceived).

Pestilent city with the stench of death!

On the blackwater of the Danube and the filthy oil fields in the distance:

Let me remind you of the brilliance of a day I
 once saw, green and white and sober,
after a fallen rain,
when the city was washed clean and pure,
when the streets emanated from a star in the
 city center,
from its stalwart heart, they stretched outward,
 cleansed,
where children from ground level to the
 top floor
all began rehearsing new etudes,
when the street cars returned from the
 Central Cemetery,
laden with wreathes and last year's bouquet
 of asters
because there was resurrection
from death,
from oblivion!

He kept quiet about the end of his trip. He didn't want it to end, but rather to simply disappear in the end, without a trace, nowhere to be found. He had finally found the means to close on a secret contract for a job that would have sent him on his way to Indonesia. But war broke out in Indonesia by the time he went to book his flight, so the contract fell through and he was no longer inclined to secure another one just to get away to some other distant country. He took that as a sign that he wasn't supposed to go. So he stayed in Rome. This is what he had in mind: going away with her, whose name he never dared utter. Fleeing with her—never returning to Europe again, simply living with her where there was sun, where there were fruits; living with *her* body, without another connection in the world and far removed from everything that had been. Living in her hair, in the corner of her mouth, in her lap.

He always loved the absolute and any step taken in that direction, and "she" was the first person to have inspired in him, with regard to a fellow human being, the desire to set out in that direction and take that other person along. In all those moments when thoughts of that outer extreme came to mind, when it was almost close enough to grasp, he fell prey to fever, became speechless, and consumed himself with a yearning to find words for it. He consumed himself in the attempt to take one single step toward the place which was, for him, the outer limit, and sought to act accordingly—ruthlessly.

But then someone always came along, delivered a letter reminding him of some previous obligation—of someone whose health was failing, some relative, some transient traveler passing through or of some appointment he had to keep for a job. Or, just when he was about to throw off all the shackles, someone came and clung to him like a drowning victim.

"Give me some peace! Just give it a rest!" he would say then and go to the window as though there were something special to see outside.

"But, we have to settle this today. Who started it? Who was the first one to say…?"

"I don't remember all that I said. Just finally leave me in peace!"

"And why did you come home so late, why did you slip through the door so quietly? Do you mean to say you had nothing to hide? Maybe you were even trying to hide yourself?!"

"I had nothing to hide. Now leave me alone!"

"Can't you see that this is killing me, that I'm crying?"

"Great! So you're crying, so it's killing you. But why?"

"You are simply awful and don't even know

what you are saying!"

No, he doesn't know. He had pleaded for peace so many times, but so often without knowing why, just so that he could finally lay to rest, could finally just put out the light, let his eyes adjust to the darkness in the distance that everyone tried to distract him from.

Just give me some peace, damn it, just once, give me some peace! He would at least like to be able to think about why he had abandoned the attempt to disappear and make himself invisible. He can make no sense of it. But someday the answer will out.

Like every other creature on earth, he can come to no conclusion. He doesn't want to live like just anyone, nor like someone special. He wants to go with the times and take a stand against them. He is tempted to praise some time-honored expediency, to defend some ancient splendor, some parchment, some pillar. But he is equally tempted to play out the things of today against those of yesterday, a reactor, a turbine, synthetics. He wants to keep the fronts and he doesn't. He tends to have some understanding for weakness, confusion and stupidity and at the same time wants to fight them, denounce them. He is tolerant and intolerant. He is hateful and without hate. Cannot tolerate and cannot hate.

That is another reason to disappear from the world.

His diary from this year contains the following statements:

"I love freedom which, of course, comes to an end in all that is firmly established and I wish for a planet scorched black and catastrophes brought on by light. But even then, freedom would come to an end, I know."

"Since there is no such thing as an innate human interdiction and no natural order, we are permitted to do not only what pleases people, but what doesnt (and who's to say what's to please in the world!), so there are an infinite number of possible laws and moral systems by which we might abide. Why do we restrict ourselves to these few combinations of systems no one has ever been happy with in the first place?"

"In the moral budget of humanity which we husband at times economically, at times uneconomically, piety and anarchy always both reign supreme. The taboos lie scattered in disarray along with the disclosures."

"Why is it that only these few systems have come to rule? Because we cling so tenaciously to habits, for fear of having to think without following a table of prohibitions and commandments—for fear of freedom. People don't really love freedom. Wherever freedom has ever flourished, they have recklessly thrown it to the wind."

"I love freedom, and I too am forced to betray it a thousand times over. This despicable world in which we live is the result of an unabated dismissal of freedom."

"The freedom I have in mind, the liberty that I love: taking the liberty—since God himself never defined the world and has no hand in the way it is—of creating the world anew, of giving it a new order. Taking the liberty of dismantling every form of structure, beginning with moral structures, so that all the others can subsequently dismantle themselves. The destruction of belief itself, every type of belief, in order to destroy any and every basis for conflict. Relinquishing every conventional view and every conventional state of mind or being: relinquishing the states, the churches, the organizations, the means of money and power, the weapons, education."

"The ultimate walkout: the strike that will bring the old world to a momentary standstill. Hand in the resignation on every form of work or of thinking that serves this old world order. Terminate the lease on history, not in favor of anarchy, but in favor of a fresh start."

"Prejudice—racial prejudice, class prejudice, religious prejudice and every other form of discrimination—will forever remain an affront—even when mitigated by instruction and insight. The elimination of injustice, of oppression, any amelioration of hardship and harshness, any improvement in conditions remains forever tarnished by past disgrace. Since it is retained in the words that survive, the shame of scandals may return at any given time."

"No new world without new language!"

In the meantime, spring has sprung. A pool of sunlight floods his room. On the small square in front of his building, children are cheering—and car horns, birds. He has to force himself to continue writing the letter. "Dear Sirs…" He doesn't tell the gentlemen the truth in his letter: that he is groveling at the cross in indifference and exhaustion; that, for lack of a better idea, he has finally come to Jesus. And what is "come to Jesus" supposed to mean anyway! Enough with these rhetorical acrobatics! "With regard to your kind offer…" Isn't it a kind offer after all? It seems reasonable enough and there is really no reason for him to consider himself too good to accept. "On the first of the month, as you requested, I shall be at your disposal. I hope…"

But he isn't hoping a thing. He doesn't have a thing in mind. There will be time enough to concern himself with future placement and future position. He is satisfied with the terms set forth and doesn't set any of his own. He seals the envelope quickly, without hesitation, and sends it off. He packs his belongings—the few books, ashtrays, some dishes, asks the apartment manager to come and take inventory and leaves behind the apartment where he had never felt at home. But he's got plenty of time between now and the first of the month, so he takes a circuitous route, long and leisurely, through the Italian provinces to get there. In

Genoa, he is again drive by wanderlust as he'd been in his youth, when he'd been released from captivity after the war, had taken the express train in, then found his way back on foot. He sends his baggage ahead and walks across country, wandering between the waking rice fields, heading north. And, since he's no longer accustomed to the exertion, he is dead tired on the second night and does something else he hasn't done in years: he stands at the side of the highway to Milan trying to hitch a ride. Darkness is falling and no one wants to pick him up until finally, just as he's given up hope, he signals one last oncoming car. And that car stops, quietly, almost without a sound. Awkwardly, he tells the man sitting alone at the wheel where he wants to go and, feeling dirty as a tramp and rather self-conscious as a result, climbs in beside him. He sits there silent for a long time, occasionally glancing furtively over at the man. He must be about his same age. He likes the look of the man's face, likes the look of his hands resting relaxed on the steering wheel. His gaze wanders further and gets stuck on the speedometer where the needle jumps suddenly from 100 to 120 and then to 140 kilometers an hour. He doesn't dare say he would rather go a little slower, that he is suddenly frightened by any degree of speed. He's not in any great hurry to step into an ordered life.

Suddenly, the young man says, "I don't usually pick people up." And then, as if to apologize for his driving, "I have to get to town before midnight."

He again looks at the man staring unremittingly ahead where the headlights sort out the twisted tangle of forest, pylons, walls and bushes. He has calmed down now and is feeling strangely at ease, but he would like to talk and again feel the focus of the man's light-hued eyes that had barely passed over him.

Yes, they had to be light in color, he wanted them to be and he wanted to talk now, to ask the man, for example, if this year had been hard on him too and what to do about it, what a person was to think about all this. In his mind, he began conversing with the man while the two of them sat side by side in the low-riding front seats like two schoolboys thrown together for a lesson and were carried through the night, a big night in which all the objects around them loomed large and strange. Up ahead, a truck suddenly emerged, they approached it quickly, swerved into the passing lane, but when they were on a level with it, the truck also swerved out to turn onto a side road.

They lunged forward a few yards and into a wall.

When he came to again, he noticed that he was being lifted; he immediately lost consciousness again, sensing an occasional jolt and momentarily guessing what was happening to him: He must be in a hospital, on a gurney, he was given an injection, above him, people were talking about, but not to him. It wasn't until he was already in the operating room that his head finally cleared. Preparations were underway, two masked doctors were busy working at a table, a female doctor approached him, took his arm and rubbed it—it tingled a little, pleasantly. Suddenly it dawned on him that this was serious and he thought to himself, silently, that he would never wake up again once they had put him to sleep here. He wanted to say something, his tongue groped to find his voice and he was happy to hear a few intelligible words come out. He asked for a piece of paper and a pencil. A nurse brought him both and, while the anesthesia slowly set in, he held the pencil to the paper the nurse was holding out on a clipboard for him. He carefully scratched out: "Dear Mom and Dad..." then hastily crossed out the two words and wrote: "Dearest...." He paused and thought hard. He crumpled the paper into a ball and gave it back to the nurse, shaking his head to indicate that it was pointless. If he should die before he woke, there would be no point to letters like that. He lay there with his eyelids sagging, pleasantly sedated, and waited to lose consciousness.

This was the year that broke his bones. He was lying in the hospital with a few scars artfully suffused with blue and red and not counting the days until the plaster cast that promised to heal him was scheduled to be removed. The stranger who had picked him up—as he'd since learned—had died at the scene. Sometimes, he thinks about him and stares at the ceiling. He thinks of him as someone who died in his stead and can see him, with that attentive tension in his face, those young, firm hands on the steering wheel; he sees him racing headlong into the center of the world's darkness and bursting into flames on arrival.

It is already May. The flowers in his room are replaced daily with fresh ones, each more brilliant than the last. The blinds are lowered for hours each afternoon and the room retains its fragrance.

If he could see his own face now, it would be that of a young man, and he wouldn't doubt for a moment that he is indeed young. Because he'd only felt particularly old when he was much younger, when he'd hung his head and drooped his shoulders, burdened by his thoughts and his body. When he was young, he had longed for an early death, hadn't even wanted to live to be thirty years old. But now, he was longing for life. Back then, it was merely life's punctuation marks he'd had swaying to and fro in his head, but now those first few sentences in which the whole world appeared were coming to him. At the time he thought he could think anything through to the end and he hardly noticed that he'd barely taken his first steps into a reality that wasn't readily thought to its end and one that still hadn't revealed itself fully to him.

For a long time, he didn't know what to believe and whether it wasn't an unsavory thing to believe in anything at all. Now he was beginning to believe in himself, in his own actions and his own words.

He was gathering confidence. He was learning to trust the things he didn't need to prove to himself, the pores of his skin, the taste of salt in the sea, the scent-laden air and simply everything that couldn't be reduced to generalization.

When he looked in the mirror for the first time—shortly before his release from the hospital—because he wanted to comb his hair himself, he got this first glimpse of his old familiar, yet slightly more transparent self propped up against the mountain of pillows at his back and discovered a glistening white something amid the matted strands of brown hair: He fondled it, drew the mirror closer: a white hair! His heart leapt to his throat!

He stared at the hair, foolish and unremitting.

The next day, he looked in the mirror again, fearing he would find more white hairs, but there was only the one, and so it remained.

Finally, he said to himself: I'm alive and now longing for a long life. The white hair, this pallid but palpable proof of suffering sustained and the first sign of age, how could it have shocked me so? I'll leave it there and if, after a few days, it has fallen out and not been quickly replaced by another, then

I will have had at least a taste of it and never again be frightened by the process of aging I'm now experiencing live in the flesh.

I am alive, after all!

It won't be long before he has healed completely.

It won't be long before he is thirty years old. The day will come, but no one will toll the bell to announce its arrival. No, the day will never come—it has already been there, it was in every day of this year that he has survived by hook and by crook. He is as prepared as he will ever be for whatever is to come, is thinking about work and hoping he'll soon walk out those doors downstairs, leaving the accident victims behind, the invalids and the moribund.

Verily I say unto you: Rise up and walk! You haven't broken so much as a bone!

Everything

Whenever we sit down to dinner, like two who have turned to stone, or meet at the apartment door in the evening because we both think about locking it at the same time, I can feel our sorrow like a bow stretched from one end of the world to the other—that is, from Hanna to me—and there is an arrow poised taut on the bowstring aimed to strike the impassive sky in its heart. Walking two steps ahead of me as we pass through the foyer, she slips into the bedroom without saying "good night," and I escape to my room, to my desk, where I sit staring into space with her bowed head before my eyes and her silence in my ears. I wonder whether she has lain down and is trying to fall asleep or is lying there awake and waiting. Waiting for what?—sure as hell not for me!

When I married Hanna, it was less for her sake than because she was expecting a child. I had no choice, no decision to make. I was motivated by the fact there was something in the works—something new that came from us—and by the way the world seemed to be waxing. Like the moon you should always bow to three times when it is new and tender, standing with a breath of color at the start of its course. There were moments of absent-mindedness like I had never known before. Even at the office—even though I had more than enough work to do—or during a conference, I would suddenly slip into this state in which I fixed all my attention on the child, this unknown being, this shadowy creature, and all my thoughts were directed toward it, penetrating even into the warm, lightless womb where it lay captive.

The child we were expecting changed us. We scarcely left the house and neglected our friends; we looked for a bigger apartment and settled ourselves in to better, more permanent circumstances. But it was because of the child I was expecting that everything began changing for me; I stumbled upon thoughts unawares, like one would stumble on a land mine, so explosive I should have cringed back in terror, but I persisted, heedless of the danger.

Hanna misunderstood me. Because I couldn't make up my mind whether the baby carriage should have big wheels or small, I seemed indifferent. ('I really don't know. Do what you think is best. Oh yes I am listening.') Standing around with her in stores where she was busy picking out bonnets, little jackets and diapers, wavering between pink and blue, synthetic and genuine wool, she accused me of being inattentive. But I was actually all too attentive.

How should I begin to express what was going on inside me? I felt like a savage who'd suddenly been informed of the fact the that the world he inhabits, passing from the hearth's fire to the encampment, from sunrise to sunset, from the hunt to the meal, is the same world that has been around for millions of years and will perish, a world that occupies an insignificant place among myriad solar systems revolving at a tremendous speed around its own axis and at the same time around the sun. All at once I saw myself in a different light, me and the child whose turn would come to be born and have a shot at life, at a predetermined point in time, the beginning or the middle of November, a child whose time would come just as it had for me and everyone before me.

Just imagine it! These generations of descent!

It's like counting black and white sheep to fall asleep (black one, white one, black one, white one and so on)—a thought that could dull and daze the senses and at the same time leave you desperately wide awake. It's a formula that has never helped me fall asleep, though Hanna, who got it from her mother, swears it's more relaxing than a sedative. Maybe it's reassuring for a lot of people to think about this chain: And Shem begat Arphaxad. And when Arphaxad was thirty-five years old, he begat Salah. And Salah begat Evert. And Evert Peleg. When Peleg was thirty, he begat Reu, Reu begat Serug and Serug Nahor, and each of them begat many more sons and daughters after that, and the sons begat son after son, among others, Nahor begat Terah and Terah Abram, Nahor and Haran. I tried a couple of times to think this process through, not only from beginning to end, but from the end all the way back to the beginning with Adam and Eve, from whom we are not likely to have descended, or back to the hominids, from whom we may have come, but there is, in every case and in any case, a point at which this chain gets lost in obscurity and that is why it does not matter whether you cling to

Adam and Eve or two other exemplars. But, if you would rather not cling to anything and prefer instead to ask why everyone has had his turn, each in his own time, you end up not knowing which way is up with this chain and you don't know where to begin with all the begetting and begotten, with the first life and the last. Because everyone gets only one shot at the game he finds before him and is compelled to take up: procreation and education, economics and politics, and of course he's able to concern himself with money and emotion, with work and invention and justification of the rules of the game that is called thought.

But since we are already so busy going faithfully forth and multiplying, we'll have to make the best of it. The game needs players. (Or is it the players who need the game?) I too had been brought into the world on an act of faith, and now I had brought a child into the world.

Now I tremble at the very thought of it.

I started to see everything in relation to the child. My hands, for example, that would one day caress and hold it, our fourth-story apartment, Kandlgasse, the 7th District, the roads crossing the city this way and that down to the grounds of Prater Park and finally, the rest of the world around us that I would explain to the child. It would hear the names from me: table and bed, nose and foot. Even words like: God and spirit and soul, in my humble opinion useless words that you cannot, however, keep concealed and later, words as complicated as resonance, diapositive, chiliasm and astronautics. I would have to see to it that my child learned what everything meant and how to put it to good use, a door handle and a bicycle, mouthwash and a questionnaire. My head was reeling.

When the child arrived of course I had no use for the lessons it brought. It was there, jaundiced, crumpled, pitiful, and there was one thing I wasn't prepared for—that I would have to give it a name. Hastily, I came to an agreement with Hanna and we had three names recorded in the register. My father's name, her father's and my grandfather's. But none of the three names was ever used. By the end of the first week, the child was called Fipps. I don't know how it came to that. Perhaps it was partly my fault because, just like Hanna, who was inexhaustibly inventive when it came to discovering and combining senseless syllables, I tried to call it by nicknames because its real names didn't quite suit the tiny naked creature. This name emerged from the constant back and forth in our attempts to curry favor with the child and over the course of years, it would come to bother me more and more. Sometimes I even blamed it on the child, as though it could have defended itself, as though it hadn't been a matter of sheer coincidence. Fipps! I'll have to keep calling him that, keep making a fool of him and of us till death and beyond.

When Fipps was lying in his blue-and-white bed, waking, sleeping, and the only thing I was good for was to wipe a few drops of spit or sour milk from his mouth, to pick him up when he cried in the hope of offering him some solace, it occurred to me for the first time that he had something in store for me, but that he would allow me some time to figure out what it was, that he was hell-bent on allowing me time, like an apparition that appears before you only to fade back into the dark and return again, always emitting the same enigmatic looks. I often sat beside his bed, looking down at this nearly impassive face, those eyes staring aimlessly, and I studied the lines like a script that had been passed down for generations but which you couldn't decipher because there was no key. I was happy to notice the way Hanna unerringly stuck to the obvious, giving him something to drink, letting him sleep, waking him, changing his sheets, his diapers, everything strictly by the book. She cleaned his nose with little cotton balls and dusted a cloud of powder between his chubby thighs, as though this would be of everlasting benefit both to him and to her.

After a few weeks, she tried to entice him into smiling his first smile. But when he finally did surprise us with it, for me his grimace remained enigmatic and detached. Even when he began directing his eyes toward us more and more frequently or stretched his little arms toward us, I suspected it was meaningless and that we were merely starting to look for the reasons he would later adopt. It would have been impossible for Hanna, perhaps for anyone, to understand, but it was during this time that my uneasiness set in. I'm afraid I may have already begun distancing myself from Hanna then, excluding her more often and keeping her at bay from my true thoughts. I discovered faults in myself—the child had led me to the discovery—and the feeling that I was heading for a fall. I was thirty years old, the same as Hanna who looked suppler and younger than ever before. But the child hadn't given me a second youth. To the degree that he expanded his circle, I contracted my own. His every smile, every cry of delight, every scream drove me up the wall. I didn't have the strength to nip this smiling, this giddiness, these screams in the bud. Because that is what it would have taken!

The time I had left passed quickly. Fipps sat up straight in the stroller, cut his first teeth, whined a lot; before long, he stretched himself to his feet, stood there unsteady, but steadily becoming more sure on his feet, he slid through the room on his hands and knees, and one day, his first words came. There was no stopping it and I still didn't know what to do.

What could I have done? I used to think I had to teach him about the world. But ever since those silent intimate dialogues with him, I'd nearly gone out of my mind and had since gotten wiser. Didn't I, for example, hold the option of refusing to name the things of the world, refusing to teach him how to use them, like a trump card in my hand? He was the first human being. Everything began with him and there was nothing to say that everything couldn't turn out much differently because of him. Shouldn't I leave the world to him to figure out, blank and uninscribed? I didn't have to initiate him into the points and purposes, nor in good and evil, or in what is real and what merely appears to be. Why should I draw him to my side, fill him with knowledge and belief, joy and suffering!? Here, where we stand, is the worst of all worlds, and no one has understood it yet, but where he stood, nothing had yet been decided. Not yet. How much longer?

And suddenly I knew: everything boils down to a question of language, and not just this German language created in Babylon along with the others in order to confuse the world. Because there is another language smoldering beneath the surface, a language that penetrates even gestures and gazes, even the processing of thoughts and the course of emotions, and it is here that everyone's misfortune is already sealed. Everything was a question of whether I could shelter this child from our language until it had created a new one and with that language could herald a new era.

I often went out of the house alone with Fipps and when I found out what Hanna had done to him—the sweet talk, coquetry, games—I was horrified. He was taking after us. But not only after me and Hanna, no, after humanity as a whole. But there were moments in which he was in complete control of himself and it was then that I observed him intently. Every path was the same to him. Every creature, too. Hanna and I were closer to him simply because we were constantly busy at his side. It was all the same to him. How much longer?

He was afraid. But it wasn't yet an avalanche or a dirty trick he feared, rather a leaf set in motion on a tree. A butterfly. Flies scared him out of his wits. And I thought, how would he be able to withstand the swaying of a whole tree in the wind when I have left him so much in the dark about everything!

He met with the neighbor's boy on the stairs; he clumsily snatched at his face, drew back, not realizing perhaps that this was a child standing before him. He used to scream when he wasn't feeling well, but now when he screamed, there was more to it than that. It happened often before he fell asleep or when you'd pick him up to bring him to the dinner table, or if you took away one of his toys. There was an anger raging within him. He could lie on the ground clutching the carpet, screaming himself blue in the face and frothing at the mouth. He would scream in his sleep as though a vampire had landed on his chest. These screams confirmed what I thought: that he still had the nerve to scream and that his screams were effective.

Oh, one of these days!

Hanna went around with tender reproaches and called him naughty. She cradled him in her arms, coddled and kissed him or looked him sternly in the eyes and instructed him not to aggravate his mother. She was a wonderful seductress. She stood motionless, bent over the nameless river, trying to coax him into crossing, pacing up and down our side of the bank, enticing him with chocolate and oranges, spinning tops and teddy bears.

And when the trees cast shadows, I thought I heard a voice saying: Teach him the language of shadows! The world is just an experiment and it's enough that this experiment has been repeated again and again in the same way with the same result. Take up another experiment! Let him turn to the shadows! Up until now, the result has been: a life of guilt, love and desperation. (I had begun to think of everything in general terms; that's when words like this occurred to me). But I could spare him the guilt, the love and every calamity and set him free to live a different life.

Yes, Sundays I strolled with him through the Wienerwald and whenever we came upon a body of water, something inside me said: Teach him the language of water. We stepped over stones. Over roots. Teach him the language of stones! Give him new roots! The leaves fell, because it was fall again. Teach him the language of leaves!

But since I didn't know or couldn't find a single word of these languages, all I had was my own language and couldn't get beyond its limits, I carried him silently up and down the paths and back home again where he learned to construct sentences and fell into the trap. Before long, he was expressing wishes, articulating requests, issuing commands or talking just for the sake of talking. Later, during our Sunday excursions, he ripped blades of grass from their roots, picked up worms, caught beetles. By now, they were no longer all the same to him, he examined them, killed them if I didn't take them from his hands in time. At home, he dissected books, boxes, even his puppet. He seized everything for himself, dug into it, touched and tested everything before he either discarded it or kept it. One of these days. One of these days he would know the score.

In those days, when Hanna was more communicative than she is now, she would often direct my attention to what Fipps said, she was enraptured by his innocent gazes, his innocent talk and deeds. But I hadn't been able to detect a shred of innocence in the child ever since it had been defenseless and mute in those first few weeks. And even then, it probably wasn't innocent, just incapable of expressing itself, a bundle of refined flesh and flax, with bare breath, with an enormous, blunt head that defused the world's messages like a lightning conductor.

When he was older, Fipps was often allowed to play with other children in the dead-end street next to the house. Once, when I was on my way home around noon, I saw him with three other boys collecting runoff water from the curbstone in a tin can. Then they stood in a circle talking. It looked like some sort of deliberation. (The way engineers deliberate over where to start the drilling, where to make the first recess). They were squatting there on the pavement, and Fipps, holding the tin can, was already pouring out the contents by the time they stood up and stepped three cobblestones further. But even this spot didn't seem to suit their purposes. They stood up again. There was tension in the air. What masculine tension it was! Something was about to happen! And then, just three feet away, they found the spot. They crouched down again, grew silent, and Fipps tipped the tin can. The dirty water flowed over the stones. They stared at it, silent and solemn. It was done, mission accomplished. Perhaps even successful. It had to have been successful. The world could count on these three little men to help it along. And they would help it along, I was sure of it now. I went home, upstairs, and threw myself on the bed in our bedroom. The world had been helped along, the spot from which the world could be advanced had been found, always the same direction. I had hoped my child wouldn't find the direction. And once, a long time ago, I had even feared that he wouldn't find his way. Fool that I am, I had feared he wouldn't find the direction!

I got up and splashed a few handfuls of cold tap water on my face. I didn't want this child anymore. I hated him, because he understood all too well, I could see him following in everyone's footsteps.

I went around extending my hatred to everything that men had made, to the street cars, house numbers, titles, the intervals on the clock, this whole corrupted, calculated mess they call order—garbage removal, university catalogues, the Bureau of Vital Statistics, all these pitiful institutions that you can't continue to assail, institutions no one bothers to assail anyway, these altars where I too had left my offerings, but was unwilling to allow my son to do the same. Why should my child succumb to that? He wasn't the one who put the pieces of this world in place, he hadn't caused the damage. Why on earth should this child assume a place in this world!? I screamed at the Register of Deeds' office, at the schools and the barracks: Give him a chance! Give my child just one chance before he falls into ruin! I beat myself silly because I had thrust my son into this world and done nothing to set him free. I owed it to him, I had to do something, take him on a trip, retreat with him to an island. But where is this island where a new human being can go to found a new world? I was caught with the child and condemned from the outset to be a part of the old world. That is why I finally let him go. I let him fall out of my love. This child was capable of everything but one thing—of secession, of breaking through the vicious circle.

Fipps gambled away the years before he started school. He gambled them away in the truest sense of the word. I was happy to let him play games, just not these games that later led him to other games. Hide and seek, pick and choose, cops and robbers. I wished for him different games, purer, other fairy tales not like the old familiar ones. But I couldn't think of anything new and he was hell-bent on emulation. You wouldn't think it possible, but there really is no way out for the likes of us. Again and again, everything is divided into top and bottom, good and evil, light and dark, in quantity and quality, friend and foe, and, when other creatures or animals do appear in the fables, they immediately assume human traits.

Since I was at a loss as to the how and wherefore of educating him, I gave it up. Hanna noticed that I no longer concerned myself with him. Once we tried to talk about it and she stared at me like I was a monster. I couldn't even get out everything I wanted to say in my defense because she stood up, cut me off mid-sentence and went into the nursery. It was evening and from that evening on, she who'd previously been just as unlikely to think of it as I commenced to pray with the child: Now I lay me down to sleep. Pray the Lord my soul to keep. And the like. I didn't concern myself with that either, but I presume they are likely to have succeeded in completing their repertoire. I think she thought she was somehow providing him protection. Anything would have sufficed for her, a cross or a mascot, a magic spell, anything. In principle, she was right, since Fipps would soon fall prey to the wolves and would soon howl with the wolves. "God willing" was perhaps the last resort. We were handing him over, each in his own way.

When Fipps came home from school with low

marks, I didn't say a word, but I didn't console him either. Hanna agonized inwardly. She regularly sat down with him after lunch to help him with his homework, drilling him. She served the cause as well as it could be served. But I didn't believe in the good cause. It was all the same to me whether Fipps would later attend the *Gymnasium,* whether he would assume a respectable position or not. A blue collar worker always wants to see his son become a doctor and a doctor wants his to become at least a doctor. I don't understand it. I didn't want Fipps to be any more adept or better off than we were. And I didn't want him to love me; he didn't need to obey me or bend to my will. No, what I wanted…was simply that he begin at the beginning, that he demonstrate one single gesture indicating that he wasn't compelled to replicate our gestures. I didn't see a sign of it in him. I had been newly born, but not he! It was I, after all, I was the first man and I had gambled everything away, I had done nothing!

There was nothing I wished for Fipps, absolutely nothing. I just kept observing him. I don't know whether a man has the right to observe his own child this way—the way a researcher studies a "case." I observed this hopeless case of humanity. This child that I couldn't love the way I loved Hanna whom I'd never dropped completely because she was so utterly incapable of disappointing me. She was certainly cut from the same cloth as I back when I first met her, shapely, experienced, something special but then again not, a woman and then my wife. I put this child and myself on trial—him, for dashing my highest hopes and me because I couldn't prepare the ground for him. I had hoped that this child, because it was a child—yes, I had hoped that he would save the world. It sounds like an abomination. And I really was abominable in my treatment of the child, but what I had hoped for was not an abomination. Just like everyone before me, I simply was not prepared for the child. I hadn't given it a second thought when I took Hanna in my arms, when I found refuge in the dark recess of her womb—I couldn't think. It was good to have married Hanna, not just for the child's sake, but, afterward, I was never happy with her again, just obsessed with the thought of preventing her from having another child. She would have liked to, I have reason enough to suspect so even though she doesn't so much as mention it or anything of the sort anymore. You'd almost think that now of all times Hanna would again be thinking about having another child, but she has turned to stone. She neither turns away from me nor does she come to me. She contends with me like you shouldn't contend with any human being because no one is master of such mysteries as death and life. Back then, she'd have been happy to have spawned a whole brood, and I prevented it. She conceded to every condition and I could not accept even one. Once, while we were arguing, she explained everything she wanted to do and to have for Fipps. *Everything:* a well-lit room, more vitamins, a sailor suit, more love, all the love in the world, she wanted to erect a storehouse to stockpile enough love to last a lifetime on account of the outside world, on account of people…a good education, foreign languages, ever attentive to his talents. She cried and took offense that I should laugh about it. I doubt she thought for a minute that Fipps would ever belong to those people "out there," that he was just as capable of injuring, insulting, cheating and killing, that he might be capable of even the slightest impropriety, and yet I had every reason to assume that he was. Because evil, as we are wont to call it, festered in the child like an abscess. And I certainly needn't so much as call to mind the story with the knife. It started much earlier than that, when he was only about three or four years old. I walked in on him while he was stomping angrily about, bawling; a tower he'd built with blocks had toppled. Suddenly, he ceased his lamentations and said, quietly and with resolve: "I'll set your house on fire. I'll destroy everything. I'll destroy every one of you." I hoisted him onto my knee, caressed him, promised to rebuild the tower. He repeated his threats. Hanna, who'd just joined us, was for the first time unsure. She reprimanded him, then asked him who'd taught him to say things like that. He responded firmly: "No one."

Then he shoved a young girl who lived in the same building down the stairs, was rather shaken by it afterward, cried, promised never to do it again, then went and did it again. For a while, he struck out at Hanna at every opportunity. This too passed.

Admittedly, I forget to bear in mind how many nice things he said, how endearing he could be, how he woke red and glowing in the morning. I took note of every one of those things, was often tempted to quickly take him in my arms, kiss him the way Hanna did, but I didn't want to placate myself with this or be deceived by it. I kept my ears pricked and my eyes peeled. Because what I was hoping for wasn't an abomination. I didn't have any grandiose plans for my child, but I did wish for this small thing, this slight deviation. Of course when a child is called Fipps, of all things…is he obliged to live up to his name? To come and go with a lapdog's name. To fritter away eleven years in one circus act after another. (Eat with your right hand. Walk straight. Wave. Don't talk with your mouth full.)

Ever since he started school I was more often to be found out of the house than at home. I was either off playing chess at some coffee house or, under the pretext of having work to do, holed up in my room reading. I met Betty, a sales clerk in the Mariahilferstrasse whom I brought nylons, movie tickets or a little something to eat and let her grow accustomed to me. She was quiet, undemanding, subservient and at most inordinately fond of food as relief from the apathy that characterized the evenings she spent in her free time. I went to see her rather often during one particular year, lay down beside her on the bed in her furnished room where, while I drank a glass of wine, she read magazines then accommodated all my advances without being taken aback in the least. This was the time of the greatest confusion—because of the child. I never slept with Betty, quite the contrary, I was on a quest for masturbatory gratification, for the shady, shunned-upon release from women and from generations of the human race. So that I couldn't be ensnared, so that I could maintain my independence. I didn't want to go to Hanna's bed anymore because I would have capitulated to her.

Even though I made no effort to camouflage the evenings I spent away from home over such an extended period of time, it seemed to me as though Hanna lived without suspicion. One day I discovered this was not so; she had already seen me once with Betty in Café Elsahof where we often met after closing time, and then again just two days later while I was standing in line with Betty in front of the Kosmos cinema waiting to buy tickets. Hanna behaved very oddly, looked beyond me like she would a stranger so that I didn't know what to do. I cast a nod her way as though I were paralyzed, slipped closer to the box-office, feeling Betty's hand in mine, and, as incredible as it may seem to me in retrospect, actually proceeded to go to the movie. After the show, while bracing myself for the reproach and rehearsing my defense, I grabbed a taxi for the short way home, as if I could have thus still made amends or prevented the inevitable. Since Hanna didn't say a word, I dove into my prepared text. Obstinately, she persevered in her silence as though I were addressing her with matters that had nothing to do with her. Finally, she did open her mouth and said, feebly, that I should think about the child. "Do it for Fipps's sake…" she actually said that! I was flabbergasted by her awkwardness, begged her forgiveness, got down on my knees, promised the proverbial "Never again" and actually never did see Betty again. I don't know why I nevertheless wrote her two letters that were certainly of no value to her. An answer never came and I didn't expect one either. As though I'd wanted these letters to land in Hanna's or my own hands, I bared my soul in them the way I'd never done to any human being before. Sometimes I was afraid Betty would try to blackmail me. Howso blackmail? I sent her money. Why, when in fact Hanna knew about her?

This confusion. This desolation.

I felt as though my masculinity had been eradicated, rendered impotent. I wished I could stay that way. If there were an account to be settled, the balance would be in my favor. Secede from this species, come to an end, an end, if only it would come to that!

But everything that happened was not about me or even about Hanna or Fipps, rather about father and son, about guilt, about a debt to pay and about a death.

In a book I once read the following sentence: "It is not heaven's habit to raise its head." It would be great if everyone were familiar with this statement commenting on heaven's harsh habit. No indeed, it is not heaven's habit to look down and send signs to the confused people below. At least not where a dark drama is being staged in which even He, this fabricated "High Almighty" is a member of the cast. Father and son. A son—the fact that such a thing exists is unfathomable. These kinds of words occur to me because there is no clear word to describe this sinister thing; as soon as you think about it, you begin losing your mind. Sinister thing: because there was my semen, my seed, indefinable and uncanny even to me, and then there was Hanna's blood that nourished the child and accompanied birth, altogether a sinister thing. And it ended in blood, with the resounding iridescent blood of a child flowing from the wound in his head.

He couldn't speak while lying there on the jutting cliff above the bottom of the ravine, but he managed to say to the first fellow schoolboy who found his way to him: "You." He tried to lift his hand to signal something or cling to him. But the hand could no longer be lifted. And finally, once the teacher bent over him a few moments later, he whispered: "I want to go home."

I'll guard myself against believing by dint of this sentence that he had explicitly asked for Hanna and me. After all, everyone wants to go home when death is near and he knew death was near. He was just a child with no great tidings to impart. Fipps was after all just an utterly ordinary child, there was nothing that could get in the way of his last thoughts. The other children and the teacher built a stretcher out of sticks they gathered, and carried him up to the village. Along the way, almost immediately after the first few steps, he died. Passed away? Departed? In the obituary, we wrote: "....our only child...torn from our side by an accident." The man at the printing press who took the order asked whether we didn't want to write "our one and only dearly beloved son," but Hanna, who was on the phone with him, said no, that he was beloved and dearly beloved went without saying, and that wasn't the point anymore. I was foolish enough to want to give her a hug for making this statement; that's how low my feelings for her had sunk. She pushed me away. Does she even know I still exist? What, for god's sake, does she think I've done?

Hanna, who had long since looked after him all on her own, wanders around unrecognizable, as though she were no longer lit by the spotlight she stood in when she took center stage with Fipps and through Fipps. There is really nothing left to say about her, it's as though she had neither traits nor characteristics. She used to be cheerful and alive, fearful, soft and strict, always prepared to steer the child, let him loose and then rein him in to her side again. After the incident with the knife, for example, she'd been in her prime, glowing with magnanimity and compassionate insight, she was able to acknowledge the child and his faults, she stood up for him about everything before every authority. It was in his third year of school. Fipps had gone after one of his schoolmates with a pocket knife. He wanted to drive it into his chest; but the knife slipped and hit the child in his arm. We were called to school and I had agonizing discussions with the headmaster and the teachers and the parents of the injured child—agonizing because I never doubted that Fipps was capable, not only of this, but of much more, but I wasn't allowed to say what I thought—agonizing because the opinions that were foisted upon me didn't interest me in the slightest. What we were supposed to do with Fipps was unclear to everyone. He sobbed, now defiant, now in desperation, and if any conclusion could have been drawn, he did indeed seem to regret what had happened. Nevertheless, we never succeeded in convincing him to go to the child and ask his forgiveness. We forced him to do it and the three of us went to the hospital. But I think that Fipps, who didn't have anything against the child when he threatened him, began hating him the moment he was forced to say his piece. It was no childish anger, but a very carefully controlled, very refined, very adult hatred. He'd succeeded in experiencing a difficult emotion, one he'd never let anyone see, and it was as though this earned him the honor of being dubbed human.

Whenever I think about the school field trip that put an end to everything, the incident with the knife occurs to me too as though the two were remotely connected due to the shock that reminded me again of my child's existence. These few school years appear, except for those events, like a void in my memory because I never paid attention to his growing up, to the ever increasing lucidity of his intellect and sensibilities. I suppose he was just like every other child that age: wild and tender, loud and taciturn—in Hanna's eyes, everything exceptional, everything unique.

The school's headmaster called me at the office. That had never happened before—even when the episode with the knife transpired, they'd called the apartment and it was Hanna who first informed me.

I met the man a half hour later in the company lobby. We went across the street to a coffee shop. He tried at first to tell me what he had to say in the lobby, then on the street, but even at the coffee shop he didn't feel like the place was right for it. Maybe there simply isn't any place that is right for announcing a child's death.

It wasn't the teacher's fault, he said.

I nodded. Fine by me.

The paths were in good condition, but Fipps had broken away from the rest of the class, out of exuberance or curiosity, perhaps he just wanted to look for a stick.

The headmaster started to stammer.

Fipps had slipped on a cliff and fallen to the one below.

The head injury itself had not been critical, but the doctor had found an explanation for the sudden death, a cyst, I probably was aware…

I nodded. Cyst? I had no idea what that was.

The whole school was deeply troubled, the headmaster said, an investigative commission had been established, the police informed…

I wasn't thinking about Fipps, rather about the

teacher whom I felt sorry for and I made it clear that there was nothing to fear from my end.

No one was to blame. No one.

I got up before we even placed an order, put a schilling on the table and we parted. I went back to my office only to go out again immediately, to the coffee shop to drink a cup of coffee after all even though I would have preferred a cognac or a shot of schnapps. I didn't dare drink a cognac. It was already noon and I had to go home and tell Hanna. I don't know how I managed to do it or what I said. It must have already dawned on her as we walked away from the apartment door and through the foyer. It all happened so fast. I had to put her to bed; call the doctor. She was out of her mind and screamed until she finally lost consciousness. She screamed as terribly as she had at his birth, and I trembled with fear for her, just as I had then. Once again, all I wished for was that nothing would happen to Hanna. I always thought: Hanna! Never did I ever think of the child.

In the days that followed I took care of the necessary formalities by myself. At the cemetery—I had kept the time of the funeral secret from Hanna—the headmaster gave a speech. It was a nice day, a light breeze was blowing, the bows on the wreaths rose as if for a festive occasion. The headmaster went on and on. For the first time I saw the whole class, the children with whom Fipps had spent half of most every day, a pack of little lads staring dully into space, and I knew that Fipps had tried to stab one of them to death. There is a sort of inner coldness that makes what is nearest and what is most distant seem equally far removed from us. The grave receded into the distance together with the people and the wreaths gathered around it. I watched the whole Central Cemetery drifting away on the horizon far to the east, and even when people pressed their hands in mine, all I could feel was pressure upon pressure, all I could see were the faces somewhere out there, precise and just as they appear up close, but far removed, extremely far removed.

Learn the language of shadows! You, learn it yourself.

But now that everything is over and Hanna no longer sits for hours in his room but has since permitted me to bar that door he ran through so often, I sometimes talk to him in the language I hadn't deemed worthy before.

My little savage. My heart.

I'm prepared to carry him piggyback and promise him a blue balloon, a boat trip on the old Danube and postage stamps. I blow on his knee when he has scraped it and I help him with his arithmetic.

And even if I can't bring him back to life this way, at least it's not too late to think that I've accepted him, this son of mine. I couldn't befriend him because I'd gone too far with him.

Don't go too far. First learn to keep going. Learn it yourself.

But you'd first have to know how to tear to shreds the bow of sorrow stretching from man to woman. This distance, measurable by the silence, how should it ever shrink? Because for time without end, wherever there is a minefield for me, there will be a garden for Hanna.

I've stopped thinking and would rather get up, cross the dark passage and, without saying a word, reach Hanna. I don't look at anything with this purpose in mind—neither my hands that might hold her nor my lips that could lock into her own. It's irrelevant which sound precedes each word when I approach her, how much warmth precedes every sympathy or sentiment. I wouldn't go for the sake of having her back, but rather in order to keep her in the world so that she in turn can keep me in the world. By virtue of union, benevolent and sinister. If children should proceed from this embrace, good, let them come, let them be, grow and become like everyone else. I'll devour them like Cronus, beat them like a looming, dreadful father, spoil them, the sacred animals, and be as susceptible to deception as King Lear. I'll raise them according to the demands of the time, half in the ways of the wolf and half in the spirit of civility—and I'll give them nothing along the way. Like a man of my times: no worldly goods, no words of wisdom.

But I don't know whether Hanna is still awake.

I've stopped thinking. The flesh is strong and sinister that buries true emotion beneath the booming cackle of night.

I don't know whether Hanna is still awake.

Among Murderers and Madmen

The men are on their way to finding themselves on those evenings when they gather together to drink, to talk and pontificate. And in these rounds of pointless conversation, they are following their own scent as their pontifications rise with the smoke from pipes, cigars and cigarettes and the world turns to nothing but smoke and madness in the small-town saloons, in the banquet halls, in the back rooms of big restaurants and in the wine cellars of big cities.

We are in Vienna, more than ten years after the war. "After the war"—that is the measure of our time.

We are in Vienna, evenings, and we swarm out into the coffee houses and restaurants. We come straight from the publishing houses and offices, from the practices and the ateliers and gather here; hot on the trail of something, hunting down the best of what we have lost, like wild animals—predator and prey—we are at a loss and laughing. During the pauses, when no one can think of a joke or a story that absolutely must be told, when no one has anything to combat the silence and everyone gets lost in himself, now and then someone hears the blue lament of the hunted wild game—once more, ever still.

That night, I went with Mahler to get together with the guys at the Kronenkeller in the city center. Now that evening had fallen all over the world, the taverns were full, and the men talked and pontificated and told stories like the sufferers and errant wanderers of yore, like the titans and demigods of history and storybooks; they rode out into the wild blue yonder, hunkered down around the fire, the communal open fire that they fanned at night and in the desert where they found themselves. They forgot their careers and their families. No one wanted to think about the fact that right about now their wives would be turning down the sheets at home and settling in for the night because they didn't know what else to do. Barefoot or in slippers, with their hair drawn back and tired faces, their wives were going through their homes, turning off the gas, fearfully checking under the bed and in the closets, placating the children with words of diversion or sitting sullenly beside the radio only to finally lie down with thoughts of revenge in the empty apartment. Feeling like victims, their wives lay there with eyes wide open in the darkness, filled with desperation and malice. They turned to account their marriages, the years and the household budgets, manipulating, falsifying and embezzling. Finally, they closed their eyes, clung to waking dreams, surrendering to deceptively savage thoughts until they finally fell asleep in the clutches of one last great reproach. And in those first dreams, they murdered their husbands, letting die in car crashes, of heart attacks and pneumonia; letting them die quick or slow and miserable deaths, depending on the severity of each respective reproach, and beneath those delicate, closed eyelids, the tears always welled up in pain and grief over the death of their husbands. They wept for their men—men who had journeyed out, ventured out like the blue knights and wild huntsmen who seemed to never come home—and, in the end, they wept for themselves. They had come into their own truest tears.

But we were far removed from all that, the Corona Club, the choral guild, the fraternities, league members, groups, associations, the symposia and the men's night out. We ordered our wine, placed the tobacco pouches out on the tables before us and were beyond reach of their revenge and their tears. We didn't die, instead we came to life, talked and pontificated. It wasn't until much later, toward morning, that we would stroke our wives' damp faces in the dark and insult them anew with our breath, the stringent, sour smell of wine and beer on our breath, or fervently hope they were already asleep and not another word need fall in the crypt our bedroom had become, this prison cell to which we returned every time exhausted, passionately conciliatory, as though we'd given our word of honor.

We were a long way off. We got together that evening the same as every Friday: Haderer, Bertoni, Hutter, Ranitzky, Friedl, Mahler and I. No, Herz wasn't there, he was in London that week preparing for his final return to Vienna. Steckel was gone, too, because he was sick again. Mahler said, "There are only three of us Jews here today," and he fixed his gaze on Friedl and me.

Friedl stared uncomprehendingly at him with his bulging, watery eyes and clasped his hands together, probably because he was thinking he wasn't even really a Jew and neither was Mahler, though his father may have been, or his grandfather—he didn't know for sure. But Mahler put on his haughty face. You'll see, said his face. And it said: I'm never mistaken.

It was Black Friday. Haderer had the floor. That meant that the errant wanderer and sufferer of yore in him kept silent and the Titan had his say; it meant he would no longer settle for being bullied about and boasting of the blows he'd been dealt in the past, rather he would now brag about the blows he had doled out himself. On this particular Friday, the conversation took a different turn, perhaps because Herz and Steckel were missing and because Friedl, Mahler and I didn't seem to pose a hindrance to anyone, but maybe it was just because the conversation had to be honest for once, because smoke and madness make room for everything to have its say at some point.

Nowadays nighttime was a battlefield, a platoon advancing on the frontlines, a state of high alert, and you had to look alive in that night, you had to revel in it. Haderer and Hutter immersed themselves in reminiscences of the war, they wallowed in remembrance, in manifold obscurities which neither of them ever completely abandoned until they reached the point where their bodies were transformed and they were back in uniform, until they had both resumed command, until they were both officers establishing contact with headquarters; the time they'd been flown into Voronezh on a "Ju 52" but then suddenly couldn't agree on what they had thought of General Manstein in the winter of '42, and the way they simply couldn't agree about whether the 6th Army could have been relieved or not, whether the deployment plan itself was to blame or not; as an afterthought, how they ended up landing on the island of Crete, but how in Paris a young Frenchwoman had told Hutter that she liked the Austrians better than the Germans, and when day broke in Norway and the day the partisans had surrounded them in Serbia—by then they'd finally reached the point where they ordered the second liter of wine, and we ordered another one, too, because Mahler had begun revealing to us a couple of intrigues from the Austrian Medical Association.

We drank the wines from the Burgenland and from Gumpoldskirchen. We drank in Vienna and for us the night was nowhere near an end.

That evening, after the partisans had already gained Haderer's respect and had only been castigated in passing (since it was never quite clear what Haderer really thought about them or anything else, and Mahler's face told me yet again: I'm never mistaken!), once the dead Slovenian nuns were lying naked in the woods outside Veldes, and, Haderer, nonplussed by Mahler's silence, had to interrupt the telling of his tale and leave the nuns lying there, an old man whom we'd known for a long time came over to our table. It was that itinerant, dirty, dwarflike man with a sketchpad who pestered the customers into letting him draw their pictures for a few schillings. We didn't want to be bothered and certainly not to be drawn, but the awkward silence that ensued unexpectedly caused Haderer to magnanimously challenge the man to draw our pictures, to finally get around to showing us what he could do. We each pulled a few schillings from our change purses, heaped them together on the table and slid the pile his way. But he paid no mind to the money. He stood there blissfully supporting his sketchpad on the crook of his left forearm with his head thrown back. His thick pencil hatched across the paper so quickly that we burst out laughing. His movements resembled something you'd see in a silent film—grotesque and slapdash. Since I was sitting closest to him, he turned to me with a bow and handed me the first sheet.

He had drawn Haderer:

With dueling scars on his small face. With his skin stretched too tautly over his skull. Grimacing, with a fixed and enduring theatrical expression. Hair parted with painstaking precision. A look in his eyes that strove to seduce, to mesmerize, but didn't quite succeed.

Haderer was a departmental director at the radio station who wrote excessively long dramas that were regularly staged at a loss by all the big theaters to the unbridled praise of all the critics. We all had them at home, volume upon volume, with handwritten dedications: "My venerable friend...". We were all his venerable friends—with the exception of Friedl and me because we were too young and hence could only be "dear friends" or "dear, young and gifted friends." He never accepted for broadcast a manuscript from Friedl or me, but he referred us to other stations and editorial departments and thus considered himself our patron and that of about twenty other young people, even though there was never any apparent sign to indicate just what that patronage consisted of and what kind of results his good favor produced. Of course the fact that he had to console us and at the same time embolden us with compliments that had nothing to do with him, rather with those "flea bags" as he was wont to call them, with that ubiquitous "pack of fly by day bandits", with the *Hofrats* and the other troublesome senile elements in the ministries, in the arts councils and the broadcast industry; he drew the highest possible salary from those very institutions and received from them, at carefully measured intervals, all the honors, awards and even the medals that city and state had to bestow; he presented speeches at major events; he was seen as a man ideally suited to represent them and was nevertheless considered one of the most outspoken and independent of men. He contested everything, that is, he always contested the opponent, so that what made one side of an issue happy one day made the other side happy on another because the one side had since become the other. He simply knew, so to speak, how to call a spade a spade; fortunately, though, he refrained from naming names so that no one in particular ever took offense.

Hatched out like this on paper by the mendicant draftsman, he resembled a malfeasant death or one of those masks that actors still today sometimes fashion for themselves to play Mephisto or Iago.

Hesitantly, I passed the piece of paper along. When it made its way to Haderer, I watched him carefully and had to admit my surprise. He did not for a moment seem bothered or offended by it, but instead demonstrated utmost composure, clapping his hands together—three times too many perhaps—but he always clapped, always applauded too much—and shouting "Bravo! Bravo! Bravo!" And what he was also saying with this "Bravo" was that he alone was the great man who had praises to grant here, and, accordingly, the old man reverently bowed his head, but barely looked up because he was hurrying to finish Bertoni's face.

But this is how Bertoni was portrayed:

With a handsome athletic face that bore traces of a tan. With sanctimonious eyes that obliterated any impression of healthy radiance. With his hand cupped over his mouth as though he were afraid of saying something too loud, as if he risked letting an inauspicious word slip.

Bertoni worked for the *Tagblatt*. For years now he had been ashamed of the steady decline in standards in his feuilleton and now all he could do was smile melancholically whenever anyone directed his attention to inconsistencies and infelicities, to the lack of quality contributions or accurate information. His smile seemed to say, "Just what *do* you expect—these days!" But he couldn't bring the paper's decline to a halt single-handedly even though he knew what a good paper was supposed to look like—oh yes, he knew, had known very early on and that was why he preferred above all to talk about the old papers, about the times when the Viennese press was in its heyday and the way he'd worked under its legendary kings and learned from them. He knew all the stories, all the affairs and scandals of twenty years' past and it was only in that period that he felt at home and he could bring those times to life, could carry on about them without letting up. He also liked to talk about the dismal times that followed, the way he and a couple of other journalists had pulled themselves through in those first few years after 1938, their clandestine thoughts and discussions and innuendos, the dangers looming around them before they, too, donned the uniform, and now, there he sat, still clad in his magic cap, smiling, unable to get over a lot of things. He formulated his sentences carefully. What he really thought, no one knew—innuendo had become second nature to him, he acted as though the Gestapo were always listening. What had become of the Gestapo was some sort of everlasting police state in which Bertoni remained constantly on guard. Not even Steckel could restore in him any sense of security. He had known Steckel well—even before Steckel was forced to emigrate; now they had again become best friends, not only because Steckel had vouched for him shortly after 1945 and given him back his job at the *Tagblatt,* but because they were more likely to come to mutual understanding among themselves than they were among others, especially when it came to talking about "those days." That was when they deployed a language that Bertoni must have simply learned to imitate sometime in the past, and now that was the only one he had left and he was happy to have the chance to speak it with someone—it was a light-hearted, transient, comical language that didn't quite suit his appearance or his demeanor, a language of innuendo that was doubly appealing to him now. Unlike Steckel, who beat around the bush in order to clarify matters, he beat things above and beyond the bush into hapless obscurity.

The draftsman had again placed the sheet in front of me. Mahler leaned over, glanced at it and laughed haughtily. I smiled and passed it along. Bertoni didn't get the chance to say "Bravo" because Haderer butted in and deprived him of the opportunity to speak his mind. He simply stared introspectively and wistfully at his portrait. Once Haderer had settled down, Mahler shot across the table to Bertoni, "You're a handsome devil. Did you know that?"

And this is how the old man saw Ranitzky:

With a zealous face, a flattery-will-get-you-everywhere face poised to nod his consent before it was even expected of him. Even his ears and eyelids seem to nod in the drawing.

You could always count on Ranitzky to agree to everything. Everyone kept silent whenever Ranitzky so much as mentioned a word about the past because there was no sense in being frank with Ranitzky. It was better to forget about it and better to forget about him; he was tacitly tolerated at the table. Sometimes he sat there nodding to himself, forgotten by everyone. He had, incidentally, been left high and dry for two years after 1945 and had perhaps even been in jail, but now he was a professor at the university again. He had re-written all the pages dealing with recent history in his *History of Austria* and republished it. Once, when I tried to question Mahler about Ranitzky, Mahler stated briefly "Everyone knows that he did it out of opportunism and that he's utterly incorrigible, but he knows that himself. That's why no one bothers to tell him. But he should be told nonetheless." In any case, the expression on Mahler's face told him every time he saw him or responded to him or simply said, "Listen up…" and with that, managed to set

Ranitzky's eyelids aflutter. Indeed, he had him shaking in his boots at every encounter, every listless, fleeting handshake. Mahler was at his cruelest when he had nothing to say or when he adjusted his tie ever so slightly, looked someone straight in the eye and let on at once that he remembered everything. He had the memory of a merciless angel and always remembered everything; all he had was this memory, he harbored no hatred, just this inhuman capacity to retain everything and to let you know that he did.

Finally, this is the way Hutter was drawn:

The way Barabbas might have looked had it seemed to him self-evident that he be set free. With a childish sense of certainty and triumph in his cunning round face.

Hutter was a freed man, shameless and unscrupulous. Everyone liked him, even I did and maybe even Mahler did, too. "Set him free!"—even we chimed in. Time had brought us to the point where we repeated it constantly: "Set him free!" Hutter succeeded at everything and even succeeded in preventing people from begrudging him his success. He was an investor who financed all sorts of endeavors, a film company, newspapers, magazines and recently Haderer had gotten him to back a committee called "Culture and Freedom". He joined different people at different tables throughout the city every night, seated beside theater directors and actors, beside businessmen and high level civil servants. He published books but never read a book, just as he never saw any of the films he financed; nor did he attend the theater, but he came to the theater tables after the shows. He sincerely loved the world in which things were laid out on the table and plans were made. He loved the world of preparations, of opinions about everything, of calculation, intrigues, risks and the shuffling of the cards. He liked to watch the others shuffle them and took their sides when the chips were down, intervened or watched the way the trump was laid, then intervened again. He took pleasure in everything, took pleasure in his friends, the old and the new, the weak and the strong. He laughed where Ranitzky only smiled (Ranitzky got by on a smile and mostly smiled only when someone else was being slaughtered by the group, an absent someone with whom he was scheduled to meet the next day, but his smile was so subtle and ambiguous that he could tell himself he hadn't gone along with it, but had simply smiled in self-defense, had kept to himself and to his own interests and opinions). Hutter laughed aloud whenever anyone was being slaughtered and could even go so far as to repeat what had been said without giving it a second thought. Or he could fly into a rage and defend the person in his absence, shield him from the slaughter, fend off the others, rescue the imperiled man while at the same time rolling up his sleeves and participating in the next onslaught if he felt so inclined. He was spontaneous, could work himself up into a lather and the slightest shred of circumspection, of careful deliberation was entirely alien to him.

Haderer's enthusiasm for the draftsman was dwindling now; he wanted to return to the conversation, so was grateful to Mahler for forbidding the man from drawing him, and, with a wave of his hand, sent the old man packing. The man quickly pocketed his earnings and bowed one last time before the great man whom he obviously recognized as such.

Optimistically, I hoped that the conversation

would turn to the upcoming elections or the vacant position of theater director that had already given us something to talk about for the last three Fridays. But this particular Friday everything was different, the others carried on endlessly about the war they had been drawn into, not one of them could escape its pull, they gasped for air in the maelstrom, ever louder, making it impossible for us to talk about anything else at our end of the table. We were forced to listen and stare into space, crushing our bread on the table, and now and then I exchanged looks with Mahler who expelled cigarette smoke from his mouth very slowly, blowing smoke rings, and seemed to have abandoned himself completely to playing with his smoke. He tilted his head back slightly and loosened his tie.

"It was the experience of the war that brought us closer to the enemy," I heard Haderer saying.

"What enemy?" Friedl stuttered in an attempt to join in, "The Bolivians?" Haderer faltered, he didn't know what Friedl meant and I tried to remember whether or not they had also been at war with Bolivia back then. Mahler laughed a stifled laugh, it looked as though he were hoping to retrieve the smoke ring he'd just released and draw it back into his mouth.

Bertoni was quick to explain, "The British, the Americans, the French."

Haderer had regained his composure and interrupted him vehemently, "I beg your pardon, but for me, they were never the enemy, I'm simply referring to the experiences. I had no intention of saying anything else. We're now in a better position to engage in dialogues, to have a say, and to write, too, all because of them. Just think about the neutral countries who don't have those bitter experiences and have gone without them for the longest time." He covered his eyes with his hand. "I wouldn't want to have missed out on a thing, not one of those years, not one of those experiences."

Friedl said like an obstinate schoolboy, but much too softly, "I could have. I could have done without them."

Haderer gave him an ambiguous look; he didn't show his anger—most likely he was preparing to unleash one of his you-can-please-all-the-people-all-the-time sermons. But at that moment, Hutter propped his elbows square on the table and, speaking loudly enough to fluster Haderer and thwart his plans, he asked, "Yeah, what is it really? Couldn't you say that culture is only possible as a result of war, struggle and conflict...Experiences—what is it about culture?"

Haderer paused briefly, first admonished Hutter, then proceeded to rebuke Friedl and suddenly, completely out of the blue, began speaking about the First World War in order to avoid talking about the Second. The Battle of the Isonzo River was at issue, Haderer and Ranitzky exchanged reminiscences about their adventures in the regiments and railed against the Italians who'd been enemies in the first war before they again turned to railing against their Italian allies in the second; they talked about "back stabbing," about "unreliable leadership," but ultimately preferred to return to the Isonzo and in the end they were lying under barrage on the Kleiner Pal. Bertoni took advantage of the split second in which Haderer thirstily raised his glass to his mouth, and inexorably began relating an incredibly involved, implausible tale from the Second World War. It was about the way he and a German philologist had been assigned the task of organizing a brothel in France; apparently there was no end to the blunders they encountered and Bertoni lost himself in the most whimsical embellishments. Even Friedl was suddenly shaking with laughter, which I found perplexing and even more perplexing when he suddenly made an effort to appear as though he too had been in on the operations, the charges, the dates. Friedl was, after all, my age and couldn't possibly have entered the military until the last year of the war at the very earliest, fresh out of school. But then I noticed that Friedl was drunk and I knew how difficult he could get when he was drunk, how he could join in a conversation in defiant mockery and put in his two cents out of desperation, so it wasn't long before I detected the derision in his words. For a moment, though, I had placed even him under suspicion because of the way he'd taken up with the others, the way he'd entered this world of cock-and-bull stories, of tests of courage, heroism, obedience and defiance, that man's world from which all the things that mattered to us by light of day became worthless; a world in which no one knew anymore what to take pride in and what to take shame and whether this pride or shame corresponded to anything in the world in which we were citizens. I recalled Bertoni's story about stealing a pig in Russia, but I knew that Bertoni was so proper he wasn't capable of pocketing so much as a pencil from the editorial offices. Or Haderer, for example, and the way he'd been decorated with the highest honors in the first war and how the story still goes that Hötzendorf had entrusted him with a mission that required utmost daring. But Haderer, to look at him here and now, was absolutely incapable of doing anything daring and always had been. In another world ruled by a different law, he may have had more mettle, but at least as long as he remained part of this world, he had none. And Mahler, who is cold-blooded and the most fearless of men I know, told me that back then, as a young man working in 1914 or 1915 as a medic, he had fainted and taken morphine in order to be able to stand working in the military field hospital. After that, he'd made two suicide attempts and spent the rest of his time until the end of the war in a psychiatric ward. So they all operated in two worlds, and in each of the worlds they were different—two separate selves, never united and eternally severed. All of them were drunk now, swaggering through hellfire and brimstone with their undelivered soldier selves screaming to be redeemed by their civilian selves, those endearing, social selves with wives and professions, rivalries and all sorts of needs. And they remained hot on the trail of the hunted wild game within them that been driven out of them at an early age, never to return, and as long as it never returned, their world consisted solely of madness. Friedl nudged me to indicate he wanted to get up and go, and I was taken aback by the sight of his glistening, swollen face. I left with him. Twice, we went in the wrong direction in search of the washroom. In the hallway, we cleared a path for ourselves through a group of men streaming into the large hall in the cellar. I'd never before seen such a crowd gathered at the Kronenkeller, nor did I recognize any of these faces. It was so conspicuous that I asked a waiter what was going on here tonight. He didn't know for sure, but he said it was some sort of "veteran's reunion," normally, they didn't rent out the space for this type of gathering, but that Colonel von Winkler, who, as I should surely know, was very famous, would also be in attendance celebrating along with them, the meeting was called to commemorate the Battle of Narvik, or so he thought.

It was dead silent in the washroom. Friedl leaned on the sink, reached for the towel hanging from the dispenser and yanked it one rotation.

"Do you know," he asked, "why we get together like this?"

I kept silent and shrugged my shoulders.

"You *do* know what I mean, don't you?" Friedl said emphatically.

"Yes, yes," I said.

But Friedl continued: "You do know why even Herz and Ranitzky get together, don't you? Why Herz doesn't hate him the way he hates Langer who is perhaps less guilty and is a dead man today? Ranitzky isn't a dead man. Tell me, for the love of god, why we get together like this!? Especially Herz I don't understand. They killed his wife, his mother…."

I racked my brain for a moment, then said, "I understand why. Yes, indeed I understand."

Friedl asked, "Because he's forgotten it? Or because after a certain point, he just wants to bury the hatchet?"

"No," I said, "That's not it. It doesn't have anything to do with forgetting. Not with forgiving either. It doesn't have anything to do with any of that."

Friedl said, "But Herz helped Ranitzky get back on his feet and for at least the past three years now, they've been getting together, and he's been getting together with Hutter and Haderer, too. He knows everything about every one of them."

"We know it, too. And what are we doing about it?"

Friedl continued, more urgent, as though something had just occurred to him, "But whether Ranitzky hates Herz because he helped him out? What do you think? He probably hates him even for that."

I said, "No, I don't believe so. He thinks that's the way it ought to be and at best, he's afraid that there's still something in the works, that there's something yet to come. He's not sure. Others just don't give it a second thought, like Hutter—they consider it the natural course of events, that time passes and times change."

"After 1945, I, too, thought the world was partitioned, once and for all times, into good and evil, but now the world has already fallen apart again and again it's different. It was hardly fathomable, it happened so imperceptibly, now we've come together again just so that it can part once more along the lines of differing opinions and the deeds of differing minds, different deeds. Do you understand? It has indeed come to that, whether we want to acknowledge it or not. But even that doesn't completely account for this pathetic sense of unity."

Friedl yelled, "What does then! What is behind it? Say something, will you? Is it because we're all the same anyway and that's why we're together?"

"No," I said, "we aren't all the same. Mahler was never like the others and, let's hope, we won't ever be either."

Friedl stared into space, "OK, so Mahler and you and I, we're still a lot different from each other, what each of us wants and thinks is slightly different. Not even the others are of one mind, there's a world of difference between Haderer and Ranitzky, Ranitzky who'd still like to see his Reich reinstated, but certainly not Haderer who's placed his bets on democracy and this time will stick to his guns, I can sense that. Ranitzky is odious, and so is Haderer—and will forever remain so for me in spite of everything, but they aren't the same, and there is a difference whether you sit at the table with only one of them or both...And Bertoni...!"

Just as Friedl had blurted out his name, Bertoni entered the room and blushed red beneath his brown tan. He disappeared behind a stall door, and we fell silent for a while. I washed my hands and face.

Friedl whispered, "So that means everything is in league with everything else, and I'm in it too, but I don't want to be. Even you are in league with them!"

I said, "We aren't in league with anyone; there isn't a league. It's far worse than that. I think that we're all forced to live with one another, and yet we can't live with one another. Everyone has one world in his head and one claim that precludes every other world and every other claim. But we all need one another if anything good or whole is ever to come of it."

Friedl laughed maliciously, "Need. That's it of course; maybe even I'll someday need Haderer..."

I said, "That's not what I meant."

Friedl, "Well, why not? Some day I will need him, it's easy for you to talk, just in general, you don't have a wife and three kids. And you might someday need someone else who's no better than Haderer, even if it's not Haderer himself." I didn't answer.

"I have three children," he screamed, waving his hand about three feet from the floor to show how small his kids were.

"Stop it," I said, "that's no excuse. This is getting us nowhere."

Friedl got angry, "Oh yes it is an excuse, you have no idea how strong an excuse it is, for just about everything. I got married at 22. It wasn't my fault. You haven't a clue as to what that means, not a clue!"

He made a face and propped himself with full force against the basin. I thought he would sink to the ground. Bertoni came out, didn't even bother to wash his hands and left the room so abruptly it seemed he was afraid of hearing his name mentioned again and more than just his name.

Friedl staggered and said, "You don't like Herz?

Am I right?"

I hesitated to answer, "What makes you think that?...All right then, no, I don't like him. Because I take issue with the way he associates with them. Because I will always take issue with that. Because he is complicit in preventing us from coming to a different table with him and a few others. Yet he sees to it that we can all sit at the same table."

Friedl, "You are crazy, crazier than I. First you say we all need one another, and now you're damning Herz for the very same thing. I don't have an issue with him. He has every right to be friends with Ranitzky."

I said, incensed, "No, he doesn't. No one has a right to that. Not even he."

"Yes, after the war," said Friedl, "we all thought that the world was partitioned, once and for all times, into good and evil. But I'll tell you one thing—I'll tell you what the world looks like when it is neatly partitioned.

"Back then, when I came to London and met Herz's brother. It knocked the wind right out of me. I could barely breathe, he didn't know anything about me, and it wasn't even enough for him that I was so young; the first thing he asked me was, 'Where were you in those days and what were you doing?' I said that I'd been in school and that my older brothers were executed as deserters; I also told him that in the end I was forced to go along with it, just like everyone else in my class. He didn't ask anything more about that, but he started asking about a few people whom he'd known, about Haderer and Bertoni, among many others. I tried to tell him what I knew and so it came out that some of them were sorry, that some of them felt badly about it, yes, there really wasn't much more to say about it, no matter how hard you tried; some of the others were dead after all, and most of them denied it and sought to cover it up, I told him that, too. Haderer will always deny it, will always falsify his past, don't you think? But then I noticed that this man wasn't even listening to me, he was completely mesmerized by one thought, and when I started talking about the differences again and said, for the sake of being fair, that Bertoni probably never did anything bad in those days and, at worst, had been cowardly, he interrupted me and said: No. Just please don't differentiate. For me, there is no difference, and there never will be. I will never again set foot in that country. I will never ever walk among the murderers."

"I can understand it, I understand him better than Herz. Although," I said, slowly, "it really doesn't work that way either, that can only last as long as the world's worse is at its worst. You can't remain a victim all your life. It doesn't work that way."

"Seems to me there's no way anything in the world works! We're busy knocking ourselves out here and aren't even capable of clarifying for ourselves this dismal little situation, and there were others before us who grappled without being able to clarify anything and ran themselves into the ground, either as victims or henchmen, and the deeper you delve into history the more intractable it becomes; sometimes I am lost when it comes to history, don't know where to hang my heart, which parties, groups, forces I can cling to because it's clear that the world is governed by the law of infamy. And all you can ever do is to side with the victims, but that will get you nowhere because they can't point the way either."

"That's what's so terrible about it," Friedl cried, "the victims, the many, many victims, cannot in any way point the way! And for the murderers, the times change. Victims remain victims. That's all there is to it. My father was a victim of the Dollfuss era, my grandfather, a victim of the Monarchy, my brothers were victims of Hitler, but that's no help to me, you see what I mean? They just fell in line, or fell in the line of duty, were overrun, shot down, placed before the firing squad, up against the wall, little people who never took a stand or thought too much about anything. Actually, two or three of them did have thoughts of their own, my grandfather saw the First Republic coming, but, can you tell me what the point was? Couldn't it have come about just as easily without his death? And my father had his own thoughts about social democracy, but tell me who can lay claim to his death, certainly not our workers' party with its sights set on winning the election. No one needs to die for that to happen. Not for that. Jews were slaughtered because they were Jews, they were just victims, so many victims, but certainly the point wasn't so that people today finally get around to telling the children that Jews are human? It's a little late for that, don't you think?

No, that's exactly what no one understands—namely that the victims serve no purpose! Precisely that is what no one understands and that's why no one is offended by the fact that these victims are the ones who pay the price for our insights. There's absolutely no need for these insights. Who in the world doesn't know that killing is wrong? That's been common wisdom for two thousand years. Is there anything left to be said about it? Oh, but in Haderer's last speech, there was plenty left to say about it, as if it were only then being discovered, the tangled snarl of *humanitas* rolling off his tongue, offering up quotes from the classics, summoning the church fathers and the most recent metaphysical platitudes. That's simply insane. How can anyone spout off about that? It's either completely imbecile or completely malevolent. Who the hell are we if we need to be told these things?"

And he started in again, "Would someone please tell me what the hell we're doing getting together like this. Someone should tell me and I will listen. Because this is really unprecedented, and whatever comes of it will be equally unprecedented."

I don't understand this world anymore!—we often told ourselves that those nights when we sat drinking and talking and pontificating. But for each of us, there were moments when the world seemed to make sense. I told Friedl I understood everything and he was wrong for not understanding. But then I suddenly didn't understand anything anymore either and thought for a moment I couldn't live even with him, and of course even less so with the others. And you absolutely couldn't live in the same world as a man like Friedl either, a man with whom you might agree on many things, but for whom having a family was an excuse, or with Steckel, for whom art was an excuse. Sometimes I couldn't even live in the same world as Mahler whom I liked better than all the rest. Did I know whether or not he would come to the same decision I did next time I had to decide? "Looking back," we were in agreement, but as far as the future was concerned? Maybe I would soon part ways with both him and Friedl—we could only hope that nothing would come between us before then.

Friedl whimpered, straightened his back and staggered to the next stall door. I could hear him vomiting, gurgling, coughing up phlegm and saying, "If you could only get it all to come out, if you could just spit it all out, everything, everything!"

He came out beaming, with a twisted look on his face, and said, "Soon I'll drink to fraternity with those guys in there, maybe even with Ranitzky. And I will tell them…"

I held his face under the faucet, dried it off, then took him by the arm. "You will say nothing to them!" We had already been gone too long and had to get back to the table. As we passed by the big hall, the men at the "veteran's reunion" were making such a racket that I didn't catch a word of what Friedl said after that. He was looking better. I think we were laughing at something, probably at ourselves, when we entered the door to the back room.

The air was even thicker with smoke now, and we could barely see as far as the table. As we approached and made our way through the smoke and cast off our madness, I saw a man I didn't know sitting beside Mahler. Both of them kept silent while the others talked. Once Friedl and I had taken our seats and Bertoni gave us this bleary-eyed look, the stranger stood up to shake hands; he muttered a name. There wasn't an ounce of cordiality in him, nothing to render him in any way accessible, his eyes were cold and dead, and I looked questioningly at Mahler, who must have known him. He was a very tall man in his early thirties, though at first glance he gave the impression of being older. He wasn't poorly dressed, but it looked as though someone had given him a suit that was bigger than he needed, even at his size. It took a while before I was able to gather anything from the conversation in which neither Mahler nor the stranger participated.

So Haderer says to Hutter, "But then you must know General Zwirl, too!"

Hutter, elated, to Haderer, "Of course! From Graz."

Haderer, "A highly educated and refined man. One of the most knowledgeable experts on Greek. One of my dearest old friends."

So now we had to worry that Haderer would hold our deficiencies in knowledge of Greek and Latin against Friedl and me without giving any consideration to the fact that he and his kind prevented us from acquiring such knowledge in due time. But I was in no mood to address one of Haderer's pet topics or to challenge him in any way, I just leaned over to Mahler as if I hadn't heard. Mahler quietly said something to the stranger, who answered loudly, staring straight ahead. He answered every question with one sentence alone. I guessed he was one of Mahler's patients or in any case one of his friends who let Mahler treat him. Mahler always knew all sorts of people and fostered friendships we knew nothing about. The man was holding a pack of cigarettes in one hand and smoking with the other—smoking like I'd never before seen anyone smoke, mechanically puffing the cigarette at regular intervals as though smoking were all he knew how to do. He lit the next cigarette from the butt of the last, burning himself on the short stub without batting an eye and smoking like there was no tomorrow.

Suddenly, he stopped smoking, held the cigarette in his huge, unsightly, reddened hand and gestured with his head. I could hear it now, too. Even though the doors were closed, you could hear the bawdy strains of singing blaring from the big hall across the corridor all the way to where we were seated. It sounded something like, "and it's home, boys, home, that's where we will be when we come from 'cross the sea…"

Hastily, he drew on his cigarette and hollered over to us in the same tone of voice he'd used when answering Mahler's questions, "They're still trying to find their way home. I guess they never quite made it home."

Haderer laughed and said, "I'm not sure exactly what you mean, but that's really incredibly annoying and my venerable friend, his Honor Herr Colonel von Winkler, could better keep his people in check…If this keeps up, we'll have to look for some other place to meet."

Bertoni added that he'd already spoken with the proprietor who said this was an exception, this veteran's reunion, that they were celebrating some big anniversary. He didn't know exactly…

Haderer said that he didn't know exactly either, but his venerable friend and one-time comrade…

I didn't catch what the stranger said to us as he kept talking while Haderer and Bertoni drowned him out—Friedl's the only one who might have been able to hear him—so it wasn't clear to me why he suddenly claimed to be a murderer.

"...I was barely twenty years old, and already I knew," he said like someone who wasn't making his first attempt at telling his story, but rather who couldn't talk about anything else and for whom it didn't matter who was listening—he was content in telling anyone who would listen. "I knew I was destined to become a murderer in the same way others are destined to become heroes or saints or just ordinary people. There was nothing I lacked in order to fulfill my charge, not a single character trait, if you will, and everything drove me to one aim: to murder. The only thing missing was a victim. Back in those days, I went running through these very streets at night"—he waved his hand through the smoky space before him, and Friedl leaned back to escape the path of his hand—"I ran through these very alleyways, with the scent of chestnut blossoms wafting in the air, the air was always filled with the scent of chestnut blossoms, here in Vienna's Ringstrassen and in the narrow lanes, with my heart wrenching and my lungs pumping wildly like wings stayed by a straitjacket, with my breath escaping in gasps like the breath of a wolf on the hunt. I just didn't know how I should kill or whom. All I had were my hands, but would they be strong enough to strangle someone? I was much weaker and undernourished then. I didn't know anyone I might have hated, I was alone in this city and almost went mad nights because I couldn't find a victim. It was always at night that I had to get up and go down there, go out and stand on the abandoned, winding, wind-swept dark street corners, waiting. The streets were so quiet then, no one came by, no one approached, and I waited till I was freezing and whimpering with weakness and the madness in me dissipated. But that only lasted a short while before I was called up for the army. The first time I held a rifle in my hands I knew I was a goner. One day I would fire the shots. I surrendered to the barrel of the gun, I loaded the bullets as though I'd been stupid enough to have invented the gun and the gunpowder, that much was certain. At target practice, my shots were off, not because I couldn't aim, but because I knew this black bull's eye-like thing wasn't an eye at all, it was but a substitute, a practice target that didn't result in death. It irritated me; it was just seductive eyewash, not the real thing. I fired, if you will, with deliberately dead-shot inaccuracy. I sweated profusely during these exercises; afterward, I often turned blue in the face, vomited and had to lie down. I was either a madman or a murderer, I was sure of that, and with my last ounce of resistance to this fate, I told the others about it, hoping they would protect me, hoping they would protect themselves from me and that they knew who they were dealing with. But those farm boys, carpenters and office workers in my barracks paid no heed to what I said. They pitied or ridiculed me, but they didn't take me for a murderer. Maybe they did? I don't know. One of them, a postal employee who spent too much time at the movies and reading, called me 'Jack the Ripper'; a smart guy; but I don't think he really believed it either."

The stranger put out his cigarette, hastily lowered his eyes, then raised them; I could feel his long, cold gaze directed at me and didn't know why I felt the desire to withstand his stare. I withstood it, but it lasted longer than the looks lovers and enemies exchange; it lasted so long I could no longer think or form an opinion and was so empty that I flinched the next time I heard his loud, uninflected voice.

"We landed in Italy, Monte Cassino. That was

the biggest slaughterhouse you can imagine. The way meat was made into mush there you'd think it would have been a murderer's delight. But it wasn't, even though I was quite convinced of the fact that I was a murderer and had already been toting a rifle in public for half a year. By the time I reached my position in Monte Cassino, there wasn't a shred of soul left in me. I took in the stench of corpses, firebrand and bunkers like I the freshest mountain air. I wasn't afraid like the others. I might have celebrated my first murder as you would a wedding. Because what was a theater of war for the others was for me a staging ground for murder—a murder scene, as it were. But I want to tell you how it turned out. I didn't fire a shot. The first time I took aim, it was when we had a group of Poles before us; you know there were troops positioned there from any number of countries. I said to myself, 'No, not the Poles.' This pig Latin-labeling of people didn't sit well with me—Polacks, Yanks, Blacks. Alright, so no Americans and no Poles. I was just a simple murderer; I didn't have any excuse and my language was candid, not florid like the language spoken by others. 'Eradicate,' 'wear 'em down,' 'smoke 'em out'—words like that were out of the question for me, they nauseated me, I couldn't even bring myself to say them. My language was clear, I told myself, 'You must and you will kill a human being.' Yes, that's what I'd wanted for the longest time; for exactly one year it had been my feverish desire. To kill a human someone. I couldn't shoot, surely you must understand. I don't know if I can quite explain it. The others had it easy, they did their stints, mostly without knowing whether they'd hit their intended targets and if so, they never knew how many and didn't want to know. These men weren't murderers after all, you know? They just wanted to survive or to be decorated with honors, thinking about their families or about triumph and the fatherland, which they certainly weren't doing now, hardly more than they did then, they were themselves caught in the trap. But I thought incessantly about murder. I never fired a shot. Once, a week later, when the slaughter let up for just a moment, when we lost sight of the allied troops, when alone the air fleet sought to put an end to us and still all the human fodder had not yet been reduced to flesh and bones, I was sent back to Rome and court-martialed. I told them everything about me, but they apparently had no desire to understand me and I was thrown in the brig. I was convicted on charges of Cowardice in the Face of the Enemy and of Sedition and a couple of other infringements—I can no longer recall exactly what they were. Then I was suddenly released, taken up north for treatment in a psychiatric clinic. If I remember correctly, I was cured and returned six months later to join a different unit because nothing remained of the previous one, and we proceeded to the East to fight the battles in retreat."

Hutter, who couldn't stand to sit through a speech as long as this and would have liked to animate someone else to tell stories or jokes, said, as he broke a pretzel in his hand, "Well, mister, did you ever finally fire a shot?"

The man didn't look at him, and, instead of taking another drink like everyone else did at this moment, he shoved his glass to the middle of the table. He looked at me, then at Mahler and once more at me, and this time I turned my eyes away.

"No," he said, finally, "I'd been cured. That's why it didn't work. Surely you understand, gentlemen. A month later I was incarcerated again and spent the rest of the war in a camp. You have to understand, I simply couldn't shoot. If I couldn't even shoot a real human being, how in the world should I be capable of shooting at an abstraction, like the 'Russians'? I didn't have the slightest clue about what that was supposed to mean. And you had to have some sort of clue about what you're killing."

"A strange bird," Bertoni said quietly to Hutter; but I heard it nevertheless, and I was afraid the man had heard it too.

Haderer called for the waiter and asked for the bill.

From the big hall you could hear now a swelling men's chorus, it sounded like the chorus in the opera when it's banished behind the curtain. They were singing: "Home, the stars in your sky…"

And the stranger again tilted his head to eavesdrop on them, then said, "It's as though not a day has passed." And he said "Good night!" Rising to his full height, he stood up and lumbered toward the door; Mahler got up too, raised his voice and said "Listen up!" It was one of his pat expressions, but I knew that this time he really did want to be heard. And yet it was the first time I'd seen him unsure of himself as he looked toward Friedl and me as if to seek our advice. We stared at him; there was no advice in our eyes.

Paying the bill cost us some time, Mahler paced back and forth, somber, ruminating, importunate, until he suddenly turned to the door, flung it open and we followed him, and, because the choir had broken off abruptly, all you could still hear were a few straggling, decaying voices. At the same time, there was a bustling activity in the corridor that bespoke some sort of altercation or disaster.

In the corridor, we ran into several men who were all shouting at the same time; others stood in shocked silence. We couldn't see the stranger anywhere. Someone was arguing with Haderer, presumably the Colonel, now white-faced and speaking in descant. I heard scraps of the sentences "….unbelievable provocation…I beg your pardon…old frontline soldiers…". I shouted to Mahler, telling him to follow me, ran to the stairs and bolted in a couple of leaps up the dark damp steps leading like a mineshaft into the night and the open air outside. Not far from the entrance to the cellar he was lying there. I bent over him. He was bleeding from multiple wounds. Mahler kneeled beside me, took my hand off the man's chest and let me know that he was already dead.

Night echoed within me and I was in my madness.

When I came home that morning and the inner turmoil had subsided, when I just stood there in my room, stood and stood, unable to move or even find my way to my own bed, fallow and at a loss for a single thought, I noticed the blood on the palm of my hand. I didn't cringe. It seemed to me that this blood offered me some kind of protection that would not render me invincible, but rather would keep the vapors of my desperation, my thirst for revenge, my outrage from escaping my body. Never again. Never more. And even if those vengeful homicidal thoughts that had risen within me should consume me, they would never harm anyone else, just as this murderer never murdered and in the end was himself a victim—victim without a cause. But who knows what I'm talking about? Who would dare presume to say?

A Wildermuth

"A Wildermuth always tries to tell the truth!" This was the bombastic sentence chief justice Anton Wildermuth had so often heard from his father Anton Wildermuth the teacher, and which he now had on his mind as he hung up his robe and cap. He took a glass of water from the tray that the court usher Sablatschan held out to him; he pulled a little tin pill box from his pocket, shook out two tablets, put them in his mouth and followed them with a couple swigs of water to help force the bitter bits of the Saridon pills down. His headache had now spread to every inch of his skull and his head was capped by a crown of pain. Wildermuth stared into space with this booming sentence echoing in his head, then gestured to Sablatschan, who was on his way out, indicating that he should stay. Gingerly, as though his head might otherwise fall off, he lowered himself into the chair and thought that it was finally time to retire the truth forever! He craned his head, listening to hear whether this silent standoff could be heard out on Court Street and in the rest of the city, even the rest of the world—

"What did I say, Sablatschan?"

The old man remained silent.

"Was I screaming?"

The old man nodded.

Shortly thereafter, a couple of gentlemen dressed in black robes entered the room, silently, like avenging angels; Wildermuth was surrounded by the swarm and escorted downstairs to a waiting taxi which took him home to his apartment. He was tucked into bed where he remained for several weeks, supervised by his family physician and a neurologist. In those hours when the fever subsided, he read the papers that had reported on the Wildermuth case. He read all the articles and opinions, soon knew them by heart, and tried, like a disinterested third party, to recreate for himself and subsequently shoot down the story of the event as the press had presented it to the public. He alone knew that no story could be compiled from those elements and there was no evidence of any coherence there, but rather that the blow from the collision of someone else's spirit with his own ineptitude had quite obviously caused an accident whose consequences were no more sufficient than to bring about but a brief, mindless confusion in the world.

1.

A farmhand named Josef Wildermuth had killed his own father with an axe, absconded with what little money his father had saved, then squandered and drank it away the night of the murder before turning himself in to the police the next day. The police records indicated that the man was guilty by his own admission and, since there was no reason to doubt the accuracy of his statements, he was the only suspect and his records were soon remanded to the examining magistrate. But the magistrate, Anderle, former schoolmate to chief justice Wildermuth, ran into considerable trouble with the defendant who suddenly began denying his guilt—to be more precise, who dared—as ineptly as possible—to maintain that everything the police had recorded was false. Nonetheless, the examining magistrate was able to close his books just a little while later and pass the case along because Josef Wildermuth confessed to having killed his father, though not in a premeditated act or just for the sake of the money, but rather out of sheer hatred; he had always hated his father, even as a kid, because his father had abused him, kept him from learning and encouraged him to lie and steal, so there was plenty to be read in the file about a troubled youth, a calloused, bestial father and a mother who had died prematurely.

When chief justice Wildermuth was assigned this case, he was asked, for the record, whether a kinship relationship existed between himself and this Wildermuth. He refuted it; even the most distant relation could be ruled out because his family was from Carinthia, but the defendant was of Alemannic descent. The murder had barely been covered by the press because it was too insignificant and commonplace to arouse any interest and notice was taken of the trial only after a journalist from the boulevard press happened to have spoken at length with the Head of Public Relations in the police department at the time and found out that Wildermuth's trial was in the hands of chief justice Wildermuth—that the Judge and the Defendant, then, shared the same name. Because this likeness of names amused the man and sparked his curiosity, he wrote about the case in a sensationalist and sententious tone for his paper, thus prompting other papers to send in correspondents post haste.

The judge was grateful for this case which looked like it would be a cakewalk, and a welcome respite because the last few times he had presided over proceedings laden with political implications: he had suffered the intrigues of government officials and other men in positions of power and had seen parliamentary inquiries initiated; he'd received threatening letters from members of the political underworld prophesying his imminent death and had been reduced to a state of complete exhaustion as a result. During the short vacation he was finally able to squeeze in, there was a death in his family that left the thought of rest inconceivable and so, toward the end, after driving back and forth to and from the countryside, after the burial, after the estate had been settled, he was probably in even worse shape than he had been before. The Wildermuth Case, a so-called routine case, but one which nevertheless reminded him of the first cases he'd conducted independently in Vienna (and hence, of happier times), thus commenced to actively concern him in all its unswerving clarity and simplicity. If you had quizzed him about it, he'd have confessed to no longer having an interest in a stunningly brilliant, unerring performance in a monstrously complicated trial and that he was increasingly galled and appalled by a world in which murders, robberies and rapes were not merely committed, but in which the crimes became ever more impersonal, more dastardly and senseless. Indeed, he would prefer a world where someone killed his father with an axe and turned himself in to the police; then there was no need to bother with psychoanalytic probes, no terminal diagnoses about the deep, dark drives underlying mass murders and war crimes; there was no need to hang the dirty linen of an entire social class on the line to be laundered by the hypocritical hue and cry of the press; the people and places in the upper echelons of public life needn't be handled with caution or acrimony, there was no need to walk a tightrope, no need for savvy political tact, and for once there was no danger of falling. All he would have to confront would be one single human being and his gruesome little misdemeanor, and he would again be allowed to simply think and believe in justice and the pursuit of truth, in the verdict and the sentence.

But while he was studying the Wildermuth file, Anton Wildermuth became increasingly aware of an uneasiness rising within him simply because he was forced to read his own name in that of a stranger again and again. He remembered the time when, as a student in Graz, he had frequently been invited to a building where, among the name-plates hanging next to the doorbells at the gate, there was a sign bearing the name Wildermuth. This sign had always disturbed him in a similar fashion. Every time he passed the door to the apartment of those unidentified Wildermuths, he'd stopped in his tracks, trying to get a whiff of the smell emanating from this apartment—once it was a soapy, steamy smell and another time it was the smell of sauerkraut. Both of these smells now wafted to his nose again, and he could see himself standing there in this dead silent building fighting back the urge to vomit.

Now, he had to read this name again and again in conjunction with a bloody axe, a leftover loaf of bread, an overcoat and, most importantly, a button that had once been attached to the overcoat and which would prove to play a very specific role in the case—with a light left burning in the kitchen that somehow went out, with time delineated in terms of "22 hours 30 minutes" and "23 hours 10 minutes" and thus barred from inclusion in any real sense of time, with objects spoken of as though the world were just waiting to hear the tales out of school these things had to tell—an axe of this specific make and an overcoat of that specific model. And here was his name in this terrible tale, linked to events just as senselessly as it had once been linked to the smell of sauerkraut, the smell of steam or the sound of music blaring from a radio suddenly filling the staircase. Events described in court documents had never affected him this way. At any rate, he had never questioned the way a murder, a wrecked car, a case of embezzlement or adultery came into its name. To him it seemed self-evident that the names themselves disclosed this information and that occurrences attached themselves to names which clearly identified defendants and witnesses.

When the trial began and he got his first

glimpse of the defendant, and in fact had to look at him again and again, he felt an even more stifling sense of unease than he had during his preliminary study of the case—a mixed feeling of involuntary shame and revulsion. This time, he had to feign the calm and cool composure for which he was renowned. Once, in the course of but an hour, he had forgotten what he'd asked and the answer he'd been given. On the second day, when the trial should have proceeded from the tedious preliminaries into a more lively phase, it stayed as lifeless as it was. The witnesses responded as though they'd rehearsed their roles—there wasn't an ounce of uncertainty or ambiguity. The defendant seemed impassive, gawky and dull—a picture of sincerity that didn't seem to discomfit anyone. The judge was the only one to suspect something was amiss, the only one frequently leafing through his papers, clasping his hands together, unclasping them, throwing up his hands too often, then lowering them again, spreading his fingers apart, closing them, clutching the table's edge in his trembling grip as though seeking support.

It was before they recessed for lunch on the third day that it happened, and the judge's hands finally came to rest. With a slight, timid gesture the defendant rose and said: "But that isn't the truth!" And added, in the great silence that ensued, softly: "Because that wasn't what happened. That's not the way any of it happened."

When asked, this Josef Wildermuth responded by saying that he had in fact killed his father, but since he was being probed so precisely, he thought he had to be more precise in his answers and admit that what happened was something else altogether. This story consisted merely of words the police put in his mouth, and he hadn't always dared to contradict the examining magistrate either. So, for example, he and his father hadn't gotten into a dispute over the money, and the button found at the scene—it couldn't have been the one missing from his overcoat ripped off by his father in a scuffle because his button had already been missing for weeks; the button must be from some other overcoat, that of his neighbor, the one who was a witness here, he was the one who'd had a dispute with his father.

The man didn't get any further than that because the prosecuting attorney jumped to his feet and geared up for a short, sharp speech in which the word "stratagems" appeared and made the defendant turn pale, even though or perhaps precisely because he had presumably never heard it before.

That afternoon, though, the judge commenced to review the questions again and to drive this Wildermuth to book; Wildermuth obligingly recounted everything again, reporting quietly what had happened and embellishing the report with new details. What remained of page upon page of transcript was not a single useful discovery. So far, neither the course of events appeared to have been accurately described, nor had anything remotely resembling a plausible supposition been written in the register concerning a possible motive. So many mistakes had been made that proceedings were adjourned in order to procure additional expert opinions.

When the trial resumed, it was guaranteed widespread public interest. Expert witnesses had been called in, among others, a specialist with an outstanding reputation, a European button- and thread specialist to answer doubts cast by the defense about the accuracy of the scientific expertise supplied by the police laboratory, and the course of events could only be ascertained beyond a shadow of doubt once it could be established whether the button came from the defendant's overcoat or from the neighbor's.

But before the expert witness was called to the stand, another day would pass; the witnesses were questioned again based on new developments in the case and the defendant tried to explain the way this, that and the other detail which only now came to light fit in and what had in fact driven him to commit the act. Up until now, he'd given straightforward answers without becoming evasive, but this time he started to stutter or fall into confused silence. No, he didn't remember exactly whether his father had seriously threatened to throw him out of the house; no, he wasn't sure whether he'd always hated his father, probably not; as a child, he hadn't hated him because his father had often given him animals carved from wood to play with, but, of course, on the other hand—something else seemed to occur to him; he scowled into space, remembering was hard for him, he had so little practice at remembering, you could see that just by looking at the man.

But the court-appointed defense counsel intervened copiously, though he appeared not to know exactly how to best defend the man now, but he suddenly saw in it a task to take on for its own sake, sensing the increased activity, the expansion of the trial, the enthralled anticipation in the court room: "We must patiently extricate the truth from this poor, martyred soul," he repeatedly beseeched the court, veritably inviting them to join in a team sport, not a jousting match. He was a very good and old-fashioned defense attorney capable of eliciting both annoyance and clemency from the court because he worked with words that younger attorneys would have refused to use and which would have sounded ridiculous coming from their mouths anyway: tortured soul. Hapless, ransacked childhood. Tender seedling. Even the word "subconscious," coming from his mouth, haltingly, took on something touching, heart-rending. And the truth he was making such an ado about seemed like a solid old commode with plenty of drawers that rattled when you pulled them out, but where all the lesser truths that could possibly be deduced were lying snow-white, serviceable, shipshape and near at hand. The heart the defendant had hung on his mother's early passing was lying there, and lying there too was the confused relationship he had to money and all the cravings of honest working men for a glass of schnapps, for a taste of humanity and warmth; and, on the other hand, there was the punctual and loyal fulfillment to obligation, the employer's stamp of approval. Then again, though, the blood-spattered axe was lying there, too, causing the law-abiding citizen to shudder and society to cry out for protection. An oppressive, knowing silence ensued and lent the old man an unusual eloquence and, when the expert witness—the European button specialist—was called to the stand, even he started to get the feeling that this trial was gaining significance, that even he was again gaining significance and that this case was not without subtleties, surprises and manifold meaning. And even though he would ultimately turn out to have erred since the surprise came from a different quarter than he'd expected, his feeling proved right.

The specialist approached the attentive court, not without confidence that his moment had come:

"Your Honor," he commenced, holding up a sheaf of papers like a petition. "while the concordance I have had the honor of examining contains many conclusions and commendable conjectures, it unfortunately contains very few established facts. I don't know whether you are fully cognizant of what, in light of current state-of-the-art technology, must be done and taken into account to produce a reliable button analysis. What is required in obtaining such an analysis is, just to cite the most important factors: a determination of the button's degree of brilliance, the consistency of its surface, the space between holes; but the inner walls of its thread holes must also be photographed, the distance between the holes and the rim must be measured, its circumference must be determined. But that's not all. In addition, we must ascertain the following: the exact weight of the button, the thickness of its raised edge…". The faces protruding above the robes and the faces of the jurors took on an expression of impenetrable puzzlement. The expert briefly looked around, then continued with his voice raised, "Your Honor, in order to determine the weight of the button, I worked with precisely trued scales, both Swiss and American!"

A man in the courtroom let out a stifled laugh.

The judge leaned over and said, smiling, "Professor, sir, if I have understood you correctly, you are demanding of this button a proper confession and, you are accusing the local laboratory of not having been able to extract a confession from the button."

The whole courtroom was now shaking with laughter.

Enraged, the defense attorney leaped to his feet and said, with the tremor of elderly aristocratic authority in his voice, "The audience's role in this room is—to be silent!"

The judge conceded, apologized for having incited the laughter and asked the expert to continue. The expert looked around, aghast, as though he couldn't comprehend the episode and the laughter.

Later, the director of the laboratory was called to the stand to help the expert clarify the question of whether the threads attached to the button were identical to the threads on the defendant's overcoat.

"Gentlemen," the expert exclaimed with great consternation, "I keep hearing the word 'identical'! You can't possibly claim that these threads are identical. The word 'identical' itself expresses the utmost degree of probability. One could perhaps—but only perhaps!—say that two photographs of the same image are identical. But one cannot possibly maintain the same about these threads. Doesn't anyone here understand that? Doesn't anyone understand what I am saying?!"

The laboratory director introduced another report compiled by the Trier of Facts and read aloud the passage that referred to the "absolute compatibility" between the threads.

"No, no," the expert murmured, exhausted, then flared up again: "But that does not by any means indicate that the individual threads must have come from the same stock. Think about it. There are only a few manufacturers of button threads in all of Europe, and, for years now, they have all been producing their wares using the same methods. The same applies to the buttons themselves. I don't know what you are trying to imply, gentlemen, but I see it as my obligation to make clear to you that you cannot speak in these terms with regard to a button, that you cannot speak in these terms with regard to the threads. The truth—even the truth about a button—is not as easily ascertained as you might think. For thirty years, I have been diligently concerned with the task of finding out everything there is to know about buttons and I can see now, that for you, dear sirs, even a half an hour is too much to devote to a serious consideration of the subject…" He retreated, lowering his head as if in deference to a higher authority.

This time, no one laughed.

The festive atmosphere had dissipated and an insufferable one set in. They moved on to different questions. But, it seemed as though neither the witnesses for the prosecution nor for the defense were able to provide any more solid or rational answers. Ever since the button had been introduced as evidence, ever since everything about the button had been made public, a contagion of uncertainty had spread. It was as though everyone sensed that the button had brought to light something that one generally needn't expect to reckon with. So it was extraordinarily difficult to say anything specific at all about the button, and learned men feared that they didn't know everything there was to know about the button and hence dedicated their lives to researching buttons and threads. The witnesses were compelled to think they had been reckless with the answers they had given and that their statements regarding a certain time or a certain object had simply been irresponsible. Words fell like dead moths from their mouths. They couldn't even believe themselves anymore.

But, just as everything threatened to dissolve and disintegrate, the prosecuting attorney, who remained immune to the soporific lulling of the truth, took the floor. He began by expressing, ironically, almost with a grin, his gratitude for the expertise that had been offered on the button, which, "as astounding and equally irrelevant" as it was, had only cost them time; then he reminded them, at which point his grin receded, of the "obvious, hard, cold facts."

He pierced the courtroom with his voice, time tested and exacting, employing the full brunt of his authority to call the assembly back to some semblance of reality. He immediately won over the audience and the jurors, both of whom had been rendered incapable of interpreting this simple crime by the flurry of renderings. He cried out for the truth. The defendant nodded in agreement. Even the defense attorney nodded involuntarily.

Contrary to what the papers reported, it was neither at the conclusion of the settlement nor during the dispute about the button but rather at this very moment that chief justice Anton Wildermuth struggled to rise from his seat, supporting himself with his hands, and screamed. His scream stunned the whole court. For days, it was the talk of the town and was written in stone in the headlines in all the newspapers. It was a scream that was exceptional only because it had nothing to do with the trial, because it was so out of place and had nothing to do with anyone. Some say what he screamed was: If one more person dares speak the truth here…! Others say what he screamed was: To hell with the truth, just knock it off with the truth…! Or: Will you just knock it off with the truth, for Pete's sake, just stop…! Whatever it was he said, he is said to have repeated the words several times in the dreadful silence before he shoved back his chair and left the courtroom. Others say he collapsed and had to be carried out of the courtroom.

One thing remained indisputable: his scream.

2.

Let someone else rack his brain over why I come along, stop him and scream in his face, and let someone else ask, where to, which way I'll stumble with my thoughts when I rise again after this fall. What color my eyes are? How old I am? What's my shoe size? How I spend my money? When I was born? For a moment, I toyed with the thought of stating my hat size, but then figured it probably about average. And my brain will weigh little once I am dead.

After all, for me, everything revolves around the truth, just as for others everything revolves around God or Mammon, around fame or eternal bliss.

My world revolves around the truth—always has, or at least for the longest time now.

Back home on the farm where my father was a teacher and my grandfather a farmer, when we were kids, there was still this huge faded inscription running across the whole front wall of the house: THIS HOUSE IS NOT OUR EVERLASTING HOME. My grandfather, a Wildermuth with a more stalwart heart than his children or his children's children, had had the words painted there. He ruled and was ruled by this weighty, unerring sentence. After his death, the inscription was whitewashed away from the wall. But since this was the sentence conferred on my first home, and since our time on earth is not, in fact, everlasting, I suppose I'll be forgiven for my single-minded pursuit of this one thing and one thing only; and since there isn't time enough to bag the beast as prey, only to hunt it down, to pursue it with perpetual passion, my empty hands will give no cause for ridicule—at least no more than anyone else's empty hands.

All of everyone's empty hands.

My father, who was a teacher for thirty years in H., the small town where I'd served as a young district judge, is Protestant; in fact, my whole family is Protestant and always has been, with the exception of my mother, a Catholic who never attended mass. As far back as I can remember, my father, burdened as he was by the task of educating so many children, never concerned himself much with my sister and me, but still, he gladly stopped reading the newspaper or correcting papers whenever one of us had something to say or when mother offered a secondhand report of some mischief, some fight or something of the sort. Then, inevitably, he would ask: Is it true? He had invented the word "true" in all its adhibitions, with all its implications and applications. "Truly, "truthfulness," "truth," "the Truth," "true to the truth," "for the love of truth," "in love with the truth"—all these words were his creations, and he was the author of the awe these words had inspired in me ever since I was little. Even before I could begin to comprehend their meaning, I fell prey to the overwhelming fascination these words exerted over me. Much in the same way other children that age strive to be precise about putting building blocks together in a certain pattern, I struggled to assemble the pattern for "telling the truth" and I sensed that this was what my father meant when he said I should tell him "precisely" what happened. Surely I had no idea what the point behind it was, but, inasmuch as my little brain permitted, I soon came to always tell the truth—less for fear of my father than out of sheer dark desire. Thus, they called me "an honest child." Before long, though, I was no longer content with simply satisfying my father—saying, for example, that I had been late for lunch because I'd dawdled on the way home from school or had gotten into a scuffle—I started telling an even truer truth. Because I suddenly understood—it might have been in the first or second grade—what was expected of me, and I realized I was justified in my actions. My desire coincided with a wish, a good wish that surpassed all the others the adults foisted upon me. An easy, wonderful life lay before me. Not only was it my privilege, it was in fact my duty to tell the truth under all circumstances! So, when my father asked why I came home from school so late, I was compelled to say that the teacher had made us stay after school for fifteen minutes as punishment for talking and creating a stir. And I had to tell him that I'd also run into Frau Simon on the way home and was even later as a result.

But no, I had to say: Toward the end of math class, probably five minutes before the bell, the teacher said, because we'd been so fidgety…

No: Because there was a disturbance in the back row, because Anderle and I were making paper airplanes in the back row, because we'd torn the paper from the notebooks and folded it to form paper airplanes and had made two wads of crumpled paper besides, two paper planes and two wads from the paper we took from the notebooks, from the center where you can loosen the staples so the teacher won't notice…

Then I tried to recall the exact wording of the sentences the teacher had issued, and I explained, in hairsplitting detail, what Frau Simon had told me, the way she took me by the sleeve, the way she had suddenly appeared standing there before me on the bridge. But after I had explained everything in hairsplitting detail, I began again at the beginning because I'd noticed, in that heightened state of excitement, that I still hadn't gotten it quite right and besides, everything I'd just described was intricately linked to a previous occurrence, an object situated outside the objects I'd described. It was so hard to render an exhaustive report, but it was all a matter of will and I had the will, so I tried again and ardently pursued this task that seemed so much more attractive than the tasks we were assigned as homework. I had a will for the truth and, back then, that still meant first and foremost, to "tell the truth."

One day, when my sister Anni and I had instigated some silly prank with some of the neighbors' children and set the whole neighborhood astir, for the first time in my life I worked myself up into a frenzy for truth that I wouldn't emerge from for years to come. Even before my father called me to the carpet, I sorted out the details of the event, placing them in painstaking order and memorizing them: First, Edi said we should waylay Frau Simon on the way home from school. Together we walked to the corner of the house to lie in wait for her. We wanted to scare her. Edi said, I said, Edi said, and, while Edi was the first to have said we should do it, even before that I had already thought of scaring her with a frog I had caught and was planning to put in her shopping bag, but the frog had escaped. When Frau Simon didn't show up, Anni went to look for some stones, Anni and I placed the stones in front of the garden gate, Edi placed his stick in front of them, five big stones, a stick from the forest—we put the stones in place, then the stick, so that Frau Simon would stumble on the stones or the stick, then Herma brought a big cobblestone, Herma said, I said, Edi said, yes, that's what we said, then Anni said she didn't want Frau Simon to fall flat on her face, but I said, Edi said…

I knew that I would get off scot-free if I told my father this first, hastily thrown together version of the story, but I asked him for permission to think about it and revised the tale until it seemed complete and accurate down to the last detail, but all I can remember now is its deathly verbosity. My father didn't want to show how deeply satisfied he was with my accomplishment, but I could sense his clemency when he let me go with the words: "The truth will take you far. Tell the truth and scorn the devil."

After that, I began describing every incident this way, even the ones that caused me the most discomfort. My mother was often too impatient to listen to my confessions in their entirety and she often gave my father a look that I couldn't quite decipher; but my father remained attentive, he relished these interrogations, and afterward I had less and less reason to fear his scorn. What is more, I was intoxicated by the pleasure I was thus able to give him. As long as I stated the truth in my boring little tales from the schoolyard, boyish pranks, nonsense, my first thoughts of good and evil!—As long as it was the truth, everything was fine! There was an aura of magnificence surrounding the truth in my childhood, surrounding these recounts, recitations and renditions. It became something of a religious regimen that had a lasting effect on me, making me more adept at dissecting in atomic detail every incident, every emotion and every object in a scene.

Only much later did it occur to me that there had of course been a lot of things I had never been asked, many things I had never been called to account for—that I hadn't told the truth about everything in my life. No one had ever asked me what I thought about the things that weren't worth confessing, about my feelings and my faith. Between the ages of thirteen and eighteen, while I may have continued the practice of telling the truth to excess, on the other hand, I wandered about freely in a world I didn't share with my family—as though I were a character on some dim-lit backstage of life where I retreated after I had made my appearance on behalf of the truth. It was there that I recovered from the strenuous performances and compensated for the loss of strength that telling the truth was already costing me. Everything was beginning to cost more and would cost more and more with each passing year. Breathing, yearning, speaking. It was on this backstage that I played out the dream adventures, dream dramas, fantastic figments no one dreamed I was capable of dreaming up, and they soon ran to seed as rampant as truths in the footlights. Circumspect and scoffing, I sometimes called this world my "Catholic" world, even though there was nothing more to the expression than an attempt to describe a world that was sinful, colorful and rich—a jungle where you could relax, sheltered from searching the qualms of conscience. For me, it was a world I associated with my mother's world. A world I held her responsible for—this mother of mine with her long and beautiful strawberry blond hair who passed unsuspectingly through our house only to raise her eyebrows in amusement when we children complained one ice-cold Sunday because we had to go to church, as if she were puzzled by this insurgence, she, who was so free...that nonchalant mother of mine who bathed in a hot wooden tub and washed her hair while we were at church and who was still standing there in her underclothes radiating rejuvenation and utterly pleased with herself when we returned. Anni was afforded the privilege of helping her comb her hair then and I wrapped the fallen red hairs around my fingers and took on the role of advisory counsel while she put up her hair. Yes, this was the form my mother's Sunday pleasures assumed and she was exempt from something—from the truth, of course. She had no way of even knowing what it was. Father was the only one who had anything to do with the truth, and not just on Sundays, when he spoke directly to the truth and paraded its virtue before our eyes. Whatever goals other people may have set for themselves—the Wildermuths, as I soon realized, always had and always would aspire to seek the truth, to speak the truth, to tell and to stick to the truth. *The Truth*—it sounded to us as kids like it were some place you could set out *in search of,* like China; it sounded like you could find it and carry it home with you in a basket the way you might go looking for mushrooms in the woods in a balmy summer and bring home a basket full.

Our house resounded with the truth, with this word and the others surrounding this royal prince of a word like train bearers. And raising a Wildermuth—well, that meant raising him to tell the truth. And becoming a Wildermuth, that meant becoming a tower of truth.

But then I left this house and abandoned that first truth just as I abandoned my parents' house, the Sundays, the articles of faith. I became acquainted with a different truth when I entered college, with the truth spoken by scholarship, a higher truth you might say. Anderle had come with me to Graz and at the university we joined forces with two students from the city, Rossi and Hubmann, who also saw in the study of law something more than the easiest way to get a degree and embark on a typical career as a federal civil servant. We weren't satisfied with the lectures; we discarded the handouts we were given to make things easier and to cram for exams. We had our minds set on something else, so we spent our evenings going beyond the course material in search of the underlying principles supporting the material. For two or three years, then, night after night we carried on heated discussions about basic premises, constitution and law, and this occasioned many a garrulous debate. But I noticed that each of us had certain tendencies—more than that, that some things just stuck to us like the smell of our skin, our way of walking, of keeping quiet, of turning in our sleep—and whatever Hubmann tended to hold true, I tended to think the opposite was true and Rossi infuriated us both by pompously tearing our extreme points of view to shreds, measuring them against what he called reality and pointing out once and for all that the truth lay in the middle. But how could the truth lie in the middle? It was simply preposterous to thrust the truth into the middle or to the right or to the left or into the void or into time or out of time. It would be pointless, I think, to mention which points of discussion could rile us into a frenzy because anyone who, whether by choice or by force, has ever read ten books on any given subject—as we had in the case of the philosophy of law—knows exactly what I mean. Our commentary was less than original; we simply lifted statements or ideas from books and dissected or intersected them with others: at times, we would see the truth here and at other times there, sometimes we'd see it somewhere else altogether. We tussled with the truth, like young dogs over a bone, with the full force of youthful agility, pugnacity and lust for ideas. We considered ourselves the originators of those fabulous great ideas that Hegel, Ihering and Radbruch had had, but the dissension among us was at best proof of the fact that the dissension had been there all along. We screamed ourselves dumb over the relative and the absolute, the objective and the subjective. We dealt our deities and those first foreign concepts like cards, or we shot our truths across the others' goal line to score a point.

We parted ways in our last years of study. We had too many exams to prepare for to keep arguing about the infinite number of problems we'd seen flash briefly into view. We had love affairs that took up our evenings and pre-test jitters that left us sleepless. The truth got short shrift, the higher truths recovered from our probes while we, our attention diverted from them, rushed headlong toward the finish line of a fast and furious course of study in the hope of securing a place for ourselves as productive members of society in the end. We settled down, wrote opinions for the courts and shed the arrogance of youth only to trade it in on another, and we realized that there was no time for seeking the truth in the law offices and the long, long corridors of the Court of Justice. We learned to draft documents, file records, type, greet our superiors, and let ourselves be greeted by secretaries, law clerks and ushers; we learned to deal with depositions, discoveries, staplers, binders, file cabinets. The truth had flown the coop and who would follow its flight and find it?

But a Wildermuth, someone whose world revolves around the pursuit of truth, a Wildermuth can never lose its trail—there's no doubt in my mind about that! And even if it means getting caught in the grind, if it means going through the wringer that everyone has to go through…

We started families. We formed cliques. We furnished apartments. I married Gerda, the girl next door in our small town. We hadn't known each other as children, but later, when I returned home as a young judge, I often ran into her at the lake when I went swimming on the weekend. Gerda, the woman I live beside in dulled amazement…I don't know anyone close to me who has so little regard for the truth as my wife. A lot of people like her, her family idolizes her, my friends prefer her company over mine. She must have some kind of magic. Because everyone admires her for her ability to craft a story around even the most insignificant event, the most incidental occurrence. She never stops amusing herself and others at the expense of the truth. I've never once caught her in the act of reporting an incident exactly the way it happened. She immediately transforms everything into a minor work of art—be it a vacation, a trip to the dairy, a conversation at the hairdresser's. Everything she says is rife with allusion or wonder and there's always a punch line. You simply can't help but laugh, be taken aback or brought to the verge of tears when she gives something her best shot. She makes observations I'd never be capable of making, rambles on and on as though no one would ever dare take her to task. She lies, and most of the time, barring a few exceptions, I'm not even sure she's aware of it herself. After she's gone to pick up her passport, she'll say: We were sitting there, maybe thirty, oh, what am I saying, forty people…(whereby I'm sure that means four or five people!) and I waited for hours on end. (But I checked the time, and she'd actually waited for a half an hour!) When she starts unpacking childhood recollections, sometimes she'll have spent weeks at the seaside, another time, it might be just one; or she boasts about the way she only played with boys, always wearing pants, but I have seen photographs from that time and all she is ever wearing are skirts. She claims she had a short haircut, that she had her hair "bobbed"—but I know she wore her hair in braids for at least two years.

I have only one life story to tell, but Gerda must have several because even though I pretty much know the details of her past and know enough people who've known her since childhood, when she talks about herself, there are always an infinite number of deviations—in fact, they aren't even deviations because there is no straight line she could deviate from, just myriad different renditions and interpretations of her life. When she's in a good mood and feeling particularly talkative, no sooner does a single detail occur to her than her life takes a different turn. As a young girl, all she wanted to do was play the piano—you couldn't tear her from the piano—she wanted to drown in music, live and breathe music; but then I learn that she'd have preferred to study medicine, that she'd wanted to go to Africa to work in a hospital helping the poorest of the poor—that her only desire was to defy danger and risk and fulfill some mission in the Congo or among the Mau-Mau.

Sometimes I get superstitious and am convinced that each of us is destined to put up with precisely the thing he cannot stand, that we are forced to throw in with the one person who is sure to make a shambles of our deepest yearning. Gerda, praised by everyone for her magic, is precisely the one woman I could have been sure not to have been able to live with. "Your charming wife..." Kaltenbrunner still dares to write me—for Kaltenbrunner, her kind of charm would have been just right, would have fit him to a tee, that bogus charm—I'd like to tear it out by its roots in my wrath and impotence.

But what a wonderful life Gerda leads, even at my side, what a wonderful life I lead with her beside me! That one should live such a wonderful life even without the truth, that's what I find so amazing! I once thought she was on the verge of death, and she thought so too, when she had a stillbirth and I thought her spell had perhaps lost its charm and her true colors would be laid bare—that from hopelessness perhaps hope for both of us would now emerge; she lied even then and to this day keeps spouting profound or melancholy witticisms and lies about the most miserable hours she has ever endured, hours that drove her body to the brink. She can make a spellbinding tale of it, can shoot off observations like fireworks, sacrificing everything that I deem important to say about it—the truth of the matter, or what was more or less true about it. Oh, I know hardly anyone aside from myself who would so much as consider incriminating her as a liar. She has, after all, like Herr Kaltenbrunner says, a very intimate way of seeing the world. I hate this intimate manner because of the price you pay for it, because of the way it obfuscates the world. Because the world is not there to be decorated and desecrated by Gerda's narrative arabesques, it's obscure enough as it is not to have to be subjected to further obfuscation by her.

For me, everything revolves around finding the truth, and not just in my professional capacity, rather because I simply can't concern myself with anything else. And even if I should never stumble on the truth…

A Wildermuth, who can't do otherwise, never

could, never will...

One who knows how far the truth can take you...

But do I really want the truth to take me even further?

Not since I screamed, no, ever since then I don't want it anymore, there have often been times when I no longer wanted it. Why should I want to get anywhere with the truth? Where to? To the boondocks of Buxtehude and back, to the heart of the matter, behind the scenes, to heaven or just beyond the seven hills...? I don't want to put these distances behind me because I've long since lost the faith. And now I know: All I want is for my own spirit and flesh to come together. I'd like to come together endlessly in an endlessly insatiable fit of lust, but since absolutely everything is out of kilter and I can't even come close to making things come together, I am about to scream.

Scream!

I searched for the truth about myself, but what's that supposed to prove—my own vivisecting self-informed opinions about myself, in detail or in mournful sweeping generalizations. What should I even begin to do with these banal revelations that could have occurred to just about anyone? I am thrifty, but sometimes generous; I have compassion for a lot of people, and no compassion for many others. I suspect I may be predisposed toward vice, but I'm not sure what you can in clear conscience describe as vicious and maybe I'm a stranger to vice just because I never developed my natural predispositions—first because I didn't have the nerve, later because I didn't have the time and it didn't seem to matter anymore whether I developed them or not. I'm ambitious, but only under certain circumstances. I'd have given my eyeteeth to have gotten a leg up on Rossi while we were still in school and even for a while later when we were both on the same career paths; but I was sincerely pleased to see Hubmann finish with grades that far surpassed my own and continue on to make a career for himself in the Ministry of Justice. I considered both of them my friends, and liked them both, and I don't quite know why there is a difference in the way I feel about them. Perhaps the fact that I begrudged Rossi his successes didn't have as much to do with me as it did with him or with some third factor that didn't rest with either of us, but rather with the nature of our friendship—something that no longer pains me today. I am loyal and disloyal, I often feel helpless and yet am quite capable of seeming resolute. I am both cowardly and courageous and most often see both these qualities in myself, in varying degrees and dispensations. But there is one thing I've always noticed about myself, and that is my singleminded search for one thing: the truth. But it isn't as though I lay claim to the truth for my own sake, it doesn't have to have anything to do with me. It's just that I am simply compelled to concern myself with it.

I have to concern myself with the truth the same way the blacksmith must concern himself with fire, the way the polar scientist must concern himself with eternal ice, the way the sick have to concern themselves with the night.

And someday when I simply cannot concern myself with it anymore, I'll lie down just as I did after I screamed and will never get up again and will live myself to death in the ensuing silence.

Indeed, just what is the truth about me, about anyone? You can only speak the truth about this point or that, about the minutest moments of action, stations in emotional processes, about drop for drop in the stream of consciousness. But then you wouldn't be able conclude that someone had such rough-cut qualities as 'thrifty,' 'kind-hearted,' cowardly,' 'foolhardy.' All those thousands of thousandths of seconds of attraction, fear, desire, revulsion, calm, excitement that a person endures—what can they possibly mean? And must they mean anything? Just one thing: that he gained and suffered much...

But seeing as how I can't even get a grip on myself and since even I am capable of seeing, feeling and understanding in such a variety of ways, what about the truth of the world!? A table, one single object like my desk! Just take this as one example! How many times have I sat down at this desk, indifferent to it, or touched it; I've groped its surface in the dark; I've sketched its outline in a letter to a friend—reduced it to a couple of strokes of pencil lead; sometimes when it reeks of long hours of work, I smell it; I look at it in amazement when all the papers have been cleared and it stands there before me, free and clear, a different desk—above and beyond all that, what else could this big bulky desk be! A mass of firewood for the stove, a form reminiscent of a certain style; as cargo, it has a certain weight, and there was a price attached to it once and it would have a different one today and yet another after my death. The truth about this desk alone is endless. A fly will see it differently than a budgerigar and I wonder whether Gerda has ever seen this desk the same way I do? I don't know. All I'm sure of is that she knows precisely the place I burned a hole in its top with a cigarette. For her, it is my desk—the one with the burn hole; she also knows about its lathed legs because they are "dust collectors." It was only through Gerda that I became aware of the fact that it is a dust collector, but on the other hand, I know something she doesn't: I know the sense of well-being generated by sitting at this desk with your elbows propped up and the way the wood's grain can capture a glimpse of reflection and I know what it's like to sleep on this desk because I've let my head fall forward on its surface and fallen asleep over my work a time or two.

Since so much can be said to be true about any single object, how much can be said to be true about the whole world and how much must be taken into consideration at any given point, and how much must be true of a human being who, after all, lives and breathes and thus far surpasses any object just by virtue of the fact that he is alive?

I sought the truth in the flesh. I wanted to make something come together, to make my living body resonate on the same frequency with another living body. I wanted to exact a confession from the flesh—it should tell its truth since nothing else wanted to tell the truth, my spirit wouldn't tell, the world wouldn't tell. For I had long since sensed that my body was host to a desire that went way beyond the desire for a woman. I suspected my body of coveting a truth and I relied on it to fill me in on something very simple and miraculous. I sent my body astray, to the women; I let it learn its lessons and let it teach someone else's body a thing or two. I tried to be honest with my body, but that was the most difficult thing of all and at least as difficult as being honest with the mind. Now that all my memories of my first encounters with women have been falsified and forged and so much has been abandoned, so much transfigured, but most things that may have been better suited to transfiguration have been merely disregarded—now, all that's left for me to do is to solve the mystery of my marriage which is so void of mystery—my marriage, on such an even keel, so good and so full of trust. Where's the mystery in that, people say. And yet there are times when our conversations and embraces seem like something horrific, something ignominious, iniquitous because there is something lacking in them—the truth, I suppose. Because there is something systematic about our displays of affection, we don't bother to keep searching, don't go beyond what we have because everything is dead and dying, forever dead and done for. It's not for lack of surprise when I take Gerda in my arms because I know her gestures and mine inside and out—no, the surprise is there, but it's just that there's no bolt of lightning between us, that neither of us is struck by thunder, that she doesn't cry out in ecstasy and I don't throw her down, that neither of us rages against this happy little lifelong liaison that is dampening and desiccating our bodies—so much so that no amount of infidelity, no unfulfilled desire, no measure of perverse fantasy could seriously impinge upon our extinction. Neither of us has anything new to say about our bodies, about whatever it was that our bodies thought was love. What is more, when I look around at our friends and acquaintances, I get the sneaking suspicion that we aren't the only ones at a loss in this regard and that it serves all of us right. We dismiss the few isolated incidents and episodes of passion ironically, as though they were punishment; we let them bleed out in telling silence or shatter them in barrages of backbiting calumny. And to me it seems like the few cases that remain are only to be found in court records; they seem to have migrated to the register of "Crimes and Misfortunes" in the papers.

But I had been meaning to speak about the truth my body coveted and about the only time I almost lost sight of myself and nearly stumbled upon this truth one summer many years ago.

That summer, while working as a judge at the local district court, I drove every other week with a student who was clerking for me in the summer semester break to the even smaller town of K. where, because in the years after the war there was such a shortage of judges whose records were unblemished by the past, we held only one day-long session of court every two weeks to hear minor cases like traffic accidents, child custody cases and boundary disputes between farmers. A waitress appeared before the court, I believe it was a paternity dispute over an illegitimate child; she was hard-pressed to express herself, but then again uttered such candid, crass statements that I had to strain myself just in order to remain stoic, friendly and impartial since I wasn't, at the time, accustomed to hearing unfamiliar regional dialects. My memory of the court record is sketchy and I wouldn't have any recollection of it if it weren't for the indelible image of Wanda: that flowing black hair, those delightfully moist lips, those strands of hair cascading over her breasts, hair tossed behind her back, hair everywhere: down to here, down to there, down to where it gets in the way of a body hell-bent on exploring every last opportunity to spread itself out, to buckle and bend, to move; her arms are there in the picture, insisting on being arms each and every minute, ten fingers, ten live-in-the-flesh fingers, each of which could have set the skin ablaze, could have sunk in its claws or delivered a message from her body—a body that did not try to conceal its search, its struggle, or its bitter defeat.

On my way to lunch, I saw Wanda standing there in the corridor, acknowledged her and nodded politely in her direction, then turned once more toward her while the student went on ahead of me. She just stood there—she wasn't waiting for anyone, you could see that just by looking at her. She stood there in the courthouse as though the space were sacred because it was the site of some significant event in her life, leaning against the wall with her hands clasped together as if she were in a church, not in weakness or in tears, but like a human being not yet prepared to leave behind an arena that was so important to him.

The day before had been *kermis* and the dancing was still going on Monday night at the local inn where we were staying. Any thought of sleep was out of the question, so we decided to join in the festivities. We were invited to sit at the best table, but since we felt like we were constantly being watched because of our social position, we weren't able to relax or fall in with the festive spirit. I had to raise my glass with the doctor and the dentist, the proprietor and a business man; I was "Your Honor, the Judge" who couldn't afford to compromise himself. In the end, the student danced, and I stayed back like a wall-flower, an ever more taciturn observer. I was engaged to Gerda at the time and was about to be transferred to Vienna and hence, about to be married. For me it was self-evident that my only choice was a woman like Gerda. And even later, I never once felt the slightest shred of doubt about the decision. But, I didn't know at the time what I know now and have successfully managed to repress: that neither she nor any woman like her would ever be able to bring my body to its truth, but this waitress certainly could, and that there was perhaps one or another Wanda in the world—other women with this faculty: a whole race of dark-haired, pale-faced women with big, doleful eyes, short-sighted and almost dumb, veritable prisoners of their own speechlessness—a whole race of women to whom I confess my loyalty without ever being able to admit it. It's not as though there were some law forbidding me from loving these women, as though I were the victim of a society that might think ill of me for professing my loyalty to them—it's just that there is a trace of highly stupefied grief in me over the fact that the truth serves me little purpose at the time and place it appears. I would have had the nerve to live with Wanda and talk Gerda out of our marriage, to burden myself for all the world to see with a woman who was mute, who didn't even know where to start when it came to dealing with this world and who would have been tolerated, but never fully accepted, by my people. But I knew right away that it was completely out of the question for me to even consider living with her, not with her, and I knew I'd never have been able to stand the truth that invaded and ravaged my flesh back then.

Wanda was sitting with a few men at a table opposite me. One of them had her by the arm, another put his hand on her shoulder. They all knew each other, were all talking at once and intermittently roaring with laughter. She rarely laughed, but when she did, it was loud, short and hideous. She had a way of laughing I could never have come to terms with. How gloriously Gerda laughs. Of course, she doesn't laugh because she has to; she laughs in order to win people over with her laughter. But Wanda was simply bursting with laughter.

By midnight, everyone around me was drunk and I was able to slip out of the place without attracting attention. I went out in the fresh air and saw her standing there before the gate. I stopped and stood beside her in what little light still staggered in the wind. While the building behind us staggered with music, salvos of laughter, singing and stomping, I looked in her eyes the way I'd never before looked someone in the eyes, I looked at her as though I would never again be able to look away and she looked at me in that same here-to-eternity way. I remember her stare like the stare on the face of a deadly intent bird of prey, and the moment we locked eyes and we walked away together without a word, without a touch, calls to my mind something shamefully solemn. We walked very slowly, with a distance between us we set for ourselves before the first step. Her skirt was not allowed to touch me, not even in the wind, she wasn't allowed to look around, I was not allowed to look back, not allowed to hurry or catch up to her, just walk, behind her, down the street, up the path, into the dark house, up the stairs. Don't ask, don't tell. By the time we reached her room, I was almost unconscious. I couldn't have taken another step. I didn't recognize my own body and yet understood it this one and only time.

We never laughed, and the few times I'd been with her when I came to K., we said only what was necessary, sometimes we smiled, a faltering smile. Everything between us remained serious and darksome, desperately serious, but how else would it have been congruent with my yearning? How would love have been worth anything to me if I hadn't exhausted it in my search for compatibility? This pale, patient body of Wanda's came so completely together with mine, I consummated the act of love so perfectly that a single word would have spoiled it and there wasn't a word in the world that would not have spoiled it.

Gerda with her flowery speech—how could she ever prevail against all those silences spent! If you could just cut out her tongue, break her of the habit that keeps me at such a distance from her. Darling, I'm so happy. Do you love me? Don't do anything to hurt your sweetheart. Do you really still love me? Am I not your wife? Is my sweetheart already sleeping? Every word written in rose-colored ink, everything immaculate, never a hint of vulgarity, never a step out of line. Does Gerda know how much or how little of what she says coincides with what she feels? What is she trying to cover up with her language, what shortcomings is she trying to compensate for and why does she try to force me to talk that way? She settled us into this language just the same way she settled us into our house with the furnishings she brought from home—things as comfortable to her as the words: "I love you" and "Do I get a kiss?"

We almost never fight, and we never take recourse to pulling the plug on this language we adopted right from the beginning and which has served us so well all this time. It's only now that I've grown recalcitrant toward Gerda, and one evening last week, when she wouldn't let me get up, I found myself in the throes of my first nasty quarrel with her. That Kaltenbrunner who passes himself off as a poet and would like to marry one of her friends came to visit her again and poured out his heart to her—about what, I don't know. Gerda gave me a little black book in which he had written, on the first page, the highly suspect and ingratiating little dedication: With many thanks to you, forever sincerely yours, Edmund Kaltenbrunner. After dinner, Gerda pressured me into leaving my own books lie and reading this one instead. Even though I usually read quickly and with ease, I struggled immensely in an effort to sort through these moidering sentences. After a few pages, I was nearly falling asleep, but then Gerda sat down at my bedside and demanded that I tell her what I thought of the book. Evasively, I muttered some excuse, alluding to a recurring fever or ailment. Her poet was not my concern. "You have to admit," Gerda said officiously, "there is such truth in the statements and images! Such uncommon truth!" I was outraged and turned hostile because it was news to me that truth so much as existed for Gerda. And it was just like her to have thought she'd stumbled on the truth in a book, in a book like that. Here, where the world was fermented into an enigmatic concoction spiked with mystery, here she could hobble the truth between sentence monstrosities. "It's just that it's a different truth, a higher truth!" she exclaimed, incensed.

Immediately, all the other higher truths I had ever encountered came to mind, the higher and the highest. So now it was happening right here in my own house, someone was in league with the higher truth and kidding herself into believing she understood something about it. Gerda, of course, got upset and said I simply was incapable of judging the book. Because my only concern is the common, not the uncommon truth? I asked, insidiously. Indeed, I'd finally let out a single word of truth—me, the sober jurist, know-it-all and cynic with my dry, desiccated truth!

How true! How true!

I was relieved. We spent the rest of the time until midnight fighting just for the sake of fighting, repeating ourselves, and in the end, when it occurred to her that she ought to go easy on me, and she turned out the light, she squeezed my hand firmly, tugged and tore it to her side and pressed it to her breast, like Gerda always does when she's ready for reconciliation. Oh and then the caresses and sweet nothings that always followed!

I'm tired of these games and this talking in tongues!

I searched for the truth in the highest of heights, in the great, grandiose words said to have emanated from none other than God Himself or at least from those few who lent Him an ear, but the great words must have been too prolific or too contradictory, because the one big word goes under amidst the multitude of great words. Which word might be the one to cling to? I tried to cling to so many great words, to all of them at once and to each and every one of them, and still, I fell to the ground, and, grazed, pulled myself up again, smoked, ate, slept, went back to work with a word or two less, back to the few tomes in which some truth that might serve a practical purpose was supposed to have stood.

But is the truth there to serve a purpose? And if so, what might that be: the purpose of accuracy, of precision? What purpose would it serve? Is it true when we say we took the train at ten o'clock in the morning when we did in fact take the train? Certainly. But what's the point! There is no point except that what we said corresponds with what we did. It would have been a lie to say: We didn't leave until 10 o'clock in the evening. Not if we left in the morning. If it doesn't come together, there has got to be a lie involved. What's wrong with a lie? It can have consequences (but doesn't the truth have consequences?), and by telling a lie I bring confusion into the world (but can't the truth bring about confusion as well?), and perhaps I deceive someone, well then, so what?

What is so different about us telling the truth? I left at 10 o'clock in the morning. There you have it: the truth! An event demands the truth, a fact demands that I tell the truth about it. And the facts remain what they are, regardless.

But why on earth do we have to tell the truth, dear friends? Why do we really have to opt for this damned truth? So that we don't fall prey to a lie because lies, after all, are human handiwork and the truth is only half human handiwork because it must, after all, correspond to something on the other side, where the facts lie. There has to be something there before a truth can even exist. Truth does not stand alone.

What, dear friends, is a higher truth? Where can there be a higher truth if there is no corresponding higher process! My dear friends, there is something dreadful about the truth because it points to so little, only to the most commonplace of things, and it produces so little, the uncommonly common. In all these years, I have gleaned nothing from the truth but this conclusion, this confession, this unburdening confession of facts. There was really nothing more to be had from the truth. I was compelled to seek the truth about people, about so many of them who were found guilty in the eyes of the law and others who were found innocent—but what's that supposed to mean! How can the law lie in truth…

Why? Why? We asked the murderer why, but all he could tell us was that it happened and how it happened. It was only in the act itself that the blood-spattered truth came to light, in the axe, in the knife, in the firearms. Truth strolled in on a thousand trivialities. But it didn't come running when beckoned by the question of "Why?". Here we have the full force of an experienced court squabbling to get a single truth to come strolling along. But absolutely nothing comes strolling our way.

(Oh why did I do this and not do that? Why has everything been so nasty and so nice? There's no truth coming my way, and what should I say, I mean I don't dare or care to say anything and the best I could say, just to keep you satisfied, would be that I had to do it, it felt like the thing to do, that's what I thought at the time anyway…).

I'm telling you, friends, I'm not as sick as the doctors claim and I'm certainly not an aging invalid and no longer need be handled with kid gloves. There was a man who spent thirty years thinking about buttons and everything remotely related to buttons, so I suppose I'm entitled to sit a spell and ruminate on the truth. I'm inviting you, friends, to think about it for once! What do you really want from the truth—assuming that, since most among you are respectable people, your world revolves around the truth as much as mine does. Surely you have no intent of cashing in on something with the truth. Perhaps you hope to get to heaven? Just because your tongue didn't slip and say 10 o'clock at night when you should have said 10 o'clock in the morning? Just keep it up. But ask yourselves whether anyone in heaven will put stock in that?

(But, there is some risk involved in saying 10 o'clock because of course there is no such thing as 10 o'clock, as I'm sure you are aware: telling time is just something we adopted, there's nothing to back it up, but, if it makes you feel better, placate yourselves by comparing the time on the clock with the time that has actually passed!).

Oh and yet how profoundly satisfying it is to finally come together, to finally find coincidence, finally create correspondence. To say: It is raining when it rains. To say: I am in love…when you are in love.

But there is again some risk involved, you start entering the gray zone all over again because how can you maintain: I am in love. Are you really in love? How do you know? Has your blood pressure increased? Do you feel elated, confused? What is the matter with you? So you think you've fallen in love. That's what you think, *think*. And what else do you think? That's just the way it seems to you. Alright, then, if it seems to you as though, if that's what you think, if you think you can cite this or that reason for it.... Go ahead and cite them, feign them, your flattering, profoundly intimate reasons. Do people believe you or don't they? OK, so you can't prove anything anyway, but there is something out there that might come to your rescue: the "inner" truth. As far as I'm concerned, let each of you have an inner truth enter the bargain. Just keep piling them up. Truth upon truth.

I searched for the inner truth. For the color-pocked poisonous mushroom in the deep woods.

But, once again, dear friends, we have contented ourselves with, for the longest time now, hearing the news that this president met with that president and released the following statement. The text, verbatim. Of course we would like to have the reassurance that this thing we just heard corresponds to something because our interests are such that we'd always like to profit from our own course of action—and the economy and industry and the political virtue keepers must be able to profit all the more, of course. When all our speculations prove false, inextricably bound to false hopes and false fears, when the big bombs are no longer lying stockpiled in the depots, when we are taken for fools, even then…that way madness lies!

But, let us rather stick to being harmless and talk about the first of April instead. When we were still kids, we'd run to our parents' rooms in the wee hours of the morning and scream: "Come, look! The cherries are ripe!" It was meant to be a joke, but surely you know it wasn't a particularly good one. A far better joke would be to look someone in the eye and say to his face: Sir, I'd like to slap your face. Or:

You know, Sir, I've always considered you a jerk. That would come close to the truth that the great jokes reveal. I tried to do it that way sometimes, just for the sake of telling the truth, but I wasn't comfortable with it, and I wasn't any nearer to the truth that I'd set my sights on.

I've paid my respects and am leaving. I am the one who screamed.

I suddenly couldn't get over it: the button and the man who is also a Wildermuth and would have had a right to see more truth come to light than the truth that serves our purposes. After all, he did say: "I did it," and for that, he was off to the penitentiary for twenty-five years. I cannot come to terms with the fact that the one truth that is permitted to come to light suffices and the other truth doesn't come strolling along, doesn't come running, doesn't flare up like a bolt of lightning. That we take from the serviceable truths the one fag-end that might best serve our purpose and use it to hang a noose around someone's neck because he said: Yes, it was at 23 hours, 30 minutes. Or because he forgot to say: It was at 10 o'clock in the morning.

I'm off to seek the truth. But the further I go in

pursuit of it, the further it recedes into the distance, flickering like an aurora borealis over every moment in time, every place and every thing in the world. It is as if you could only grasp it, as if it only materialized when you stayed completely still, without asking too many questions, and let yourself be satisfied with the crudest outline. It has to be set at moderate temperatures, a moderate perspective, a moderate word: everything in the middle. The result then is an ongoing catchpenny correspondence between word and object, word and emotion, word and deed. Oh you well-bred word, called to a halt for the sake of granting clemency to the silent world of buttons and hearts. Phlegmatic, sedated and sedentary all-purpose word for congruence, for compatibility.

But beyond that, there is only a plethora of opinions, strident contentions, opinions of opinions and an opinion about the truth that is worse than the opinions about all the truths for which you could be put before a firing squad at certain times, or burned at the stake because there is something dreadful about an opinion, and even more dreadful about the truth—

But that's no good either,
this high opinion I had of the truth
and that I no longer hold it in high esteem,
not since I finally retired it—

All it left was a dent in my soft hot-and-cold head—a head that doesn't fare well in moderate temperatures. Who the hell spent the night in my head? Who spoke with my tongue? Whose scream was it that I screamed?

Please, will you tell me the tale of the snow-white woman who lived beyond the seven hills? Please, I'm begging you!

I'm ready to hang up my robe and cap, ready to squat in any spot in the world, lie down in the grass and on the asphalt and listen to the world, touch it, test it, turn it topsy-turvy, take it in my teeth and then coincide with it, completely and endlessly—

Until finally, it dawns on me: the truth about the grass, about the rain, and about us:

A silent introspection compelling us to scream, to scream bloody murder about all the truths.

A truth no one, not even in his wildest dreams, would want.

Undine Quits

Men! You monsters!

All you monsters named John. John, John, John. If there is one name I shall never forget, it is this.

Every time the ramifications diverged and I entered the clearing; whenever the boughs brushed the moisture from my arms and the leaves lapped the droplets from my hair, I stumbled upon someone named John.

It has been a great lesson in logic: your name will *always* be John because each of you—each and every one—bears the same name and that name is John. And yet, there is never more than one. Just one J.O.H.N. is ever written on my memory in indelible ink. Even if I were to forget you all; if I were to erase your memory from my mind as completely and as wholly as I have loved it; even after the weight of the Earth's great waters—the torrents of rains, rivers and oceans—have long since washed away your kisses and your cum, the name would linger, reverberating beneath the waves because I cannot cease the calling: John, John.

You monsters with your heavy, disruptive hands; with your stubby, pallid paws; your grazed nails and their blackened cuticles; your white-cuffed wrists; your baggy sweaters and suits of uniform gray; your rugged leather jackets and casual, loose-fitting summer shirts! Let me make no mistake in exposing you for the disparaging monsters that you are because I will not come again. I will not heed your call—your invitation to a glass of wine, a vacation, a trip to the theater. I will never, ever come again. Never again will the answer be yes and you, yes, only you and yes, I do. I do. All these words will no longer be spoken, and I'll tell you why: because you know the questions, and all of them begin with "why". My life is void of such uncertainties. I love the water—its impenetrable transparency, its green hues, its taciturn creations (and I'm about as dumbfounded as they!), my hair under water, immersed in its justice, the mirror of indifference preventing me from seeing you in any other light. Water—the liquid reef between me, myself and I.

The reason I never bore your children was that I didn't understand the questions, the demands, the motivations and the precautionary measures. Your future was beyond my grasp and I never quite figured out how to make a place for myself in someone else's life. I had no use for the alimony and the alibis, the insurance policies, the guarantees. All I ever needed was air: night air, sea breezes and fresh, frontier winds—that I might breath anew the kisses, the incessant confession, "I do, I do." Once the verdict was in, I was sentenced to love; after I'd extricated myself from its throes, I was compelled to go back into the water—to return to that one element in which no nests are built or roofs raised and no one covers himself up with a tarp. Water—where there is no place to run or to hide. Where there is only diving, cradled by the sway of effortless motion and the sudden coming to senses, surfacing in the clearing only to find him standing there and utter it once more: John. To begin at the beginning,

"Good evening."

"Good evening."

"How far is it to your place?"

"Far, very far."

"And it's a long way to mine."

The perpetual repetition of that one mistake

which marks us for life. And what's the use, then, of experience, of having been washed clean by all the waters in the world: the Danube, the Rhine, the Tiber and the Nile? The bracing depths of the Arctic oceans and the spectral splashes of the highest seas? The puddles and pools of fairy's tales? Fiercer females of the species hone their tongues and flash their furious eyes while more docile breeds let silent tears do the talking. And the men are without comment as they run caressing hands through their wives' and children's hair. They open the evening paper, leaf through the bills or turn up the radio. But the gusty fanfare penetrates the dial tone and is still audible later, when the houses are dark and they get up from their chairs to steal down the back alleys and through the gardens where the eerie strains, the tenor of agony, the cry from afar is clearly discernible: Come! Please come, just once, come!

You monsters with your women!

And wasn't it you who said it is hell on Earth with her and no one knows quite why you stay? Wasn't it you who said your wife is a wonderful woman? Yes and that she needs you and couldn't go on without you? And didn't you laugh, imperiously, and say, "Don't take it so hard. You should never take these things so hard"? Didn't you say this was the way it should be, forever and always? That anything else was sheer insanity? You monsters with your hackneyed epithets—empty promises echoing the ways of women's words—that you might never want, that the world would be one, that you might be whole. You who have taken women for lovers and made them your own. You who have sold yourselves to chivalry, let husbands be made of men. (The fact that you did is worthy of a rude awakening in itself!)

You, jaundiced in envy of your women, condescendingly forbearing, tyrannical, relentless in your search for refuge in women's arms. You with your monthly allowances and the intimacy of your pillow talk, your bedtime stories—buttresses to fortify the illusion of your own moral integrity. You, with your pitifully adept, helplessly diverted embraces. I was flabbergasted by the way you give your women money for the groceries and clothes and the summer vacation. Always, you were the ones who invited them (you "invite" them—that means you pay). You buy and let yourselves be bought. All I could do was scoff, laughing incredulously: John, John.

The quaint little college kids and the industrious blue collar men who let their women work beside them. You progress and are promoted in separate faculties and chairs, climb the ladders of his-and-hers factory jobs. Still, you struggle to succeed as one. You pool your resources and brace yourselves against the future, employing your women like epoxy to the prospect of posterity, forcing them to bear your children. And when they stroll about—timorous and bursting with the weight of bubbling babies in the womb—then your clemency blooms. Or perhaps you forbid them from having children for the sake of rushing unimpeded into the golden years on the tails of your unspent youth. There's a lesson to be gleaned from that, that much is certain. The swindlers and the swooned! Don't try it with me. Not with me.

You, with your muses and your mules. With your educated, compassionate and comprehending mistresses and how you let them speak. But the sound of my laughter has rippled the water for ages. It is that gurgling cackle you have often mimicked in the dark horror of the night. Because you have always been cognizant of the lunacy and audacity of it all and have known that you were satisfied with your lot even though it was not yours by choice. And that is why it is better not to go out into the night, not to proceed down the paths, auditioning the courtyards and the gardens because that would amount to nothing less than acknowledging the temptation inherent in the sound of pain, its timbre, its seductive beckoning—admitting that man craves, above all else, ultimate betrayal. Never did you ever concede to the big houses, the firm foundations. Secretly, you were jubilant over every brick that flew, every impending collapse. You reveled at the very thought of fiasco, of escape, of vilification and of the solitude which might have offered some reprieve from the insistent clutches of the status quo. You were all too willing to toy with the thought of it. When I came, when the wind announced my arrival, you jumped from your seats and knew that the time was near: defilement, derision, decay, disintegration and the unfathomable end. The call to end it all. The end. You monsters! For this I have loved? That you let yourselves be beckoned, knowing full well what the cry meant, and can still maintain that you never agreed to the things you have become? And me? When did I ever consent to this? Not until you were alone, completely alone, and your thoughts drew no constructive conclusions of their own; not until there was nothing left which might be of use to you in your lamp-lit room; when the clearing emerged and the air was sultry and damp; not until you stood—lost for eternity, utterly forlorn in your remorse—then, and only then, was there time for me to enter with the admonishing eye that said: Think! Be! Speak!

I have never understood you, nor why you thought the rest of the world somehow did. I said, "I don't understand. I just don't get it. It is beyond me." And it lasted for a good long while: no one understood you and even you could not fathom the why of this or that—why the walls between nations and people, why the politics, the papers, the banks, the market exchange and the commerce and so on and so forth.

I understood perhaps all too well the diplomatic mission behind your political policies, your ideas, convictions and beliefs. This, and so much more— the conferences, the entrenchments, the threats and the cases against us were so perfectly clear that I could make no sense of it. Ultimately, it was that very inanity which compelled you to act. The truth of the matter is, this was at the core of your grand design. I merely elicited from you concepts that were already there—your impossible plan in which time and death erupt, inflamed, and burn the whole thing to the ground. It was that perception of the world in which order is cloaked in a blanket of crime and the night is vilified with sleep. You have infected your women with your presence, committed your children to a future of damnation—even they could not bring you to plunge into the abyss of death—they could only give you a cursory glimpse of its edge. But, there in the midst of your perfected and brightly blazing rapture, I taught you all with one piercing stare. I told you, "Your room is filled with death" And I said, "The time has come," and in saying it, I said, "Death, be gone! Time, stand still!" This is what I had to teach. But you persisted, my beloved; your tongue, heavy with the weight of this pristine and cathartic epiphany—free from all that had gone between—punctuated the tragedy and pronounced the pathetic truth of this, your great spirit, which is the spirit of all men—a spirit void of purpose. And, because I was destined to partake of that same absence and you could not so much as imagine the presence of purpose, all was well between us. We were in love. We were of one mind.

I met a man once whose name was John. He was quite unlike the rest. I knew another, and he, too, was different. Then there was yet another exception to the rule. His name was John and I fell in love. I met him in the clearing—we departed, defying all direction. It was there on the Danube. We rode the Ferris wheel, meandered down the boulevards beneath the towering plane trees in the Black Forest and drank Pernod. I was in love. We stood at the station where the train pulled out just before midnight. I did not wave good-bye. Instead, I took my hand and drew the sign that said, "the end". The end that is without end. It was never quite over. But one should not hesitate to give the sign. It's not as tragic as it seems. It doesn't envelop the train stations and highways in smut—not like the sleight of a hand waving good-bye that so often puts an end to these things. "Be gone, death! Stand still, time!" No magic oracle can do the trick, no tears, no wringing of hands that intertwine and devour, no vows, no prayers. None of this will do. There is but one commandment in the world: trust that four eyes will suffice, that the green is enough, that the ease of simplicity will prevail. Obey the law of the land, do not follow the path of the heart lest you fall headlong into solitude: that lonely path upon which no footsteps echo but your own.

Don't you see what I mean? I cannot share your solitude because I have my own more ancient and infinite one. I was not born to bear the burden of your sorrows. Not these sorrows! How could I ever own them without compromising my beliefs? How could I ever attach any significance to these, the tangled sheets of your affairs, as long as I remain utterly convinced that you are more than your feeble, conceited dictums, your despicable deeds and your suspicious reasoning? Always, I have believed that you were more: knight in shining armor, adonic idol, not far removed from a soul deserving of the highest imperial honor. When you could make nothing else of your life, then you spoke with veracity. Then and only then did the dams finally break and the raging rivers rise—water lilies blossomed and drowned by the hundreds and the sea heaved a heavy sigh. Empowered, it struck out against the earth—battered, rammed and tore at her shores until they were livid with the rabid frothing of white foam.

Traitors! When you saw no other recourse, you invoked the power of defamation and infamy. Suddenly, you knew what it was about me that seemed so sinister—water and vaporous veils—all that defies definition and cannot be bound by shackles and chains. Suddenly, my presence posed a threat which you recognized just in the nick of time and I was anathematized—vexated by your disobliging vituperations. Then, in the bat of an eye, you were suddenly smitten with regret. Compunctious and penitent, you bowed down in the church pews before your women, your children, your admiring and public audience. How valiantly you paraded your contrition before the benches of justice and authority in your gallant courts—all for the sake of indemnity. How quickly you erected the altars and sacrificed my blood in the ritual ligation of the insecurities that had grown within you. Did you savor the taste of my blood on your tongue? Was it a culinary delight, like the blood of the doe hind and white whales? Was there a tinge of their sepulchral silence in it?

Bravo, good men, showered with adoration and

forgiveness. Just do not forget that it was you who conjured my presence in the world. It was you who contemplated my existence: the Other, conceived of your same spirit but not of your gestalt. The Unknown, the estranged alter-ego whose plaintive plea set the tenor of objection and rose in protest at your weddings. The Other who walked on dampened feet and whose kiss, you feared, was filled with death and the promise of that final end you sought but never found: a disordered death, rapturous, orchestrated according to the principles of highest reason.

Why in the world shouldn't I finally speak my peace?

Don't worry, I'm on my way out the door…

Because I caught one last glimpse of you. I heard you speak in a tongue better reserved for someone else, not me. My memory is ruthless. It has retained every act of treason and depravity. I returned to the scene of your crimes. I went back to the places we'd been and saw you again. Those sites, once luminous and light, are desecrated now—enshrouded in the dark shadows of all that you have done. I stood, silent; not one word fell from my tongue. You should say it yourselves. I sprinkled a handful of water on the ground, hoping that it might again grow green like the grassy graves. Hoping that, in the end, the light would return to this spot.

But, this is no way to say good-bye. So, let me call into account some of the better things you have done, that this might be a fond farewell. That there might be no parting of ways between us. That we divorce ourselves from nothing.

In spite of it all, your talk has been good—your mental meanderings, your zeal, and your willingness to sacrifice the whole truth for the sake of those self-evident partialities shedding light on that barely perceptible glimmer of being that permeated the fabric of your blind enthusiasm. So full of valor you were, so resolute in your struggle to keep the others at bay—and, of course, you could cower and sometimes covered your cowardice behind an intrepid charade. Even when the disastrous consequences of your policies of conflict and strife loomed before you, still you persevered. You stuck to your guns, knowing it was a losing battle and there was nothing in it for you. You fought bravely in defense of your possessions and against the principles and properties that would secure them. You fought for peace and for war, for the old and the new, for the rivers and those who would contain them. You took your vows, disavowing the administrators of oaths. Know, too, though that even as you struggle to keep your peace, your silence gives you away—that is perhaps laudable!

Every ounce of tenderness that survives the weight of your cumbersome bodies is a delicacy, indeed. One solitary act of kindness or generosity executed at your hands can exude an aura of stupendous magnitude. Even the most sublime sensitivity of your gentle women's deeds wanes against the backdrop of one sincere word issued from your mouths or one iota of compassion, comprehension or understanding that penetrates the surface of your deadened eardrums. You sit, tethered to the weightlessness of your leaden bodies; the slightest display of emotion—pathos or pleasure, even a simple smile crossing your face—is enough to momentarily deprive the wells of doubt rising in your friends' eyes of all sustenance.

How praiseworthy that your hands sometimes manage to handle the gift of frailty with care and to cherish fragile things, tending them so as to keep them from breaking. How noble that you should bear the burdens and clear the path from the weight of grievances. And the way you diagnose and treat human and animal life, cautiously wiping the salt from the wounds. So, really, in spite of the constraints you have constructed around your lives, your hands have done perhaps enough good to insure your redemption in the end.

It's amazing, the way you hover beneath the hoods, bent over motors you have built and know inside and out, explaining away their bodily function and moving parts until the meaning is lost amidst the subterfuge of extrapolations and exegeses and you have yet another great mystery on your hands. What was that you said? This principle and that property? It was all well and good that you said what you did. Never again will anyone have spoken so eloquently of the currents and catalysts, of magnetics and mechanics, of the core of all things.

Never again will anyone have spoken thus of the elements, the universe, and the sum of all heavenly bodies.

Nor has anyone before said such things of the

Earth, her matter, her ages, her depths. Everything was stated so clearly in your letters to the world: the icy crystals, volcanic eruptions, and the molten ash.

Never have the peoples of this Earth spoken thus of the circumstances surrounding their lives; of the human condition, the things that bind them, what they have built, bought and sold; of their perception of themselves as inhabitants of this Earth, some more ancient one or some future planet. It was right to have said all that you did and to have taken so much into consideration.

For never before did words exert such enchantment over the things of this Earth—never was language so superb, so sublime, so sodden with superiority, so capable of inculcating insanity or revolt. Words could swell and rise in rebellion on your tongue. You did it all with the words and the sentences, took every liberty in employing them to express the inexplicable; transformed and reversed them to make yourselves heard; you re-defined the neologisms and the logic; and those things which could comprehend neither the even nor the odd words were nearly swept up and away in the verbiage.

No one in the world could play the games as well as you, monsters, because they were yours by design—you invented them, each and every one: plays on words, mathematics and probability, passion plays, the sleep of dreams and the book of love.

No one has ever spoken this eloquently of himself. It is as close to the murderous truth as one comes. Bent now over the water, almost lost to yourself—the world has grown bleak. But I cannot throw you a line. There will be no clearing, not this time. You? Different from the rest? I'm going down. Deep beneath the waves. I am under water.

And above me someone treads who hates water and all that is green. One who does not understand and never will. Just as I have never done.

Almost dumb,
Almost numb.
Nearly deaf
to the call.
Come. Just once.
Come!

Manners of Death

Ladies and Gentlemen!

There is nothing more awkward than reading a few fragments from a novel which is subject to sometimes vague, sometimes more concrete ideas submitted by the author. The book is called "Manners of Death" and what I'm about to read has been compiled for your consideration and not with an eye for the work as a whole because I neither dare nor care to put it in words after all. Just this much: There's a lot of wrangling to reconcile the past going on today, by novelists, poets, and journalists, and I must admit that while I, too, am of course horrified by the gruesome occurrences we all know about, I haven't let that hinder me in embarking on a quest for something else. Without seeking to curry favor with compatriot geniuses, I *do* come from a country that has always concerned itself with that unknown entity, the human being, against the backdrop and the abyss of its darkest depths and most cryptic secrets.

Nor do I have any explanation for the fact that

my country has been host to several revolutionary scientific discoveries. I can only ascertain that it is so. Stretching from the unacknowledged Sacher-Masoch to the greatest pioneer, historically dated though he may have since become, Sigmund Freud, this line of research has never been severed. In recent years, I have followed with piqued interest the work of another fellow scholar, Konrad Lorenz, the zoologist and behavioral scientist. Still, that explains nothing, because writers discover *a conto suo* and it is at best a quivering delight to discover discoveries even remotely related to your own. Direct correlations never exist. But, ever since I was forced to realize that, contrary to what we might like to believe, 1945 was not a date that gave us reason to suddenly sleep soundly at night, I have wondered where the quantum criminal activity, the latent murder, has remained. You should not infer from this an attempt to *escape* the past. I just want to know what is happening now and this is a book about the "post-zero" hour. The here and now is difficult to discern because everything is shrouded in cotton, but only for appearance's sake. Murder and cruelty *are* to be detected in our society .

These manners of death would be the extension of a society that washes its hands clean of culpability and simply has no outlet for bloodletting, torture and gassing. But people—they just aren't like that—to be transformed suddenly into a herd of disarmed and indignant lambs. Our literature feigns to be daring at the expense of the past but I have found out that it, too, is predicated upon a subliminal deception. Unwittingly, it conceals the dramas, the methods of murder, at play here.

The protagonist, whom you will hardly notice here, a young Viennese historian whom I will have to make into a central figure by means of a slow and circuitous process, barely appears in these scenes. Just before he is to depart for North Africa to study (though the rest of the book takes place exclusively in Vienna), he is confronted by his older sister whom he cannot understand but who obtrudes upon him after escaping from a Viennese clinic when she realizes she is incurable. The grotesque victim of a well-known psychiatrist who, with her assistance, has fabricated a book that successfully "masters" the aforementioned past and wins him the highest distinctions, but at the same time destroys his wife—it is a dialectic process beyond good and evil.

The book begins in a village in Carinthia, between Galicia and Tschinowitz: the brother takes his sister along against his will; she is ill-equipped for the trip, which ultimately, if only by virtue of coincidence and analogy, assists her in coming into her own manner of death. It is but one of many and the person whose death and demise I portray here is but one precedential case that never surfaces again.

So, please bear with me...

Manners of Death

The professor, the Fossil, had driven his sister into the ground. He'd formed that opinion long before he had the slightest shred of evidence in hand because on the train to Vienna all he held was her telegram, two-pages long; typical of Franza, as he'd say to himself in his own manner of speaking, who either never wrote—incapable as she was of expressing herself in writing—or preferred instead to stutter together telegrams that were far too long, too expensive, too unexpected and too rare. Martin may have misplaced his train ticket a few times, but he never let the telegram out of his hand, reading compulsively between the stops—guessing, inventing, imagining. And it wasn't until he'd returned and hailed a late-night taxi from Villach nearly all the way to Tschinowitz, where he simply *had* to head toward Galicia on foot, or at least thought he did, after that asinine trip, sensing that the missing Franza must be near. He felt her presence like a misplaced object you'd forgotten somewhere and sought desperately in vain until suddenly, just before you find it beneath a pile of papers or laundry or in an unused drawer—suddenly, just a moment prior, you know—it's here, it has been here all along. This is the place. You're getting hot, hotter.

From that moment on, he calmed down, and at the same time felt himself growing annoyed with Franza because this all had to happen before his departure, because now he would have to keep Nemec from coming, the woman he'd already reserved a room for at the hotel Warmbader Hof and who would never, ever believe this was because of his sister and he wondered if he shouldn't spend at least one night with Nemec before sending her back to Vienna or whether he'd have to wire her a telegram right away. Following the path of the Gail River, a route he knew like no other, the river's unique, but familiar intonation, he tried to come up with some story about himself and Franza, but absolutely nothing occurred to him. At any rate, he wanted to be alone before he entered the house they owned together, their grandmother Nona's stuffy, unaired house he couldn't even subject Nemec to and where Franza probably was, where she had to be, simply *must* be there. Or there would be news from her, or—as it occurred to him for the first time—he might even be confronted with news of her death. He took in increasingly deep breaths of night air, 2 AM air, to purge himself of the railroad air and to put behind him the criminalistic search in Vienna and Baden and, above all, the demeaning phone conversation he'd had with his brother-in-law—what a disgusting word, "brother-in-law"—his brother-in-law who had treated him as though he were a patient suffering from some nonexistent disease, or one who was a credit risk and best brushed off with sanctimonious pandering. Recalling the conversation, it occurred to him that he hadn't acted differently than any member of an antiquated family, and that at a time when families no longer existed and never would again. What did he have to do with Franza whom he had rarely seen more than once a year in Vienna, first at this Fossil's house, where the man surrounded himself with low-level medical specialists, assistants and students so that he could rise like a central solar star emitting opinions and schoolmasterly advice? What had repulsed him most, though, was the way the man would gently pat his sister's shoulder in order to let everyone know she belonged to him—that she was his creation—and there was no way Martin could have taken a liking to that creature with those skimpy black dresses clinging to her emaciated little body: like a high-society bitch with blind attentiveness in her face, Franziska this and Franziska that, they called after her, Franziska here and Franziska there passed out glasses and babbled faculty gobbledygook. He suspected, and broke out in a cold sweat because of it, that later, when everyone had left—even this stoic brother who had since become so seldom seen—she would be called "my little mouse" or "sweetie-pie" or even "honey bunny." Martin was glad that even in spite of occasional threats to do so, the Fossil had at least never set foot in this house, had never seen the humble abode, had never known the Franza that he and only he knew, the one he was last to know, the one who had paraded through the village with a burning candle in a carved pumpkin head. He had never known the one who'd gone hungry for his sake and his mother's, who'd buttered up to the captain—what was his name?—but at any rate a fourteen year-old who was capable of anything, who conjured up fantastic games with him and the kids in the hay loft and who had inspired in him as a half-pint child but one thought: to be with her when he "grew up," to live with her, to wander through the world like a vagabond, her initiate in everything, with her slanted, brooding eyes, a *Gitsche*[1] with an expressionless gaze and a body that articulated all she was. The girl remained for him the epitome of all Gitsches, even though he no longer called her that in Café Herrenhof; calling her Franza was the closest he could come to retaining some of what had been, though he could never quite account for it because he had more important concerns, nor did he know why he and his *Gitsche* had grown so far apart and had nothing left to say to one another. Effortlessly and without an accent, this little lady, with her linguistic gift, had taken that giant leap most country girls never take—she'd simply fallen prey to Viennese social life and become the galley slave imprisoned by a city and a milieu that he despised. He listened to her talk, converse, or better put, carry on in a

---

[1] Slovenian dialect for "girl."

conversation as he'd never imagined possible. Whereas he hardly knew his parents anymore, Franza was forced to recollect everything and missed her father and went into hiding because it wasn't just that he was missing from the missing person's lists, missing in Crete or in the Balkans. She missed and was looking for something he didn't understand, with one exception. His father must have had two warts on his face, just like the Fossil had two warts on his face. He noticed it immediately and back then, as a student, he'd had the distinct feeling—supported by half-digested scholarship—that Franza had married a father figure and was seeking shelter, and now, ten years later, Martin again contemplated the warts as possible grounds for marriage: he arrived at their home and opened the door—he didn't need a key. She was there after all—the door was unlocked. The kerosene lamp was burning in the hallway and he proceeded into the bedroom with its two beds, one against each wall. At first all he saw of Franza were two feet sticking out from the bed with rolled up stockings still on; she started to get up, but then retracted her feet, hoisted herself up and propped herself on her elbows, and he hoped she wouldn't notice his horror at the sight of her bloated face. He hurried over to her, and, because she pulled away from him, kissed her on her hair that reeked of dirt and sweat. She'd simply turned away too abruptly, had tried to smile, but failed; tears were already streaming down her face. This wasn't his *Gitsche,* it wasn't even the little lady in the skimpy black dress with her epithets and figures of speech, the woman lying on the corn husk bed that rustled relentlessly was rather a complete stranger, unwashed, swollen in the merciful semi-darkness while he tried to think of something rational. I knew it, that's why I'm still awake, you know. He knew she couldn't keep talking and would immediately switch over to Italian, the secret language they both shared from an earlier time when they learned it from the Walsian workers, supplemented by librettos, official bureaucratic Italian and border crossings. Alfin sei giunto, she said, with her faced nestled in the pillow, *Sai. Sono finita, e stanca e morta e muta.*

He kissed her again on the head, then picked up her glass from the floor and drank from it. Cheap wine from the Burgenland. *Alla tua. Alla tua,* she said again and then once more, as though she wouldn't be able to convince him. You know, I'm at the end of my rope. She just kept repeating that sentence. He twisted the screw on the kerosene lamp in the hall shut, then turned on the lamp in the room, occasionally casting a furtive glance her way. He'd never seen someone so seriously ill before, no one so terminally ill, but the certainty about how bad off she was set in immediately, as if by reflex; he simply knew, he didn't need a doctor or his diagnoses. This wasn't his sister anymore, it was someone with only a few days left to live. He started undressing, as though he were but a child and she a young girl, surrogate mother, big sister; she watched him and he told her, profusely, far too profusely—and without ever actually naming the Fossil by name—about the odyssey of the journey: details that only occurred to him now; he didn't turn out the light and put on his pajamas under the constant watch of Franza's attentive eyes. She's dying, he thought, but hopefully, not today, that's the last thing I need. But he also thought that now he really would have to send Nemec back because—family schmamily—this was beyond comprehension for an unemployed pin-up girl, and he couldn't even let her get as far as Villach. Since he'd come to the end of his story about the odyssey and couldn't think of anything else to say, he said, just in order to do something about the silence, you know, of course, that I'll pay for the hospital, and he wasn't saying it just for Franza's sake, but out of pride and anger at the Fossil for having brushed him off on the phone—on the pretense that he had important work to do, and surely he did—but without comprehending that a brother and sister relationship could mean something and that ten years of marriage could mean nothing. Martin nonetheless wanted to prevent Franza from uttering one more word tonight, into his weariness; but, before he said good night and spread-eagled himself on his back as he always did before falling asleep, while she cowered, tiny, in her bed on the other side, thinking something to herself, he asked: whatever happened to the money, I mean, do you still have the money from Nona? He had relinquished his portion to her, and he would at least like to have some idea what she did with it after she married—that is, after Nona's death. Franza was silent, then she said, in the voice of that woman who'd become a complete stranger to him: I don't have it any more, that is, uh, we, no—it's not there anymore, that is, I still have a little, but hardly anything, otherwise I'd have paid myself, but I still have some, what I would need for you to take me along.

What? What did you say, Martin said as though he weren't falling asleep, but was in that little lady Nemec's living room instead.

You are taking me along, Franza said. He was sure she wasn't crying, her voice sounded so dry. I'm going down there with you. That's why I took off, I've prepared everything, I even have a visa, I knew you were going. You have to take me along.

It was hard to argue with her in the dark, but suddenly he was wide awake. I'm taking you to Vienna tomorrow; I have a week's time left, you have to see the best doctor, go to the best clinic. I'm going to call Alda right away. Let me take care of it. You have to get out of here. This is insanity. You can't stay here.

Yes, she said, as wide-awake as he, I have to get away from here, but I'm not going to Vienna.

Now she belonged to him, for the duration; now

she'd come home, much too late, and this was no time for coming home. He dragged her, since she wanted so much to go, over to the Zündhölzel bridge along the softly sodden paths in the faint April sun. On the soccer field next to the hovels—those slipshod little houses strewn along the river—they greeted everyone; sometimes they stopped and said they'd be going away, but would be returning again soon: after all, they'd always gone and had usually come back, too. And they always went to the little cemetery in Galicia, where they had to do some weeding of the graves because it turned out every time that old Bohan didn't take weeding very seriously and drank up all the money for flowers. But there was nothing they could do about it now that they'd commissioned out the care of the graves because they were too busy studying and marrying.

So they went to the desert.

Light spewed out over them, heaven's hot eruption, with a heated, almost sanitary smell. The great sanatorium—huge, inescapable, but open on all sides, purgatory, Arabic, Libyan, with subdivisions, fine-grained, solid as stone, stockpiled into rocky cliff grown granular again. She had been taken in, admitted.

The desert bus drove for nine hours, stopping only once briefly in Suez, where the festering wounds had already burst open and a liquid discharge, a white something from the Whites, started seeping out. Franza bought a pita bread and Martin ordered two glasses of tea; they'd stopped talking to each other, it wasn't that they had said all there was to say, but he had been looking at her skeptically ever since she'd swaggered out of the bus. If you could still speak in terms of a study tour—a thought that might have cost him a chuckle if he'd been able to laugh in this heat—so this eyes-glued-shut start was the grandiose beginning of his *studium generale*. Would she collapse: what did you do in Suez when a white woman suddenly collapsed or started screaming, or, since she'd grown so silent now, died without a word still clutching a pita bread in her hand? He saw her approach him, seat herself in front of this ramshackle shack; she had a glazed look he couldn't quite decipher—he hoped that she wasn't in Vienna right now, not haggling with a surgeon and begging him to let her take her fetus home in a canning jar. What had horrified him so on the ship, what he'd considered completely preposterous, was the fibrous solemnity of her plans—the unleashing of an archaic appetite for something that came naturally to her but not to the others, the recognition of ancient laws that she still knew and were inapplicable in this day and age; for the first time, that didn't seem as crazy to him as it had just a few days ago. While she drank her tea and stared at the street—alternately, over at the bus as though she were afraid she might miss it—he repeated her words more calmly to himself. He bit his lips because the tea was too hot—everything was too hot here; and so Franza had screamed at a high-titled individual, presumably the Chief of Medicine, with sterilized hands, a mask, and in a white climate-controlled room, she had screamed and asked him to at least let her eat this thing she thought was her child—to eat it, not throw it way, not to burn it or relegate it to the Viennese sewage system, not to let it end up where everything else landed. He studied her from the side and knew she was always in Vienna, not here—she had simply chosen the right equivalent of a space where she lived with her own ideas; indeed, it was less than that—not a remembrance, nothing like that—but with a constant reoccurrence of an event you would describe as having happened. Nor was it the recapitulation of a story and there wasn't any change of place for her; nor did she travel—she was always there in a place that was one and the same, whether in Baden or Vienna—because for her, both these places were entwined with Suez, and the time two or three months ago wasn't past, it engaged itself like a cogwheel in this day, in every day, and only the calendar could have contradicted Franza, but not here, here where time didn't speculate about the clock, not in this region that had produced fever, hallucinations, icons and religions.

At the military station just before Hurghada, there still wasn't anything in sight, but they entered the rest house as though they thought it perfectly normal that a building with running water and water pipes should be situated there, together with a gathering of thirty Arabs in an amicable no man's land. Chairs, tables, coffee and a long corridor where half the men at a time stood waiting in line to use the latrine; a mere six hours ago, at a stop along the dusty route, they'd left the bus and gone off into the desert and, their faces facing the desert, had stood there fumbling with their galabayas and pajamas. Franza had stayed back at the bus, had said to

Martin: so just go on, will you; at first she didn't know where she should look, so she looked at one side of the desert—inasmuch as the desert can be said to *have* two sides—but then she simply turned toward the men, holding the empty coke bottle in her hand. Europe, then, was at an end: it was all over for a White woman with her habits, taboos, social deformities.

Ever since Suez, there had been—beneath the baggage in a box next to the driver—a couple bottles of yogurt, some fish and some vegetables, viewed skeptically by everyone because once the two ice blocks surrounding them had melted, the fish were all that remained worth mentioning and immediate cause for ritualistic exclamations and prayers, and Martin saw that Franza was staring at the box; it was the first sign of interest she had shown: a concern for nourishment she'd never had to worry about—about fish and, above all, a field flask with water, one that a passenger passed around from time to time. The first time, Martin and Franza declined with an overly polite thanks, but no thanks; the second time, Franza took a swig from the cup and Martin just gestured as though he were drinking before he returned the cup. He slid the book over to Franza. He was outraged.

> Not advised outside better hotels
> Fresh fruit, peeled if possible
> if not possible, wash with soap
> let it stand for ten minutes in
>   potassium permanganate.
> Don't drink tap water anywhere outside
>   major cities
> Boiled water only, weak tea
> Prophylactic measures after severe mosquito
>   bites, 2 tablets of Resochin by Bayer
> Schistosomiasis, Egyptian tapeworm and
>   intestinal parasites, miliaria rubra, sometimes
>   called prickly heat, occur frequently
> Change sweat-soaked underclothes frequently,
>   wash once daily with soap

Never shower more than three times a day, one part mercuric chloride per thousand ml., Ace bandages, razor blade to cut open snake bites, Eldoform dye-works Hoechst, Behring pharmaceutical division, 10 ml.

They laughed while the letters and words were flagged through the dust squadrons and slithered away before their eyes.

Sure, the dye-works Hoechst and Bayer and Ala, Franza said, I'll just hop out here and run to the nearest pharmacy.

Who around here is afraid of the bacteria developed by Whites? Who would wash out a cup, who would boil the water, who would delouse the lettuce leaves, x-ray the fish? No one. Hunger, thirst: rediscovered; the danger: rediscovered; the goal: recognized. A roof over one's head, a camp for the night, a shadow, a patch of shade. There should be enough gas, no flat tires, no clogged spark plugs, no broken axle. The path should stay in sight—it is narrow, barely visible, there's just enough room for the wheels to fit on it.

The wind rose for the first time, gripped into the sand and the threatening ground dissolved itself in the air, revealing its true texture. The eyes and the desert found one another: the desert in the eyes—for hours, days—the halting, faltering eyes cleansed themselves in base instability; they purge themselves—ever emptier the eyes, ever more attentive, wider, in the only landscape just made for the eyes.

The subdued persuasion of the desert, with its delicate sketches. What are you seeking in the desert? said the voice in the wilderness where there is nothing to hear. Why hast thou forsaken me? Why is the Red Sea so full of sharks, the fiercest of animals? And the voice that cannot be heard because there is nothing to hear in this desert doesn't answer. My god. Someone has reserved this desert for himself, and this someone was not a hotel chain or an oil company.

The supply tanker didn't come, but Hurghada has its own small reservoir of water; even so, no one is allowed to wash, but there's still food to be had in the hotel and even a couple bottles of wine, so there was something to drink after sunset. The water on this waterless coast, completely and wholly waterless, now belongs to everyone: the Bedouins who come, the *fellahs*, guests—no one can be denied it: it is the unwritten law of the desert, that water—worth more than gold or plots on the Riviera, more indispensable than the monthly salaries, the insurance policies, the right to vote—cannot be denied anyone. You see, said Franza, nothing can be denied me here. I'll get my due.

Martin, who hadn't been able to get up all day because of his sunburn and high fever, said it for the first time: *Gitsche,* you know that you will become the picture of health now; you're just as clever as you ever were, even though I don't know why you're clever and in what way—in your case, the intellect must have slid from your head into some other part of your body, into your flesh, your nerves, tendons, your vital organs, anywhere but your brain. Franza laughed, then, because the damp cloth she'd wanted to cool his skin with had already gotten hot; she started licking him, do you like that, doesn't this work, too? She'd not only been tanned brown, everything had solidified itself again in her, she carried her flesh for herself, or her flesh was smart enough to cling to her bones. Now she would just have to hold out. I don't know whether you're right or not, you understand, but do you remember: Of a hundred brothers, this one.

Martin nodded, he remembered, he was it, for better or for worse: this one, burned from head to toe, a grilled piece of meat with a reliable heart and good circulation, journeying alone with this savage who came to life here where he felt more miserable each day. He wanted to get away, at the very least to Qina or Luxor, and to a decent hotel; he wanted to see something of the country, but Franza didn't want to see anything, not even from the plane that must be coming in a couple of days to take them back to Cairo so he could see the people he needed to see. The only thing that could contain or convince her to go was the promise that she would be allowed to continue through the desert.

Salam, Ahmed, Martin turned on the light and Franza flared up: I'm already sleeping. She looked at the men standing around smoking. Martin was talking, talking about what. Do it for yourself, just do something for yourself, and stop with Vienna, I only wish you'd stop with that. Franza said, yes, but not now, I'm already asleep. Which one were you with…she motioned toward the cigarettes. With Ahmed, Martin said. I am in Aswan, am I not. No one would give her a cigarette, they regard me with such suspicion in their eyes: go on ahead to the bar, I'll come later. I don't even know where I am and they stare and stare; one of them sits down in the only chair, the others sit with Martin on the edge of her bed: give me your hand, Martin, you mustn't leave me alone. He brushed her shoulder tenderly and pushed the slender straps aside and the wrap, too heavy to be used as a blanket—why did she even bother to cover herself up here—he showed them all his sister and she kept her eyes open. She wouldn't let go of his hand, and she soon lost sight of him.

A neutral plural, *Orgia,* used by the Greeks, like Diana as a brand name for cigarettes, like Apollo as the name for a cinema, Kalodont for toothpaste— sold out, never again understood. Never again the Greeks, never again the neutral plural, nothing more that is Greek, wiped out, eclipsed in Egypt, in a single night on the Nile, taking her beyond, wiping out what was white, seceding from the rubbish of tenderness, of the proclamations, of the ideological product of love, the white hysteria of inferiority. Wanting the whole, wanting mutuality: not man wanting woman, woman wanting man, but the great act of revenge against this partition, this separation from one another—sleeping then, like never before, with solemn faces, waking, kissing each others' hands, each slave to the other. Each the other's redeemer.

Ahmed stood in the lightened room, they were all drinking tea; Franza glanced past Martin, but was hard-pressed to hide her triumph. I killed him,

I have killed all the Whites; he must have had a nasty night in Vienna or just a normal, numbed, nonsensical night.

Franza, standing erect, her head held high, no longer in Vienna: The Whites' venereal diseases will bring me to do nothing but laugh. Franza, deferent: and you, and you? Of a hundred brothers. Martin said, I was watching you the whole time, I was envious, but I don't know what that's supposed to mean, not that I was envious of you, but of what you succeeded in doing. You were so beautiful. Ha, she said, it never so much as occurred to me, but I'm sure now that I was very beautiful.

It is light in the room. The Nile rose, they walked and walked with Franza between them—a being that commanded utmost respect just by virtue of its hybrid haughtiness—they crossed over in a boat to Elephantine Island, and she didn't so much as look at the men in her pride; like a traveler between one wonderland and another, she observed the sky, the other boats, the sails. And then: Who died here? Kitchener, of course. There's always someone who has died somewhere no matter where you go. Ahmed and Sallah—unmoved by Kitchener's death, by his grave, by Elephantine and Philae—gallantly escorted Franza silently to the Nilometer where they explained to her, in bad English, what was behind the prehistoric measuring instrument. She understood only half of it and was satisfied with that; she only lent one ear—so to speak—to listening to her subordinates anyway—as we do with so much for which no name has yet been found. Even Franza stood there unnamed—with one deaf ear, swollen lips, and a white hat—on the island of Elephantine, looking toward Sudan, in the direction of the Cataracts, the Aswan Dam, looking toward an official state ceremony, the politicians' ship, and she thought: this is how it could have happened last week when the High Dam was inaugurated—when the water came, it came. An entire wasteland got to cash in on a pawned out promise for water.

Franza said, we're going back, and climbed back down to the boat, I have no interest in the dead who were buried such a short time ago. And islands under water, she pointed, and Martin corrected her, to where Philae would remain flooded for a few months yet before it could re-emerge with its Isis temple. And islands under water, that too shall pass, otherwise, I'd have to see them too.

What business did Kitchener have in this place anyway, what were these two busy looking for here, with the cry of terror ringing in their ear, *les blancs arrivent*. The Whites are coming! Franza: I'm afraid of the Whites, I've always been afraid to be alone with one of them in a room—afraid of having a pillow stuffed in my face, of being suffocated by those who consider themselves members of a superior race; they've seen through me: I am of an inferior race. Never again to live with the fear of strangulation, of poisoning at breakfast, of having to say it a thousand times: I love you; of having to gesticulate like a marionette: oh thank you, oh please, excuse me, please? No, thank you.

Pain—a peculiar word, peculiar thing, dredged up from the natural history of humanity, ferried out of the body. I'm here in the desert to get rid of the pain and it's not going away—it's raging through my head, on my breath: this insane pain that ferrets out a new field to test me every couple of hours; my jaws, so that my teeth that can't clench anymore; my hands, growing numb and letting the cup fall;

my feet, cramping; my knee, collapsing; my eyes with their dilated pupils, pitching and hankering, squinting, not seeing anything for an hour.

Hashish, *cannabis india,* the Chronic, and how many other names must the hemp plant answer to? Abdu and Ahmed were only able to procure a tiny piece, but a good one—a hard, earth-brown piece, they took turns fondling it. One of the Soviet engineers who was working on the High Dam wanted to stay but left after all; the crazy Irishman stayed. Martin donned his galabaya for the first time: you're in disguise, Franza said, that's all there is to it. Oh, just do it for me, do it for me. Do you remember: Of a hundred brothers. Martin saw the Isis-and-Osiris look in her face again—the height of hopelessness—and now more than ever, he had the feeling that she didn't even believe herself anymore and that she knew now she was lost, with one deaf ear, and death entered the room, but it didn't actually enter: something like that doesn't enter into existence, not something like death. He started twirling the tobacco out of the cigarettes, carefully, while Abdu and Ahmed crumbled the piece of hash and took on the task of kneading it into the tobacco.

Then the stuff was inserted back into the cigarette sleeve: it was all done with extreme care—it was a ritual act, a ceremony. They all started smoking at the same time. After the second joint, she looked at Martin begging for mercy, but he lit the third one for her and she smoked: she saw faces skewed inward, a slight smile for the very first time, on the Brown face and the Black. She could sense that silence was in order. Something was happening—barely imperceptible at first, but speeding up then—happening slightly different for each of the others: where are the others, where is everybody? Franza wanted to get up, she couldn't stand the thought of staying here one more moment; a moment was no longer what she knew it to be—time was up and over, space was in motion, her body poised against space and time, pointing in a new direction. Since she couldn't expect anyone to come to her aid, she crawled down from the chair, crept a ways further along the floor out to the carpet-covered terrace; she stretched out on the carpet, straining to direct her eyes toward the light emanating from the room. She had inhaled very deeply, holding the smoke in her lungs. The nausea subsided when she closed her eyes. She wanted to scream for horror because she no longer inhabited one body, but two; she had doubled herself—she clasped her hands over her stomach, but two hands clasped over her other stomach, too: I've turned into two, I am at once big, gigantic, and at the same time small, the same size I've always been, and both her bodies, lying on their backs, suddenly commenced to drift, all four feet flung upward; both her heads remained on the rug, she hung there like that, doubly incapable of becoming one again. She opened her eyes wide: everything was there, the room, the lamp, she saw Ahmed's galabaya, his dangling arm, closed her eyes again. A vise was driven beneath her body—no shift in position. Under her closed eyelids the papyrus scroll started rolling, adorned with black and white inscriptions; under cover of hieroglyphs, as yet undeciphered, a hot, dull scent from the Nile opened her eyes again—opened them in a lightning-like flash—she assured herself: this is real, not a shift in position; the mosque's minaret is still in view. The vise loosened itself, she flew forward toward the minaret, returned again, flew back, and started laughing: she could fly back and forth without a carpet after all. A flurry of thought hailed like drumfire: something thinks itself into existence with rapid-fire velocity, the scrolls come to a halt, thoughts arrive. *Arrivent les blancs.* I don't want to think, I want to fly back to the minaret, don't think, don't think. Franza didn't know when and what had been the last moment of her altered state—didn't know when she had become one, when she had fallen asleep. She woke up in her own bed next to Martin who must have carried her there. The morning was clear and light. Nothing was left—they both had clear heads, didn't even have to pinch themselves to see whether their heads were still attached. They tried telling each other about the night, but Martin didn't understand Franza, least of all her insistence on having a double body, and she didn't understand what he had heard. Heard? She hadn't heard a thing. They were both reluctant, unwilling and heart-wrenched: they'd each been sent off to different countries.

What are you seeking in this desert wasteland, in the city of the dead, where graves are desecrated by archaeologists, wandering back and forth evening for evening along the great Sphinx boulevard, a thousand rams' heads flanking your fear? What in this singular landscape that says nothing, expresses nothing—nothing can be said about it. There's purity before your very eyes, so what are you fleeing from, harrying daily into the desert. Where is the Gulf of Aqaba? Rushing still, crossing the Nile, in the sail's shadow—as though the desert would befriend a stranger—still shimmering with the nimbus of a fool, still tormented by words that echo, by acts and deeds not declared punishable by any clause in the law. The Whites have a strong alibi. Not a single effort has been spared in the attempt to sweep you out of the way, to make you step on the land mines of their intellect, their plans and their plots.

At the train platform in Idfu, Franza guarded their baggage. She sat on a suitcase, she didn't want to see the temple, but her will was wavering. Martin evidently had a future and was compelled to see the temples, and for her, the present was the outer limit, her fainting spells in the train traveling ever steady and stopping in the open desert with its coaches threatening to break apart, with the fowl and the foulness in the cabin. She stared into space, her fainting increased, just not in the desert, but she didn't know how to make it clear to Martin, and she dreaded the temples, the graves, the depths of millenia that she could only counter with a depth of little more than thirty years, her own history against the whole of this history, her own limited madness against this one great boundless insanity proven to have commenced right here, as verifiable as the testimonies to its beauty. Witnesses to the madness: the colossuses, the pylons, arteries paved with gold, calculations and imagination set in gargantuan stone, and the evaporated sweat of fear and suffering.

At the train station in Idfu, Franza saw the woman. She was on her knees, shackled by ropes bound about her feet and wrapped around her body, her hands were tied together behind her back—that's the first thing she saw—the slender, dirty feet, these hands, and it was only after that that she saw the woman's head, a narrow, elongated overstretched head like the one Echn Aton's daughters had, then she saw the big Arab man holding her hair, it too twirled into a noose. Smiling, grinding his teeth, he held the woman by the hair, she was kneeling, and because he held her knitted hair, she held her head high with closed eyes, Franza leapt up and took a few steps toward a group of Arabs, she couldn't speak, now it was happening again, she looked for Martin, who didn't return, she stared with clenched jaws at the Arabs. The woman, Martin, the woman. The man is crazy, the man, she repeated it so many times to herself that she suddenly blurted it out in halting English. The youngest of the Arabs grinned and answered, in English: Not he is crazy. *She* is crazy. The woman, the woman, at the train station in Idfu I saw a woman who was shackled and no one would help her, that will befall us too, all that will befall us too. He takes her home, doesn't he, he will shackle her again and again. But he really does take her home, doesn't he, at least he takes her home, even after all that? The man had the tickets in his hand or in his belt. Franza never tired of telling Martin this story over and over again every day. I am certain that whenever I return to Idfu, the woman will always be there. She is of course always there, I *did* see her, what I see is eternal, unshakeable, it never changes its place. The jackals and rams' heads on the boulevard aren't the only thing that's eternal. Everything is eternal, for as long as I live. She didn't tire, she said, as long as I live. That long. Now it was Martin who thought about Vienna, but in the usual sense, picking apart and deciphering, the less she spoke about Vienna, what happened there. He came to the preliminary conclusion that there were subliminal crimes and he had underestimated the Fossil. He blurted out his thoughts, I should have wrung his neck instead of talking to him on the phone, taking his condescending advice. Franza didn't answer, then laughed. She laughed often now.

In the big tent, lined with carpets, concealing a thousand and one nights in paltry poverty, even the children stayed awake all night. The wedding was for the others, even for these two, whom the children, laughing, poked with their fingers. The children had looks of love, gestures of love that would have to be cast off by the time they reached their twelfth or thirteenth year. They were in that phase, Martin and Franza recognized, of lily-white innocence and purity. The men sat around smoking incessantly and drinking coffee with barely a glance between them, without that artificial childish sanctity, talking and talking at them, darkly, you couldn't see the bride and groom. In the sand near Franza's chair, a Cretan crouched on the ground, with twisted hands, a shaved head, covered with boils, leprous, even though it wasn't supposed to be leprosy. The children kicked his feet, his hands, but brought him a bottle of coca-cola all the same and poured it into his mouth, laughing, and the Cretan laughed. Ahmed said, solemn and in English: He is a holy man. He nudged Franza several times, but she kept her eyes glued straight ahead, staring, and the girl with her forcemeat fat stomach and bovine breasts had been dancing clumsily for an hour already to the music coming from a speaker, dancing in a transparent red dress, naked, repulsive; he is a holy man, she mumbled over and over, but as she was taking her seat, she had inadvertently set eyes on him, but she didn't want to look, I just can't. Martin traded places with her. Then she cast another tortured look his way, didn't see anything, only the twisted, festering hand getting stepped on by a man in pajamas.

They left at the crack of dawn, they still hadn't seen the wedding couple. In the courtyard, Franza wanted to go see the camel that the groom had given as a wedding gift, but it was no longer there. About a hundred yards away, under one of the stable lanterns, she let out a shriek. Martin saw now too that the sand was red, Franza stood in the red sand and they waded through the bloody sand. The camel had been killed, a couple of men sliced it up with big knives. Its head lay in the sand with the very same expression that came over Franza's face.

Far off in the distance, always on the Red Sea, the red played off like land against the black shore, toward Safaga, bleeding into the oil fields, no tank, no water, landing on the loneliest stretch of beach in the world, she took off running, and then it surfaced, again and again it surfaced, and Franza, who steadfastly maintained that this was not a sea, saying over and over, this isn't a sea, it's a basin on the brink of hell, stuffed full of jellyfish, spiders, crabs, a couple miles further out the barracudas poised for attack, every square foot of the beach was a foretaste of the water's content, of snakes. She ran along the beach, first she saw a car, no, she didn't see it, there was nothing to see in the light here, a shadow, across a dirt road, yet there was no dirt road to be seen, but instead the *sound* of a car was audible, and a shadow. She screamed and ran. A car, she cried, then the dirt road and the sound and the shadow all disappeared and she kept running.

Then she stood there seeking a spot to stand between all that was crawling around her, clawing, biting, stinging, and the sun stood straight over her head, until suddenly she saw the scene. There was nothing more to see of the shackled woman, nothing more of the slaughtered camel, she sobbed suddenly. I saw a mirage. I saw what no one else saw, a scene, and they stood and the scene was staged in the distance, set in red Arabia, while her skin began to burn, I have to run, as long as I can see that scene, that's him, my father, I saw my father, I saw him, but that isn't my father, no, he's wearing a white coat, he has come from Vienna, cloaked in a coat of comfort, I saw him in it. She started running again, placing her hands over her head because her head had started to burn.

But he isn't my father and he doesn't have a white coat. What is it that I see, then, something big, black and looming erect, I have to get closer, I can see, ever more clearly, that he's coming at me, on the ground, no, above ground now. God is coming at me and I'm coming to God, too. She started running again and cried and screamed and spit the cigarette phlegm she coughed up from her throat out in the sand. I have seen God. Within a hand's reach, where am I, Safaga, beautiful mountains in the 2,000 meter and up range, in a tent, a military post, where is the post, the phosphate company, the former British harbor, the phosphate company has to let me get there, not even the phosphate company can stand in God's way.

She stumbled and landed on her knees, and there it was, then, lying before her, this black tree stump, a sea cucumber, a monster shrunk in on itself, this stump still containing something akin to life, barely thirty centimeters long, this is what she'd been running toward, and she was still crying when she laughed and reached for the animal that had been washed up from the ocean onto the shore, and shoved it off back into the water, let it drift out into the water to keep it from dying. I saw a scene, she was left lying there in elliptical convulsions, just as if she were lying on the floor of the corridor in Vienna, my salvation, my linoleum floor, my sand, where camels bleed to death, not here, but at some point in the past, and that means everywhere.

She laughed and laughed—and in her laughter, in that imaginary event horizon for decomposition, who am I, where am I from, what am I doing here in this desert, didn't enter, didn't enter, how is anything supposed to enter into existence here? since no event can enter in—with a deaf ear, half-dead, half-a-head, half animal, half human, having half of five senses, the sister, according to her passport anyway, was a woman, for lack of a better term, the scorched, executed flesh of something recognizable, not entirely accessible to the sciences of zoology and the humanities.

She screamed.

The fringe of the Arabian desert is wrapped in a wrack of broken faiths.

Voyage Out

Smoke is rising from the ground.
Keep an eye on the tiny fishing hut,
for the sun will set
before you've put ten miles behind you.

The dark water, thousand-eyed,
opens its white-foamed lashes
to peer at you, wide-eyed and long,
for thirty days.

Even when the ship pitches hard
and takes an uncertain step,
stand steady on deck.

They are seated at the tables now,
eating the smoked fish;
later, the men will kneel
and mend the nets;
nights, though, they will sleep,
an hour or two,
and their hands will soften,

free from salt and oil,
soft as bread of the dream
they have broken.

The first wave of night hits the shore,
the second has already reached you.
But when you cast your gaze beyond,
you can still see the tree
raising a defiant arm
— the wind has already robbed it of another
— and you wonder: how much longer,
how much longer
will the twisted timber weather these storms?
There is no land left in sight.
You should have dug into the sandbank with your hand
or tied yourself to the cliffs by a strand of hair.

Blowing into conches, sea monsters float
on the crests of waves, they ride and slice
the day to pieces with bare sabers, leaving a red trail
in the water, where sleep overcomes you
for the rest of your days
and your senses leave you.

Suddenly, something has happened to the ropes,
you are called, and are happy
to be needed. Best of all
is to work on ships
that sail far away,
tying knots in the ropes, bailing water,
caulking walls and guarding the freight.
Best of all is to collapse in exhaustion
when evening comes. Best of all, at daybreak,
with the first light of dawn, to awaken,
to stand against an immovable sky,
ignoring the impassable water,
and to lift the ship above the waves,
sailing toward the ever recurring shore of the sun.

The Mortgage on Borrowed Time

There are harder days to come.
The mortgage on borrowed time
is pending on the horizon.
Soon you must lace your boots
and chase the hounds back to the marsh farms.

For the fishes' entrails
have grown cold in the wind.
The paltry light of lupines' burns.
Your gaze presses on in the fog:
The mortgage on borrowed time
is pending on the horizon.

Over there, your lover sinks in the sand
rising around her flowing hair,
he cuts her short,
demands her silence,
thinking her mortal
and willing to depart
after every embrace.

Don't look around.
Lace your boots.
Chase back the hounds.
Throw the fish in the sea.
Put out the lupines!

There are harder days to come.

Wood and Shavings

I will not speak of hornets
because they are so easily recognized.
And the ongoing revolutions
present no danger.
Death has always followed
close on the heels of noise.

Yet beware the dayflies and women,
beware the Sunday hunters,
the beauticians, the undecided, the well meaning,
those untouched by contempt.

We carried brushwood and logs from the forests,
and it was a long time before the sun rose above us.
Intoxicated by the paper on the conveyer belt,
I cannot make out the branches,
or the moss, fermented to a darker tint,
nor the word, carved into the bark,
impudent and true.

Wasted paper, banners and slogans,
black placards…by day and by night
the machinery of faith quakes
beneath these stars and others. But
as long as it is still green, and bitter with gall,
I would write into the wood
what was in the beginning!

Make sure you stay awake!

The trail of shavings that flew follows
the hornets' swarm, and at the fountain,
the seduction that once
sapped our strength
now just makes our hair stand on end.

Theme and Variation

That summer there was no honey.
The queens led their swarms away,
the strawberry bed dried up in a day,
the berrypickers went home early.

All that sweetness, swept on one ray of light
off to sleep. Who slept this sleep before his time?
Honey and berries? He is a stranger to suffering,
the one with the world at his hands. In want of nothing.

In want of nothing but perhaps a bit,
enough to rest or to stand straight.
He was bent by caves—and shadows,
because no country took him in.
He wasn't even safe in the woods—
a partisan whom the world relinquished
to her dead satellite, the moon.

He is a stranger to suffering, the one with the world
    at his hands,
and was anything not handed him? He had the beetle's

cohort wrapped round his finger, blazes
branded his face with scars and the wellspring
appeared as a chimera before his eyes,
where it was not.

Honey and berries?
Had he ever known their scent, he'd have followed it
long ago!

Walking a sleepwalker's sleep,
who slept this sleep before his time?
One who was born ancient
and called to the darkness early.
All that sweetness swept on one ray of light
before him.

He spat into the undergrowth a curse
to bring drought, he screamed
and his prayers were heard:
the berrypickers went home early!
When the root rose up
and slithered after them, hissing,
a snakeskin remained, the tree's last defense.
The strawberry bed dried up in a day.

In the village below, the buckets stood empty
like drums waiting in the square.
Then the sun struck
and paradiddled death.

The windows fell shut,
the queens led their swarms away,
and no one prevented them from fleeing.
Wilderness took them in,
the hollow tree among ferns,
the first free state.
The last human being was stung
and felt no pain.

That summer there was no honey.

Early Noon

The linden tree greens silently in summer's
 grand opening,
far removed from the cities, the dim radiance of the day
moon shimmers. It is already noon,
the fountain's stream is already astir,
already the flayed wings of the fairy bird
rise beneath the shards
and the hand, crippled by the casting of the stone,
sinks in the wakening grain.

Where the German sky blackens the soil,
her beheaded angel seeks a grave for hatred
and offers you the basins of her heart.

A handful of pain recedes beyond the hill.

Seven years later,
standing at the water-well before the gate,
you suddenly remember everything,

don't delve too deep
lest your eyes brim over with tears.

Seven years later,
in the house of the dead,
yesterday's henchmen
empty the golden cup.
Your eyes would sink for shame.

It is already noon, and the iron
cringes in the ashes, the flag is hoisted
on the thorn and the eagle remains
welded from now on to the cliff
of an ancient dream.

Hope, blinded by the light, is all that cowers.

Release her from the shackles, lead her
down the steep incline, place a
hand before her eye, that she might
not be scorched by the shadow!

Where the German soil blackens the sky,
the cloud seeks words and fills the crater with silence
before summer heeds them in the tremble of sparse rain.

The unspeakable crosses the country, softly spoken:
it is already noon.

Every Day

War is no longer declared,
merely perpetuated. The outrageous
has become commonplace. The hero
stays far from battle. The weakling
is transferred to the firing zone.
Patience is the uniform of the day,
the order of merit a wretched star
of hope stuck to the heart.

It will be awarded
when the action has ceased,
when the drumfire dies down,
when the enemy has receded from view
and the shadow of eternal armament
enshrouds the sky.

It will be awarded
for deserting the flags,
for bravery in the face of a friend,
for the betrayal of ignoble secrets
and the disregard
of every command.

Message

The sun steps from the corpse-warm atrium of the sky
where not the immortal reside, but
rather the fallen—so we are told.

And brilliance is not troubled by decay. Our godhead,
history, has ordered for us a grave
from which we shall never rise again.

Night Flight

The sky is our field, an acre
tilled to the engine's sweat
in the light of night's toiled brow,
in the deployment of a dream—

dreamt at the sacrificial sites of skulls and the pyres of
   the stake,
beneath the world's roof with its shingles
carried off by the wind—now there is rain, rain, rain
in our house and in the mills
the blind flights of bats and bombers.
Who lived there? Whose hands were clean?
Whose light shone in the night,
a ghost to the ghosts?

Secure in a nest of steel feathers, instruments
interrogate the air space, time clocks and dials probe
the thicket of clouds and love caresses
the lost language of our hearts:
short and long, long…an hour-long

pummel of hail stirs the recalcitrant eardrum
to eavesdrop, it winces, then recovers from its recoil.

Sun and earth have not gone under,
they have merely wandered as stars out of sight.

We ascended from a harbor
where neither the return,
nor the freight nor the catch amounts to anything.
India's spices and Japanese silks
belong to the traders
like fish to the nets.

And yet, in the forward wake of comets,
you can detect a certain stench and the tapestry of air is
torn apart by fallen comets.
Call it the status of solitaries
where astonishment occurs.
Nothing more.

We have risen, and the convents are empty
since we merely endure, this monastic order that cannot
   heal or teach.

It is not the pilots' job to act. They have airbases in sight
and the map of a world with no room for anything new
spread across their laps.

Who lives down there? Who weeps…
Who has lost a house key?
Or cannot find his bed, who sleeps
on the thresholds? Who would dare
to interpret the silver stripe of morning's arrival: look,
above me…
Who will dare remember the night
when water once again churns the wheel?

Psalm I-IV

I

Abide with me in silence, as all bells abide!

In the afterbirth of horrors,
the vermin forages for sustenance.
Good Fridays, a hand hangs on display
from the firmament; missing two fingers,
it cannot swear that all this,
all this has never been and nothing
shall ever be. It dips into scarlet skies,
dislodges the fledgling murderers
and is set free.

Nights on earth,
open the windows and throw back the linens,
to expose the secrets of the sick,
a tumor rife with nourishment, infinite pain,
something for everyone.

The butchers' gloved hands
cut short the breath of the naked,

the moon, framed by the door jamb, falls to the floor,
let the shards lie, and the handle…

Everything was prepared for the last anointment.
(The sacrament cannot be administered.)

II

How vain it all is.
Waltz into a city,
pull yourself up from its dust,
assume public office
and adopt a pose
to circumvent exposure.

Redeem the promises
before a blind mirror suspended in air,
before a closed door in the wind.

The paths along heaven's steep incline remain untrodden.

III

O eyes, burned by the solar silo, Earth,
fueled by the fill of rain from everyone's eyes,

entwined now, enwrapped
by the spiders' tragic webs
of the present…

IV

Place a word
in the hollow of my silence
and raise the forests high to either side
so my mouth
rests wholly in their shadows.

In the Storm of Roses

Wherever we turn in the storm of roses,
the night is lit by thorns, and the thunder
of leaves, once so quiet in the bushes,
now nips at our heel.
 Viennese Panorama

Spirits of the plains, spirits of the swelling current,
called to our end, do not halt before the city!
Take with you, too, the grapes clinging to the
brittle edges of the bank, and direct anyone in search
of scapement to the trickling stream, and open
 the steppes!

The naked joint of a tree withers nearby,
a flywheel springs to life, oil rigs drive springtide from
 the field,
the depraved torso of green yields to a forest of statues,
and the iris of oil presides over a well beneath the ground

What is it? We don't strike up the dances anymore.
After a long interval: dissonances plucked, unraveled,
almost resolved, still, just barely cantabile.

(And I can't feel their breath on my cheeks anymore!)
The wheels grind to a halt. Through the dust and
   cloud husks,
the Ferris wheel slurs the coat that covered our love.

Nowhere are last kisses guaranteed before the first
as they are here. You simply carry on in silence with the
sound of their aftertaste on your tongue. Where the crane
perfects its arc to land amid the reeds encircling
   shallow waters,
he is struck by his hour's tenor sounding above the wave
   in the cane.

Asia's breath lies beyond.

The rhythmic rising of seeds, the harvest of ripe cultures
on the brink of demise; still, I would write their testimony
on the wind. Beyond the embankment, there are
calmer waters to cloud the eye and I am overcome
by the drunken sentiment of *Limes'* limits;
beneath the poplars at the Roman obelisk, I dig
for the buried arena of multi-national tragedy,
for the smirking yes and the smirking no.

All of life has migrated to the tenements,

where there is a sterile stilling of the newly needy,
the chestnut tree blooms scentless on the boulevards,
the air will never again sample the candles' smoke,
a head of hair unfurls in solitary above the breast
    of a parapet
in the park where the balls sink, untouched
by the child's grip, to the water's bottom
and the dead eye meets the blue, once one and the same.

The miracles of disbelief are without number.
Does a heart insist on being a heart?
Dream of your purity, raise your hand in oath,
dream of your race and its triumph over you, dream
and still, rise in protest against mystic retreat.
With another hand, numbers and analyses
manage to disenchant you.
You are what separates you from yourself. Disperse,
return, knowing, in a renewed visage of farewell.

The sun flees west before the hurricane,
two thousand years have passed, and we are left
    with nothing.
Baroque garlands rise suspended by the wind,
the cherub's face tumbles from the stoops,
bastions crumble in the sultry half-light of courtyards,

from the commodes, the masks and wreathes…

Only in the bright daylight of the square, where the chain
rests at the foot of the colonnade, leaning toward the most
fleeting moment and succumbing to beauty, can I release
myself from time and become a spirit among
    arriving spirits.

Maria am Gestade —
the nave is empty, the stone is blind,
no one is saved, many are stricken,
the oil will not burn, we have
all drunk from it—where, oh where,
is your everlasting light?

The fish, too, then are dead and drift
toward the black seas that await our arrival.
We, though, gripped by the undertow of other currents,
have long since been swept out to
where the world—long overdue—
failed to appear and there was small matter of joy.
Towers on the plains rise in posthumous praise of
our passive arrival and the way we fell down the ladders
of melancholy, deeper and deeper, acutely attuned to
    the fall.

Curriculum Vitae

The night is long,
long for the man
who cannot die, his
naked eye staggers long
beneath the street lamps
blinded by drunkenness, and the scent
of wet flesh under his nails
doesn't always numb him, o God,
the night is long.

My hair will not whiten,
because I crept from the womb of machines,
Rose Red smeared tar on my forehead
and in the strands of my hair; someone had
strangled her snow-white sister. But I,
the Indian chief, marched through the city
of a million souls, and my foot
trod on the souls' isopods beneath a cowhide sky,
drooping with
the weight of a million peace pipes
gone cold. I often long

for the angel of repose,
and happy hunting grounds filled
with the helpless cry
of my friends.

With its legs and wings spread,
filled with clichés, youth clambered
over me, over pig-swill, over jasmine it crept
into the gargantuan nights with the secret of
   the square root,
the saga of death breathes down my window by the hour,
give me wolf's milk and empty
the laughter of ancients
into my rasp, when I
fall asleep bent over the folios
shamefaced in the dream
that I might not be worthy of thoughts,
but play instead with tassels,
fringing with snakes.

Our mothers, too, dreamt
of their husbands' future,
envisioned them powerful,
revolutionary and alone,
still, after the memorial in the garden

bent over the flaming weeds,
hand in hand with the rambling
child of their love. My disconsolate father,
why were you and yours silent then,
why didn't you think ahead?

Lost amidst the fusillades' flare, one night beside
   a cannon
that will not fire, the night is
damned long, beneath the dregs
of a jaundiced moon, in its bilious
light, above me, on the rail of imaginary power
the sled of brocaded history
sweeps by (I cannot stop it).
Not that I was sleeping: I was awake,
I took the road diverging between ice skeletons,
came home, wrapped myself arm and leg
in ivyand whitewashed the ruins
with what remained of the sun.
I observed the high holidays
and didn't break the bread
before it was blessed.

In such vainglorious times,
one must pass quickly from one light

into another, from one country
to another, underneath the rainbow,
taking night as the radius
for a compass point in the heart.
Wide open. You can see the lakes
from the hills and the hills in the
lakes, and the bells of someone's world
swing in the clouds' belfries.
I am forbidden from knowing
whose world it is.

It happened on a Friday—
I fasted for my life,
the air was dripping with lemon juice
and fish bones stuck in my craw—
then I pulled from the filleted fish
a ring; tossed away
at my birth, it fell
into the stream of night and sank.
I threw it back to the night.

Were I not taken by fear of death!
Had I but the word,
(I wouldn't misplace it),

Had I no thistles in my heart,
(I wouldn't turn my back on the sun),
Had I no greed in my mouth,
(I wouldn't drink the raging waters),
Had I not flung my eyelids open,
(I wouldn't have seen the rope).

Are they hauling away the heavens?
Had the earth not taken me in arm,
I'd have long since been lying still,
I'd have long been lying
where night would have me,
before she flared her nostrils,
and reared her hooves
to new heights,
to the beat of the hooves.
Forever night.
And no day.

Exile

I am a dead man, walking
with no registered address
unknown to the realm of the prefect
a surfeit in the golden cities
and in the country's waking green

dismissed as done for long ago
and left with no sign of remembrance

but wind, time and tone

I who cannot live amongst people

I drift through all languages
with the German tongue —
this cloud I hold around me
like a house

Oh, but the way it darkens
the sinister, the tenor of rain
only a few of them fall

Then it lifts the dead man into the lighter zones

You Words

for Nelly Sachs, friend, poet, in homage

You words, march, follow me!
and even if we've gone further,
gone too far, there's still a long way to go,
even further, there is no end to it.

It's not getting any lighter.

This word
will only
bring other words in its wake,
sentence for sentence.
That's how the world
would have its way,
be said and done,
once and for all.
She won't say.

Words, follow me,
that once and for all never comes
—not to this lust for words
and diction to contradiction!

For a while now
put emotion to rest, let
the heart muscle
move on.

Let it go, I say, let it go.

Not a word in the supreme ear,
nothing, I say, whispered,
let not one word of death in,
let go, and follow me, not gently
nor embittered,
not bursting with consolation,
without consolation,
signifying nothing,
thus not without sign—

Just spare me this: the image
spun from the fabric of dust, the empty garble
of syllables, last dying words.

Not another word,
you words!

No Delicacies

Nothing appeals to me anymore.

Should I
garnish a metaphor
with an almond blossom?
crucify the syntax
to halation?
Who would wrack the brain
over such trivialities —

I have learned one thing
from the words
that exist
(for the lowest class)

hunger
  humiliation
    tears
and

        darkness.

I will get by on the
unclean heaving of my shoulders,
on the desperation
(and desperation may yet drive me to despair)
over the widespread suffering,
the ills, the cost of living.

It's not the Word I neglect,
it's myself.
God knows
the others can help themselves
to comfort in words.
But I am not my own assistant.

Should I
imprison a thought,
surrender it to the well-lit cell of a sentence?
pamper eye and ear
with first-class morsels of words?
research the libido of a vowel,
determine the collectible value of consonants?

Must I
with a hammering head,

with this writer's cramp in my hand,
under pressure of the three hundredth night,
rift away at the paper,
sweep away these authorial operatic scraps,
with a vengeance: I you and he/she/it

we, all of you?

(Should indeed. Should leave it to the others.)

And let my part be lost.

*"she laughed as she remembered Ingeborg's laugh,
and you could see how beautiful
Ingeborg had been."*

—Rainer Maria Rilke,
The Notebooks of Malte Laurids Brigge
(trans. Stephen Mitchell)

GREEN INTEGER
Pataphysics and Pedantry

Douglas Messerli, *Publisher*

Essays, Manifestos, Statements, Speeches, Maxims,
Epistles, Diaristic Notes, Narratives, Natural Histories,
Poems, Plays, Performances, Ramblings, Revelations
and all such ephemera as may appear necessary
to bring society into a slight tremolo of confusion
and fright at least.

*

Individuals may order Green Integer titles through PayPal
(www.Paypal.com). Please pay the price listed below plus $2.00
for postage to Green Integer through the PayPal system.
You can also visit our site at www.greeninteger.com
If you have questions please feel free to e-mail
the publisher at info@greeninteger.com
Bookstores and libraries should order through our distributors:
USA and Canada: Consortium Book Sales and Distribution
1045 Westgate Drive, Suite 90, Saint Paul, Minnesota 55114-1065
United Kingdom and Europe: Turnaround Publisher Services
Unit 3, Olympia Trading Estate, Coburg Road, Wood Green,
London N22 6TZ UK

*

OUR TITLES [LISTED BY AUTHOR]

±Adonis *If Only the Sea Could Sleep: Love Poems* [1-931243-29-8] $11.95
Tereza Albues *Pedra Canga* [1-899295-70-9] $12.95
Will Alexander *Asia & Haiti* [Sun & Moon Press: 1-55713-189-9] $11.95

Pierre Alferi *Natural Gaits* [Sun & Moon Press: 1-55713-231-3] $10.95
Hans Christian Andersen *Travels* [1-55713-344-1] $12.95
Eleanor Antin [Yevegeny Antiov] *The Man Without a World: A Screenplay*
      [1-892295-81-4] $10.95
Rae Armantrout *Made to Seem* [Sun & Moon Press: 1-55713-220-8] $9.95
         Necromance [Sun & Moon Press: 1-55713-096-5] $8.95
         The Pretext [1-892295-39-3] $9.95
Ascher/Straus *ABC Street* [1-892295-87-7] $10.95
Ece Ayhan *A Blind Cat Black and Orthodoxies* [Sun & Moon Press:
      1-55713-102-3] $10.95
Ingeborg Bachmann *Letters to Felician* [1-931243-16-6] $9.95
Krzysztof Kamil Baczyński *White Magic and Other Poems*
      [1-931243-81-6] $12.95
Djuna Barnes *The Antiphon* [1-899295-56-3] $12.95
      Interviews [Sun & Moon Press: 0-940650-37-1] $12.95
Dennis Barone *The Returns* [Sun & Moon Press: 1-55713-184-8] $10.95
Martine Bellen *Tales of Murasaki and Other Poems* [Sun & Moon Press:
      1-55713-378-6] $10.95
†Henri Bergson *Laughter: An Essay on the Meaning of the Comic*
      1-899295-02-4] $11.95
Charles Bernstein *Republics of Reality: 1975-1995* [Sun & Moon Press:
      1-55713-304-2] $14.95
      Shadowtime [1-933382-00-7] $11.95
Régis Bonvicino *Sky-Eclipse: Selected Poems* [1-892295-34-2 $9.95
Robert Bresson *Notes on the Cinematographer* [1-55713-365-4] $8.95
André Breton *Arcanum 17* [1-931243-27-1] $12.95
      Earthlight [1-931243-27-1] $12.95
Lee Breuer *La Divina Caricatura* [1-931243-39-5] $14.95
Luis Buñuel *The Exterminating Angel* [1-931243-36-0] $11.95
Olivier Cadiot *Art Poetic'* [1-892295-22-9] $12.95
Francis Carco *Streetcorners: Prose Poems of the Demi-Monde*
      [1-931243-63-8] $12.95
Paul Celan +*Lightduress* [1-931243-75-1] $12.95
      Romanian Poems [1-892295-41-4] $10.95
      Threadsuns [1-931245-74-3] $12.95

Louis-Ferdinand Céline *Ballets without Music, without Dancers, without Anything* [1-892295-06-8] $10.95
The Church: A Comedy in Five Acts [1-892295-78-4] $13.95
Andrée Chedid *Fugitive Suns: Selected Poetry* [1-892295-25-3] $11.95
Anton Chekhov *A Tragic Man Despite Himself: The Complete Short Plays* [1-931243-17-4] $24.95
Chen I-Chih *The Mysterious Hualien* [1-931243-14-x] $9.95
Dominic Cheung [Chang Ts'o] *Drifting* [1-892295-71-7] $9.95
Marcel Cohen *Mirrors* [1-55713-313-1] $12.95
Joseph Conrad *Heart of Darkness* [1-892295-49-0] $10.95
Clark Coolidge *The Crystal Text* [Sun & Moon Press: 1-55713-230-5] $11.95
Charles Dickens *A Christmas Carol* [1-931243-18-2] $8.95
Mohammed Dib *L.A. Trip: A Novel in Verse* [1-931243-54-9] $11.95
Michael Disend *Stomping the Goyim* [1-9312243-10-7] $12.95
Jean Donnelly *Anthem* [Sun & Moon Press: 1-55713-405-7] $11.95
±José Donoso *Hell Has No Limits* [1-892295-14-8] $10.95
Arkadii Dragomoschenko *Xenia* [Sun & Moon Press: 1-55713-107-4] $12.95
Oswald Egger *Room of Rumor: Tunings* [1-931243-66-2] $9.95
Larry Eigner *readiness / enough / depends / on* [1-892295-53-9] $12.95
Sam Eisenstein *Cosmic Cow* [1-931243-45-x] $16.95
Rectification of Eros [1-892295-37-7] $10.95
Andreas Embiricos *Amour Amour* [1-931243-26-3] $11.95
Raymond Federman *Smiles on Washington Square* [Sun & Moon Press: 1-55713-181-3] $10.95
The Twofold Vibration [1-892295-29-6] $11.95
Carlos Felipe [with Julio Matas and Virgilio Piñera] *Three Masterpieces of Cuban Drama* [1-892295-66-0] $12.95
Robert Fitterman *Metropolis 1-15* [Sun & Moon Press: 1-55713-391-3] $11.95
Ford Madox Ford *The Good Soldier* [1931243-62-x] $10.95
Maria Irene Fornes *Abingdon Square* [1-892295-64-4] $9.95
Jean Frémon •*Island of the Dead* [1-931243-31-x] $12.95

Sigmund Freud [with Wilhelm Jensen] *Gradiva* and *Delusion and Dream in Wilhelm Jensen's* Gradiva [1-892295-89-x] $13.95
Federico García Lorca *Suites* 1-892295-61-x] $12.95
Armand Gatti *Two Plays: The 7 Possibilities for Train 713 Departing from Auschwitz and Public Song Before Two Electric Chairs* [1-9312433-28-x] $14.95
Dieter M. Gräf *Tousled Beauty* [1-933382-01-5] $11.95
Elana Greenfield *Damascus Gate: Short Hallucinations* [1-931243-49-2] $10.95
Jean Grenier *Islands: Lyrical Essays* [1-892295-95-4] $12.95
Barbara Guest *The Confetti Trees* [Sun & Moon Press: 1-55713-390-5] $10.95
Hervé Guibert *Ghost Image* [1-892295-05-9] $10.95
Hagiwara Sakutarō *Howling at the Moon: Poems and Prose* [1-931243-01-8] $11.95
Joshua Haigh [Douglas Messerli] *Letters from Hanusse* [1-892295-30-x] $12.95
†Knut Hamsun *The Last Joy* [1-931243-19-0] $12.95
On Overgrown Paths [1-892295-10-5] $12.95
A Wanderer Plays on Muted Strings [1-893395-73-3] $10.95
Marianne Hauser *Me & My Mom* [Sun & Moon Press: 1-55713-175-9] $9.95
Lyn Hejinian *My Life* [1-931243-33-6] $10.95
Writing Is an Aid to Memory [Sun & Moon Press: 1-55713-271-2] $9.95
Sigurd Hoel *Meeting at the Milestone* [1-892295-31-8] $15.95
Hsi Muren *Across the Darkness of the River* [1-931243-24-7] $9.95
Hsu Hui-chih *Book of Reincarnation* [1-931243-32-8] $9.95
Vicente Huidobro *Manifestos Manifest* [1-892295-08-3] $12.95
Len Jenkin *Careless Love* [Sun & Moon Press: 1-55713-168-6] $9.95
Wilhelm Jensen [with Sigmund Freud] *Gradiva* and *Delusion and Dream in Wilhelm Jensen's* Gradiva [1-893395-89-x] $12.95
Jiao Tong *Erotic Recipes: A Complete Menu for Male Potency* [1-893395-85-9] $8.95
James Joyce *On Ibsen* [1-55713-372-7] $8.95

Richard Kalich *Charlie P* [1-933382-05-8] $12.95
Ko Un *Ten Thousand Lives* [1-933382-06-6] $14.95
Alexei Kruchenykh *Suicide Circus: Selected Poems* [1-892295-27-x] $12.95
Tom La Farge *Zuntig* [1-931243-06-9] $13.95
Else Lasker-Schüler *Selected Poems* [1-892295-86-5] $11.95
Michel Leiris *Operratics* [1-892295-03-2] $12.95
Osman Lins *Nine, Novena* [Sun & Moon Press: 1-55713-229-1] $12.95
Mario Luzi *Earthly and Heavenly Journey of Simone Martini*
 [1-9312433-53-0] $14.95
†Thomas Mann **Six Early Stories* [1-892295-74-1] $10.95
†Harry Martinson *Views from a Tuft of Grass* [1-931243-78-6] $10.95
Julio Matas [with Carlos Felipe and Virgilio Piñera] *Three Masterpieces
 of Cuban Drama* [1-892295-66-0] $12.95
±Friederike Mayröcker *with each clouded peak* [Sun & Moon Press:
 1-55713-277-1] $11.95
Deborah Meadows *Representing Absence* [1-931243-77-8] $9.95
Douglas Messerli *After* [Sun & Moon Press: 1-55713-353-0] $10.95
 Bow Down [ML&NLF: 1-928801-04-8] $12.95
 First Words [1-931243-41-7] $10.95
 ed. *Listen to the Mockingbird: American Folksongs and
  Popular Music Lyrics of the 19th Century*
  [1-892295-20-2] $13.95
 Maxims from My Mother's Milk/Hymns to Him: A Dialogue
 [Sun & Moon Press: 1-55713-047-7] $8.95
 [ed. with Mac Wellman] *From the Other Side of the Century:
  A New American Drama 1960-1995* [Sun & Moon Press:
 1-55713-274-x] $29.95
 see also Joshua Haigh and Kier Peters
Henri Michaux *Tent Posts* [1-55713-328-x] $10.95
Christopher Middleton *In the Mirror of the Eighth King*
 [1-55713-331-x] $9.95
Sheila E. Murphy *Letters to Unfinished J.* [1-931243-59-x] $10.95
Martin Nakell *Two Fields That Face and Mirror Each Other*
 [1-892295-97-0] $16.95

Gellu Naum *My Tired Father / Pohem* [1-892295-07-5] $8.95
Murat Nemet-Nejat *The Peripheral Space of Photography*
  [1-892295-90-3] $9.95
Gérard de Nerval *Aurélia* [1-892295-46-6] $11.95
Vítězslav Nezval •*Antilyrik & Other Poems* [1-892295-75-x] $10.95
Henrik Nordbrandt *The Hangman's Lament: Poems* [1-931243-56-5] $10.95
John O'Keefe *The Deatherians* [1-931243-50-6] $10.95
Toby Olson *Utah* [1-892295-35-0] $12.95
OyamO *The Resurrection of Lady Lester* [1-892295-51-2] $8.95
Sergei Paradjanov *Seven Visions* [1-892295-04-0] $12.95
Kier Peters *A Dog Tries to Kiss the Sky: 7 Short Plays* [1-931243-30-1] $12.95
  The Confirmation [Sun & Moon Press: 1-55713-154-6] $6.95
Dennis Phillips *Sand* [1-931243-43-3] $10.95
Pedro Pietri *The Masses Are Asses* [1-892295-62-8] $8.95
Virgilio Piñera [with Julio Matas and Carlos Felipe] *Three Masterpieces*
  of Cuban Drama [1-892295-66-0] $12.95
Nick Piombino *Theoretical Objects* [1-892295-23-7] $10.95
Edgar Allan Poe *Eureka, A Prose Poem* [1-55713-329-8] $10.95
Antonio Porta *Metropolis* [1-892295-12-1] $10.95
Anthony Powell *O, How the Wheel Becomes It!* [1-931243-23-9] $10.95
  Venusberg [1-892295-24-5] $10.95
Stephen Ratcliffe *Sound / (system)* [1-931243-35-2] $12.95
Jean Renoir *An Interview* [1-55713-330-1] $9.95
Rainer Maria Rilke *Duino Elegies* [1-931243-07-7] $10.95
Elizabeth Robinson *Pure Descent* [Sun & Moon Press:
  1-55713-410-3] $10.95
Reina María Rodríguez *Violet Island and Other Poems*
  [1-892295-65-2] $12.95
Martha Ronk *Displeasures of the Table* [1-892295-44-x] $9.95
Joe Ross *EQUATIONS=equals* [1-931243-61-1] $10.95
Amelia Rosselli *War Variations* [1-931243-55-7] $14.95
Tiziano Rossi *People on the Run* [1-931243-37-9] $12.95
Sappho *Poems* [1-892295-13-x] $10.95
Ole Sarvig *The Sea Below My Window* [1-892295-79-2] $13.95

Leslie Scalapino *Defoe* [1-931243-44-1] $15.95
Arno Schmidt *Radio Dialogs I* [1-892295-01-6] $12.95
        Radio Dialogs II [1-892295-80-6] $13.95
        The School for Atheists: A Novella=Comedy in 6 Acts
        [1-892295-96-2] $16.95
Arthur Schnitzler *Dream Story* [1-931243-48-4] $11.95
        Lieutenant Gustl [1-931243-46-8] $9.95
Eleni Sikelianos *The Monster Lives of Boys and Girls* [1-931243-67-0] $10.95
Paul Snoek *Hercules Richelieu and Nostradamus* [1-892295-42-3] $10.95
    The Song of Songs: Shir Hashirim [1-931243-05-0] $9.95
Gilbert Sorrentino *Gold Fools* [1-892295-67-9] $14.95
        New and Selected Poems 1958-1998
        [1-892295-82-2] $14.95
Christopher Spranger *The Effort to Fall* [1-892295-00-8] $8.95
Thorvald Steen *Don Carlos and Giovanni* [1-931243-79-4] $14.95
Gertrude Stein *History, or Messages from History* [1-55713-354-9] $5.95
        Mexico: A Play [1-892295-36-9] $5.95
        Tender Buttons [1-931243-42-5] $10.95
        Three Lives [1-892295-33-4] $12.95
        To Do: A Book of Alphabets and Birthdays
        [1-931243-16-4] $9.95
Kelly Stuart *Demonology* [1-892295-58-x] $9.95
Cole Swensen *Noon* [1-931243-58-1] $10.95
Fiona Templeton *Delirium of Interpretations* [1-892295-55-5] $10.95
Henry David Thoreau *Civil Disobediance* [1-892295-93-8] $6.95
Rodrigo Toscano *The Disparities* [1-931243-25-5] $9.95
Mark Twain [Samuel Clemens] *What Is Man?* [1-892295-15-6] $10.95
César Vallejo *Aphorisms* [1-9312243-00-x] $9.95
Paul Verlaine *The Cursed Poets* [1-931243-15-8] $11.95
Mark Wallace *Temporary Worker Rides a Subway* [1-931243-60-3] $10.95
Barrett Watten *Frame (1971-1990)* [Sun & Moon Press:
        1-55713-239-9] $13.95
        Progress / Under Erasure [1-931243-68-9] $12.95

Mac Wellman *Crowtet 1: A Murder of Crows and The Hyacinth Macaw*
    [1-892295-52-0] $11.95
    Crowtet 2: Second-Hand Smoke and The Lesser Magoo
    [1-931243-71-9] $12.95
    The Land Beyond the Forest: Dracula and Swoop
    [Sun & Moon Press: 1-55713-228-3] $12.95
Oscar Wilde *The Critic As Artist* [1-55713-328-x] $9.95
William Carlos Williams *The Great American Novel* [1-931243-52-2] $10.95
Yang Lian *Yi* [1-892295-68-7] $14.95
Yi Ch'ōngjun *Your Paradise* [1-931243-69-7] $13.95
Visar Zhiti *The Condemned Apple: Selected Poetry* [1-931243-72-7] $10.95

† Author winner of the Nobel Prize for Literature
± Author winner of the America Award for Literature
• Book translation winner of the PEN American Center Translation Award [PEN-West]
* Book translation winner of the PEN/Book-of-the-Month Club Translation Prize
+ Book translation winner of the PEN Award for Poetry in Translation

THE PIP [PROJECT FOR INNOVATIVE POETRY] SERIES OF WORLD OF
POETRY OF THE 20TH CENTURY

VOLUME 1 Douglas Messerli, ed. *The PIP Anthology of World Poetry
of the 20th Century* [1-892295-47-4] $15.95

VOLUME 2 Douglas Messerli, ed. *The PIP Anthology of World Poetry
of the 20th Century* [1-892295-94-6] $15.95

VOLUME 3 Régis Bonvicino, Michael Palmer and Nelson Ascher, eds.;
Revised with a Note by Douglas Messerli *The PIP Anthology
of World Poetry of the 20th Century: Nothing the Sun
Could Not Explain—20 Contemporary Brazilian Poets*
[1-931243-04-2] $15.95

VOLUME 4 Douglas Messerli, ed. *The PIP Anthology of World Poetry
of the 20th Century* [1-892295-87-3] $15.95

VOLUME 5 Douglas Messerli, ed. *The PIP Anthology of World Poetry
of the 20th Century: Intersections—Innovative Poetry in
Southern California* [1-931243-73-5] $15.95